A DEADLY
ENDOWMENT

Books by Alyssa Maxwell

Gilded Newport Mysteries
MURDER AT THE BREAKERS
MURDER AT MARBLE HOUSE
MURDER AT BEECHWOOD
MURDER AT ROUGH POINT
MURDER AT CHATEAU SUR MER
MURDER AT OCHRE COURT
MURDER AT CROSSWAYS
MURDER AT KINGSCOTE
MURDER AT WAKEHURST

Lady and Lady's Maid Mysteries
MURDER MOST MALICIOUS
A PINCH OF POISON
A DEVIOUS DEATH
A MURDEROUS MARRIAGE
A SILENT STABBING
A SINISTER SERVICE
A DEADLY ENDOWMENT

Published by Kensington Publishing Corp.

A Deadly
Endowment

ALYSSA
MAXWELL

KENSINGTON
PUBLISHING CORP.

www.kensingtonbooks.com

KENSINGTON BOOKS are published by

Kensington Publishing Corp.
119 West 40th Street
New York, NY 10018

All Kensington titles, imprints, and distributed lines are available at special quantity discounts for bulk purchases for sales promotion, premiums, fundraising, educational, or institutional use. Special book excerpts or customized printings can also be created to fit specific needs. For details, write or phone the office of the Kensington Special Sales Manager: Attn. Special Sales Department. Kensington Publishing Corp., 119 West 40th Street, New York, NY 10018. Phone: 1-800-221-2647.

Library of Congress Card Catalogue Number: 2021944907

The K logo is a trademark of Kensington Publishing Corp.

ISBN: 978-1-4967-3490-7
First Kensington Hardcover Edition: January 2022

ISBN: 978-1-4967-3493-8 (ebook)

10 9 8 7 6 5 4 3 2 1

Printed in the United States of America

To Bonnie, Carla, and Vonnie,
three amazing, beautiful women, dear friends and sisters
in writing, who helped keep me sane during the insanity
that was 2020. I don't think I could have found the focus
to write this book without you.

ACKNOWLEDGMENTS

The process of bringing a book from its initial premise to the bookstore shelves is a long and difficult one in the best of circumstances. It truly does take a village, from author to agent to editor to copyeditors, proofreaders, cover artists, etc. Attempting to do this during a pandemic, while at the same time ensuring everyone's safety, seemed, at the outset, an impossible task. I am grateful beyond words to everyone at Kensington—especially CEO Steven Zacharias, my editor, John Scognamiglio, production editor Robin Cook, communications manager Larissa Ackerman—and my agent, Evan Marshall, along with the many other dedicated professionals who made the publication of this book possible.

CHAPTER 1

The Cotswolds, England, May 1921

Sometimes a woman had to stand alone and do what needed to be done regardless of what others thought of her. Regardless of their refusal to rally around her. Luckily for Phoebe Renshaw, such was not the case. Not entirely.

But even knowing she had an ally or two didn't make sitting down to breakfast that Friday morning any easier. The family was using the Petit Salon today rather than the dining room, which had been tidied and readied for to-day's experimental event. The Petit Salon was among her favorite rooms at Foxwood Hall. However, today, even the cheerfulness of its pale green walls, crisp white wain-scoting, and the bay of windows overlooking the south gardens, a happy circumstance owing to the room being tucked into the turret of the original portion of the house, failed to calm her nerves. Likewise, the china service grac-ing the table, a unique design incorporating the Wroxly crest within a pastoral Cotswold setting, commissioned by Phoebe and her siblings as a gift for their grandparents' anniversary, did little to lift her spirits.

She put off facing the rest of the family as long as she could by going straight to the sideboard and selecting a light variety of fruit and grilled tomatoes. At the last minute she scooped a generous portion of kedgeree, a curried mixture of fish, eggs, and rice, onto her plate. She would need to keep up her strength.

There was nothing for it now but to take her seat at the table. "Good morning, everyone. Grams, Grampapa. How are you today?"

"Quite well, thank you, dear." Grampapa, the Earl of Wroxly, came to his feet and offered her a kindly smile, which Phoebe eagerly returned, as Douglas, the footman, held her chair for her. Grampapa resumed his seat. Her brother, Fox, had stood as well, but only because Grampapa insisted a gentleman always stood to greet a lady. As for the others around the table . . .

Grams pinched her lips, sparing Phoebe the merest of nods. Once he resumed his seat, sixteen-year-old Fox grunted and dug with vigor into his scrambled eggs and black pudding, as if perhaps there were precious jewels hiding within their depths. And Julia . . .

Phoebe's eldest sister, the undisputed beauty of the family, raised her perfect chin, flared her delicate nose, and from beneath her carefully delineated eyebrows pierced Phoebe with a sapphire-blue glare obviously meant to quash any further attempt Phoebe might make at pleasantries.

She retaliated by turning to Amelia. "All ready for today?"

"I'm so excited. I can hardly wait to put your plan in action, Phoebe." Her younger sister, eighteen now and newly graduated from the local finishing school, somehow managed to convey a youthful exuberance combined with the self-assured poise of a grown woman. She said to their grandmother, "You'll soon see, Grams, that Phoebe's idea of opening the house to tours will help the villagers and the tenant farmers, *and* bring enjoyment to countless more. After all, if we're merely the custodians of this estate, as darling Grampapa is always saying, why *should* we keep it all to ourselves?"

Phoebe beamed at her from across the table.

Owen Seabright had said as much last night when Phoebe spoke with him on the telephone, the crackling of the wires across the many miles between them unable to strip the warmth and reassurance from his voice. She feared she had come to depend on him rather too much in the past year, a circumstance that gave her pause. A woman of this modern age should be able to stand on her own two feet, be resilient and astute in her own right, and not need to go running to a man whenever difficulties arose.

Then again, he had telephoned *her*—not the other way around—to wish her luck and congratulate her, again, on her ingenuity in facing a growing problem head-on. He wished he could be here today, but as Phoebe well knew, his business concerns kept him in Yorkshire for the moment. She would certainly not have him drop pressing matters at his woolen mills to run down to Little Barlow and hold her hand. However much she enjoyed holding hands with him.

That left her and Amelia to face down the opposition together. "Thank you, Amellie. I could not have put it better myself."

To that, Fox snorted. Julia scowled. Grams huffed and placed her napkin beside her plate, a signal that had Douglas circling the table to gently slide back her chair as she unfolded her nearly six-foot length. "I suppose we'll see, won't we? Today may be the first and last day of these so-called tours." Then, under her breath, but still clearly audible, "One can only hope."

How Phoebe loathed making Grams unhappy, but she simply couldn't sit idly by while the rest of the world sped forward, steadfastly leaving Foxwood Hall, and those who occupied it, in a quagmire of old-world traditions that no longer served any good purpose. The estate's function had always been to help support the village of Little Barlow and surrounding farms; it must continue to do so even if it meant tucking a bit of one's pride into one's pocket.

Chin up, shoulders straight, Grams swept from the Petit Salon at a sedate pace, probably resisting the urge to storm out. But that would be undignified, and, of all the virtues, Grams held dignity in highest esteem. Once the trailing hems of her morning gown had cleared the threshold, Grampapa reached his hand out to Phoebe. She leaned toward him to place her hand in his.

"Don't take your grandmother's displeasure too much to heart, my dear. She'll come around."

"Have you come around, Grampapa?" She harbored no doubts as to his initial sentiments toward her plan. And she understood their reservations perfectly. Allowing strangers to troop through the house, gawking and staring at family heirlooms, after paying a fee for the privilege of doing so? Money, in exchange for a glimpse into the private life of an earl and his family? The outlandishness of such a notion had nearly given Grams the vapors, and Grams had never suffered an attack of the vapors in her life. She had put her foot down and adamantly forbade it; had refused to hear another word about it. Meanwhile, at the time, Grampapa had remained quiet. Contemplative. A bit brooding. And then . . .

"I do see its merit," he had quietly ventured a fortnight ago, and then fell silent while Grams had launched another argumentative assault on why such a vulgarity must never, *could* never, be permitted at Foxwood Hall. While

Grams had raged on, Grampapa had taken Phoebe's hand in both of his wide, very reassuring ones and whispered, "I shall think on it, and let you know."

For the next week there hadn't been another word said about the matter. Even Grams had carried on as if nothing had ever been amiss. Fox, home for a brief school holiday, had made himself scarce. Julia had kept herself busy. Phoebe had almost been content to let the matter drop. And then Grampapa had made his decision.

"It's certainly not the ideal solution, but circumstances these days are less than ideal, aren't they? The tenant farms need repairs. The village businesses need a new influx of visitors. And money isn't what it was before the war."

Thus the battle lines had been drawn, with Phoebe, Amelia, and Grampapa on one side, and Grams, Julia, and Fox firmly entrenched on the other. Would today end the war, or escalate it?

"Tourists . . . in our home. Good heavens, what next?" Julia drained her teacup and came to her feet, Douglas arriving at her chair almost too late to assist her. "Shall we open the dining room as a stopover for travelers? I've a good mind to take little Charles and leave. Go to Lyndale Park." She patted the perfect sweep of blond hair framing her face. "It's becoming more and more apparent that's where we belong."

"Oh, Julia, don't be like that," Amelia pleaded, truly taken aback at the threat. If Julia was the beautiful one of the family, Amelia claimed the distinction of sweetest. Ingenuous and trusting, Amelia believed the best of someone until proven wrong, and her hazel eyes, honey-blond hair, and lovely complexion mirrored her agreeable nature. But all that didn't mean she wouldn't speak up for herself whenever she deemed it necessary. "Charles belongs here, with all of us. He needs his aunties and uncle, and Grams and Grampapa, and we need him. I shall be wretched if you take him away. You mustn't do it, Julia. Promise you won't."

Charles Gilbert Townsend had been born on the eighth of January that year, the longed-for son that had settled the matter of who would inherit Julia's deceased husband's title and estate. His arrival into the world had also settled Julia's own inheritance, in question all those months since her husband's death. Whether she remarried or not, she would never need worry about the future, could lead an independent and luxurious life. Charles was now Viscount Annondale, with an estate called Lyndale Park in Staffordshire, a town house in London, and several manufactories that produced both automobile and aeroplane engines. Julia's child would never lack for anything.

Except, perhaps, his Renshaw relatives, should Julia make good on her threat. Phoebe wished to add her protests to Amelia's, but knew better than to utter a word. Julia often liked to do the exact opposite of Phoebe's expressed desires. But if Julia was the beautiful sister, and Amelia the sweet sister, Phoebe had learned, in the years since their father had died in the Great War, that she was the sister who recognized a problem for what it was and refused to sit still until a solution had been found. Hence today's endeavor.

"Exams or no, I'll be happy to get back to school. That's all I can say." Fox shoveled a last, heaping forkful of eggs and sausages into his mouth, realized his lack of decorum, and darted a glance at Grampapa. With a gulp he swallowed it all down, attempting to hide his indiscretion behind his napkin. "But since that won't be until Sunday night, I'd like to take Fairfax on an especially long walk today." He darted another glance at Grampapa from beneath a shock of tawny hair. "If that would be all right, sir?"

Fairfax, another newish member of the Renshaw family, was a Staffordshire bull terrier they had adopted back in the fall. Still a puppy at heart, he had grown to nearly full size, being all muscle and sinew and boundless energy.

"It would," Grampapa said with an approving nod. "Fairfax love his walks and I think you could both use a good jaunt about the place. Why not take him on a round of the tenant farms and see if there are new repairs to be added to the list after the recent rains." Grampapa could be strict with Fox—far stricter than he ever was with Phoebe and her sisters—but he also understood when a sixteen-year-old boy needed to be made to feel like a man, and a useful one, at that. Fox would be Earl of Wroxly someday . . . a thought Phoebe never liked to contemplate, for the loss it would mean to them all.

Her brother hurried away and Grampapa turned his attention back to Phoebe and Amelia. "Well, you two, you'd best go prepare."

Amelia clapped her hands together once and sprang up from her chair. With a little squeal of glee, she grabbed Phoebe's hand, drew her to her feet, and practically hauled her from the room. "This is going to be such fun."

Eva Huntford stood behind Lady Phoebe in front of the tall mirror in her lady's bedroom and put the finishing touches on her lovely strawberry-gold hair, coiled in a simple French twist held by a colorfully enameled comb in the shape of a hummingbird. Lady Phoebe had suggested the ornament, saying its added sparkle of semiprecious stones would serve as a beacon to keep today's visitors following her throughout the downstairs rooms of the house.

"But in the event they begin to wander off, it's up to you and Amelia to herd them back to the group." A note of worry tinged Lady Phoebe's voice. "We can't have strays meandering here and there, or Grams will put an end to this for good—Grampapa or no Grampapa."

"Between the three of us we shouldn't have a problem."

Eva smoothed the shawl collar that draped over Lady Phoebe's shoulders, the very latest styling of embroidered lawn, over a yellow silk voile dress that barely reached her calves. All the Renshaw sisters had pretty, well-shaped legs flattered by the current trend of rising hems. "You look lovely, my lady. No one will want to stray once they've caught sight of you." She turned to Phoebe's younger sister, Amelia, in violet satin with a tapering, tiered skirt. "Perfect," Eva assessed. "I'd say you're both ready. Oh, and listen! Do I hear motorcars approaching?"

Before any of them could peek out the window, Julia appeared in the doorway. Her maid, a hale and fiercely devoted Swiss woman named Hetta, stood behind her in the corridor holding baby Charles. "We going out for the duration. We'll duck out the service entrance so your gawkers won't be tempted to snap pictures of us."

Amelia brushed past her. "*There's* my nephew and godson." She tickled Charles beneath his chubby chin, eliciting a round of high-pitched giggles. "Make sure you keep him warm."

"You saw him before breakfast, so don't make it sound like it's been ages." Julia gave a roll of her eyes. "And I do know how to take care of my son, thank you."

"*Ja,* as do I," Hetta added for good measure.

Lady Amelia shrugged as she offered Charles her forefinger, which he grabbed with enthusiasm and tugged toward his mouth. The sound of tires on the driveway reverberated from outside.

Lady Phoebe exited the bedroom, kissed her nephew on the brow, and headed for the stairs. "That'll be our guests arriving."

That sent Eva and the two sisters hurrying downstairs to the Great Hall, where Phoebe planned to begin the tour once Eva had greeted their guests outside. Mr. Giles, Foxwood Hall's longtime butler, stood ready to admit them. The great door opened . . .

Outside on the drive, a good dozen schoolchildren were piling out from a rickety motor bus that surely hailed from well before the Great War. They were from the village school, between ten and twelve years old, and, goodness, their voices echoed against the house as they laughed and shouted with the excitement of having left the confines of the classroom for the morning. Their teacher, a young woman whose thin form swam within a shapeless skirt and jumper ensemble, her hair tucked up beneath a kind of beret, called out instructions in her attempt to quiet them. Her efforts had little effect. It seemed the outdoors, the trip from school, and the prospect of actually entering an earl's home—not through the servants' entrance some of their parents might frequent, but the very same door the earl himself used—proved too much for her.

"Oh, dear," Lady Phoebe murmured, "what *have* I done?"

"I'll go out now. Perhaps I can calm them down." They had agreed beforehand that Eva would explain the details of the exterior of the house and the surrounding park. She strode out to the sun-strewn forecourt, only to be engulfed in a maelstrom of voices and motion.

Several children were skipping along the front of the house, stopping here and there to examine the sculpted foliage or jumping up to peek into windows. Others made a game of kicking up showers of carefully raked gravel. A particularly errant pair of boys was tossing said gravel into the basin of the fountain to see who could raise the highest splash.

Eva peered out over the distant rolling hills, half shaded by steep banks of clouds, and reminded herself they would all be going home in an hour or two.

"Children," she called, and held her arms out as if in a welcoming embrace meant to gather them around her. To her utter surprise, the gesture worked, and she found herself surrounded by the small but high-spirited horde. "Good morning, everyone, and welcome to Foxwood Hall."

This met with an immediate question from a redhaired girl standing in front. "You're not Lady Phoebe, are you?" It was more of an accusation, really, than a question.

"You're quite right, I am not," Eva responded without missing a beat, knowing full well she could lose the esteem of these children with the faintest show of hesitation. "I am Miss Huntford, Lady Phoebe's and Lady Amelia's personal maid, and I'll be helping with the tour. Miss Carmichael, thank you for bringing your class today."

The teacher, who had held the position only for this past year, offered her a withering look. "They're very excited, as you can see." She laughed at the understatement of her own comment and cast a doubtful gaze at her charges. Then, pulling straighter, she seemed to gather her wits and her fortitude. "Children, it's time to collect ourselves. We cannot enter the Earl and Countess of Wroxly's home unless we promise to be quiet and orderly. You don't wish to climb back into the motor bus and return to school, do you?"

Ah. This had the desired effect, and within moments the children had formed two straight lines, their lips compressed with subdued enthusiasm. The resulting quiet was heavenly, and allowed the chatters of finches and sparrows, the patter of a woodpecker, and the distant cry of a kite to fill the morning air. Eva even thought she heard, from somewhere on the other side of the house, Fairfax's happy barking. She hoped the children's newfound composure would last.

"We'll wait here for the others to arrive," she told them, a bit of information that elicited muffled groans of impatience. This caused her an instant's worry that she had lost their cooperation, yet she understood their eagerness. How many children of farmers, craftsmen, and laborers ever had the chance to walk through a front door such as the one before them now, manned by a butler, no less, and see with their own eyes how the upper class lived? One might think such an experience would engender envy and perhaps even resentment, but Eva knew there existed in the local community a deep pride in their earl and his family, as if they, too, were part of that family, and in many ways they were.

This tour was intended as a trial run for future ones and not meant to make much of a profit. Hence the children were exempt from the fee. However, clouds of dust swirling at the end of the drive announced that the paying guests were arriving. Eva raised a hand to shade her face from the dapples of sunlight filtering through the trees. Two motorcars came to rest behind the motor bus. The doors opened upon two groups, each comprised of two men and two women, all of them adjusting clothing and straightening hats as they climbed out. Eva recognized some of them from the village; others were new to her. They formed themselves into a coherent assembly and marched over to where Eva, Miss Carmichael, and the children stood waiting.

The man who seemed to be leading them stuck out his hand, although whether he aimed for Eva or Miss Carmichael remained a matter of ambiguity. To clear up the matter, Eva placed her hand in his for a brisk shake. His grip was firm and to the point, rather like the image he projected in his country tweeds and neatly pointed beard.

"The Little Barlow Chapter of the Greater Costwald Historical Society, I presume?" she inquired. The organization was a new one, having formed, she understood, only in the past several months. At his nod she took in the rest of the party and continued, "I'm Eva Huntford. I work for the Renshaws. Welcome to Foxwood Hall."

"Thank you. I'm Abel Hawkhurst, president of the chapter, and this is my wife." He spoke with that husky drawl affected by so many men who fancied themselves of the upper classes. Beside him, a trim woman of early middle years thrust out her chin, pursed her lips, and tilted her head in greeting, although by doing so her toque hat, made heavy by the braiding and beading around its edges, slipped askew over her brow. It was all Eva could do not to reach out to fix it for her.

The woman also extended a hand, the fingers long and bony. "Mr. Hawkhurst and I cofounded the chapter. I understood Lady Phoebe would be conducting the tour?" Her gaze skittered over the façade of the house. "Hmm . . . yes, well." She took the opportunity to slide her hat back to its proper position, and then gazed down at the dozen or so faces peering up at her as if only just noticing them. A frown formed above her birdlike nose. "Will these be joining us on the tour?"

These? Years of being in service allowed Eva to school her features not to betray her sentiments. She turned her attention to the others in the group and hoped she wouldn't be required to remember all their names. A small but stout woman, in a sensible navy-blue suit, matching pumps, and a jaunty bucket hat, pushed her way to the front.

"Excuse me . . . *excuse* me." She nudged shoulders aside and elbowed her way through. A young man, perhaps Eva's age, followed on her heels wordlessly and without offering to help, and by their resemblance she guessed they were mother and son. Except where the mother's eyes were an ordinary hazel, his were starkly green, as green as the new spring foliage. The breeze lifted his dark hair off his brow, revealing a jagged scar above his left eyebrow that traveled to his hairline. His gaze met Eva's and skittered quickly away. He raised a hand to smooth his hair back down.

When the woman in the blue suit finally stood before Eva, she, too, thrust out a hand, far broader than Mrs. Hawkhurst's, the nails short and neat; though, on further examination, not without a smudge or two of ink. Eva also noticed the Victorian mourning brooch affixed to the lapel of her jacket. On an onyx background tiny seed pearls surrounded a smooth weave of ruddy hair, threaded with gray. A widow, she surmised.

"I'm Arvina Bell," the woman announced as if it should mean something significant. "I'm with the society, but I also telephoned ahead to explain my purpose in coming." When Eva stared at her blankly, the woman elucidated, "My book? The one I'm writing?" More forcefully, and as if speaking to a simpleton, she added, "The one about the great manor houses of the Cotswolds?"

"Ah." Whoever had taken the message must have passed it on to Lady Phoebe, who apparently neglected to mention it to Eva. No matter. It explained the ink—perhaps from a typewriter ribbon. "Well, then, we'll begin with a brief description of the park and overall architecture of the house. The Barlow Foxwood was originally a royal hunting ground dating back, some rumors have it, to the Conqueror. The land remained a royal hunting ground until the late 1540s, when it was bestowed by Edward the Sixth on the first Baron Foxwood. But more about him later.

"Now, then, the gardens we see here today were originally designed by Capability Brown in the 1760s. Before that, the park followed the much more geometric patterns of the Elizabethan era, with the inclusion of a knot garden to the rear of the house. Capability Brown had all that cleared in favor of a more pastoral and natural design, meticulously planned to appear unplanned, one might say."

She paused, hoping to hear a chuckle or, at the very

least, an airy twitter. When none came, she gestured to the front of the house. "As I said, the land was bestowed on the first Baron Foxwood in 1547, and it was he who had the house built. It was constructed in the Late Gothic Perpendicular style, but has undergone numerous renovations and enlargements through the centuries."

As Eva pointed out details of windows, the turret, and the roofline, which soared and dipped and peaked, the children became far more interested in the erratic course of a butterfly. She hurried through the rest of her speech and gestured to the steps and up to the front door. "And now we'll enter the house."

Miss Carmichael escorted the children in first. Then Mr. Hawkhurst offered his wife his arm and once more led the way, the other society members trailing behind him like a brood of obedient ducklings. To their credit, they proceeded slowly and each greeted Eva as they passed her. She took note of their appearances, not so much to consign them to her memory as to take their measure. Who would be likely to wander? To interrupt? To contradict? She had been on museum tours in the past and knew from experience people could be as eager to teach—or, rather, to show off their knowledge—as to learn.

"Arvina . . . Arvina, dear, do allow me to assist you up the steps. Here we are, righto . . ." One of the men hurried to catch up to Arvina Bell and her son, amusing Eva with the way he simpered when he reached Mrs. Bell's side. She accepted his offered arm, but not without a huff that raised and dropped her shoulders visibly.

"I'm quite all right, George. No need to fuss," she admonished, though not unkindly.

Older than his fellow society members, mustachioed, red-cheeked, and sporting a comfortable paunch, Dr. George Bishop had taken up residence just beyond Little Barlow's precincts rather suddenly last winter and hung a shingle outside his garden gate. From the surgery tucked into his home, he attended to the inhabitants of the outlying farms, who often had neither the time nor the inclination to come into Little Barlow, or the neighboring village of Redvale, for their occasional medical needs. Eva had met the doctor on several occasions in the village and found him to be an affable fellow. Once he had even insisted on carrying her parcels down the High Street to the motorcar waiting to convey her back to Foxwood Hall.

She prepared to take up the rear of the procession, when a figure appeared at her elbow and a voice spoke directly to her. "You're a lady's maid, if I'm not mistaken."

She turned to a pretty face framed by a stylish picture hat with a wide gold silk sash hugging its crown. A sweet ivory ensemble that featured a short, loose jacket with gold trim flattered a slender figure, while matching ivory shoes with stacked heels revealed a keen fashion sense. It was rather something Lady Julia would wear, though this outfit lacked the impeccable tailoring and quality of fabrics Lady Julia insisted upon. For, whereas the eldest Renshaw sister wore the latest from Paris, this woman obviously shopped at London department stores. Not that Eva held that against her. She smiled at the woman's inquiry, guessing her to be about Lady Julia's age. "Yes, I am," she replied lightly. "Can I do anything for you?"

"No, heavens, that isn't why I asked. Ophelia Chapman, *Country Heritage Magazine*." She offered her hand for Eva to shake. From the other arm dangled a small, square handbag and a box camera hung around her neck. "You've heard of it, yes? I'm writing a piece on Little Barlow, part of my Villages of England series." She spoke rapidly, in a clipped but clear manner.

"Another writer. Are you not with the historical society, then?"

"I certainly am, but I'm rather a long-distance member,

as I don't live here in your village. In fact, I belong to quite a number of historical societies. It's a great help being able to access their records for my articles, you see. I'd very much like to interview you and a couple of the other servants, if that would be agreeable."

"Interview me? Whatever for?"

"Simply to learn more about the house and the village from a . . . shall we say . . . less lofty perspective?" The woman smiled, but took on a puzzled look. "I must say you don't speak like a lady's maid, at least not one raised in the country."

"Yes, I had the good fortune of attending the local finishing school." Eva didn't bother mentioning that her time there had been cut short by an emergency at home that made it necessary to return to her parents' farm before she could complete her studies.

"Ah. Scholarship girl?"

Eva didn't take offense, even though during her school days some of her fellow students had used the term to mock her. "That's right."

"You're smart, then. Good for you. So, about the interview?"

"Yes, I suppose." But a wariness came over her. To be sure, she had heard of *Country Heritage Magazine*, but before she said a word to this woman, she intended to be certain she worked for that periodical and not some scandal rag like the *Daily Mirror*, with its sensational reporting on celebrities, aristocrats, and the like.

"It's all right if I take a few photos of the front of the house now and after the tour, yes?"

"Only the outside, I'm afraid," Eva told her firmly. "The earl and countess don't wish any photography taken inside." That had been part of the bargain, and the countess would not be budged on it.

"Fair enough." Miss Chapman raised the camera away from her torso a few inches and gazed down into the viewer, snapping the shutter when she appeared satisfied with the framing of her shot. She took several more before walking smartly into the house.

Who *were* these people, really, filing into the Renshaws' home? Strangers, all of them, and who knew what they really wanted? Perhaps Lady Wroxly had been right. Perhaps Lady Phoebe's utterance would prove prophetic. Eva hoped not. But good heavens, what *had* they done?

CHAPTER 2

A mistake. Oh, yes, Phoebe couldn't deny her lapse in judgment when a full score of visitors formed a crush in the center of the Great Hall, all eyes turned to her in expectation. And as she launched into the history of the house, explaining what dated back to Elizabethan times and which sections constituted the Georgian and Victorian additions, the children began to shift and fidget, forcing her to accept her miscalculation. Then the murmurs began, despite the not-very-discreet shushings of Miss Carmichael. Of course the studious scribbling of some of the historical society members in their little notebooks helped redeem her judgment somewhat, but something had to be done about the children before they lapsed into anarchy.

Fortifying herself by exchanging a glance with Eva, who nodded her encouragement, she segued into the history of the Renshaw family, beginning with the first baron, who had had the house built, and tracing it to the elevation of the first Earl of Wroxly during the Restoration.

When she paused, Amelia smiled as if to say "well done," but Phoebe felt her grip on the youngsters slipping away. She changed course a bit.

"Children, do any of you know how many generations of your family have lived in Little Barlow?" Phoebe raised her eyebrows as if her question was of vital importance. A small forest of hands went up, and she called on several of them, one by one. Her ruse had the desired effect of focusing their little minds on a matter that interested them.

But then the adults began to fidget.

"Time to move on," she said gaily. "Please follow me across the Great Hall. We'll begin our tour of the rooms in the library."

Phoebe was familiar with some of the members of the historical society. Abel and Vesta Hawkhurst, though not strictly of the aristocracy, had inhabited an estate some minutes outside of Little Barlow for a decade now, ever since Mr. Hawkhurst had inherited the old pile from his father, who had inherited from his father before him. Somewhere at the end of the line, there had been a baron or earl or someone of that ilk—much like Phoebe's own family.

And, of course, there was Lady Primrose Scott—who *was* to the manor born, but now the ordinary wife of a Cotswold member of Parliament. She had been a local fixture these many years, serving on numerous church committees and even helping out here, at Foxwood Hall, to collect and prepare supplies during the war years. As for everyone else, Phoebe challenged herself to put names to faces based on the list she had been provided with.

As everyone trooped along behind her, she asked over her shoulder, "Are there any questions about the history I've related so far?" Just as with the children a hand went up, prompting Phoebe to bring the group to a halt. "Ah. Yes, Mrs. Hawkhurst?"

The woman gave a little sniff. "Are there currently any plans to modernize?"

"*Modernize?*" Phoebe flicked a glance at Eva, who

twitched a dark eyebrow in response. Beside her, Amelia scrunched her features within their frame of honey-blond curls.

"Yes, to bring the house into the twentieth century," Mrs. Hawkhurst clarified. "To air out some of the Victorian stuffiness, so to speak."

Amelia gasped audibly, but Phoebe did her best to maintain a neutral expression. She had noticed, only minutes ago, how the Hawkhursts had traded murmurs throughout her introduction to the house—although it wasn't so much the whispers Phoebe had found distracting, but the disparaging looks that had accompanied them. The subtle ridge above a nose, the pull of the corner of a mouth, the slight roll of the eyes. Mr. and Mrs. Hawkhurst traded yet another such look now, and Phoebe's hackles rose.

"My grandparents are traditionalists in every way," she proudly informed them. "They enjoy the deep sense of history the house provides them."

"Besides," Amelia called from the rear of the group, "we *all* love Foxwood Hall exactly the way it is."

"To each his own, wouldn't you say, Abel?" Mrs. Hawkhurst said under her breath. Her husband nodded his agreement.

"I very much appreciate a traditional perspective." The woman who spoke up now smiled sweetly. Lady Primose Scott was tall to the point of being considered statuesque, and, though middle-aged, she had nonetheless maintained a buxom, curvy figure. Yet this she countered with conservative country tweeds, her blouse buttoned to her chin and knotted with a silk scarf, the skirt falling nearly to her ankles. According to the list of the historical society members, Lady Primrose served as its treasurer. She sent a circumspect glance at the Hawkhursts. "My husband and I are most conservative in both our tastes and our views, so I understand your grandparents completely, Lady

Phoebe. As you all know, my husband, Mr. Conrad Scott, is a conservative MP representing our lovely region, and . . ."

"Yes, Primrose, we all know," Mrs. Hawkhurst sang out in a long-suffering voice. "We needn't be reminded."

"I'm only making a point, Vesta," the woman countered, her sweet smile unwavering. "Not to mention defending this lovely house from criticism it certainly doesn't deserve."

"I was only stating the obvious," Mrs. Hawkhurst quipped in return, her nose quivering in annoyance.

"Indeed." Phoebe heard no conviction in Mr. Hawkhurst's affirmation, merely a desire to please his wife.

But good heavens, she thought, whatever antagonism existed between Lady Primrose and the Hawkhursts— and, obviously, it *did* exist—must they exhibit it here? Before she could think of a way to smooth ruffled feathers, Mr. Hawkhurst glowered at the MP's wife, rendering a complete alteration in Lady Primrose's person. One minute she had been genteelly assertive, and the next her chin tucked itself into her scarf and she seemed unduly fascinated by the pattern of the marble tiles beneath her leather pumps.

Once again, Phoebe and Eva communicated via the slightest of facial movements, forming subtle expressions familiar to each. They were, Phoebe decided, in complete agreement.

"Phoebe . . . the library?" Amelia held up a hand to point the way.

"Yes, of course. If you'll follow me, please . . ." Phoebe got no farther than a step or two before the next interruption came.

"My goodness, I'm very excited to see your library, Lady Phoebe." A gentleman stepped forward, and although his features appeared those of someone in his midthirties, his bearing was that of a much older man. Rounded shoulders, a head that leaned forward like that of a pigeon, the swirl of a cowlick at the front of his hair, and a tweed suit, years out of date, hanging as if he'd suddenly lost a good deal of weight. He motioned backward at the Grand Staircase, his spectacles flashing in the light from the clerestory windows. "Will we have also a chance to view the portraits hanging along the upper gallery? I'm simply mad about historical portraits. I assume these are of the previous earls and countesses of Wroxly?"

"They are," Phoebe replied, "but we're to stay on the ground floor, I'm afraid. It is a compromise I promised my grandmother we would honor."

"Not even a peek?"

"You may peek all you like from down here," she told him with a smile to soften the decree.

"Then let us on to the library." A gleam entered the gentleman's eyes. "Eamon Sadler, my lady. I'm a bookseller, did you know? Sadler's Rare Books Emporium, out on the Old Gloucester Road. Set up shop back in the autumn."

"Good heavens," Phoebe said earnestly. "I didn't know. I'll certainly make a point of visiting soon." She sped her steps in hopes of arriving in the library without another interruption. Mr. Sadler walked on, ahead of her. She thought to call him back, but, on second thought, what mischief could a bookseller come to in a library?

From the corner of her eye she noticed the woman beside her, younger than the others, and dressed with a modern flair. But what Phoebe most admired about her was her handbag, a darling black-and-beige patent leather affair with a metal frame—again, very modern—which contrasted smartly with her ivory ensemble. This must be Ophelia Chapman, Phoebe guessed, the magazine writer.

Beside Miss Chapman walked a woman just this side of fifty, who possessed features that had probably been pretty in her youth, but had faded to blandness. From the start

she had seemed anxious to record every word Phoebe
spoke, her pencil rarely pausing. By process of elimination
Phoebe deduced this to be Arvina Bell, another writer, this
one working on a book about the great houses of the
Cotswolds. A much younger man, perhaps Phoebe's own
age, trailed close behind her. He hadn't been on the list,
but she guessed by his resemblance to Arvina Bell that he
must be her son. She also guessed he wasn't particularly
interested in this house or any other, as he rarely bothered
to glance at the details she pointed out.

"I'm coming, Arvina. Pip, pip! Wait up!"

Phoebe and Eva traded grins. This wasn't the first time
Dr. Bishop had called after Mrs. Bell, entreating her to
wait for him. Even now, as her pencil continued its trails
across the current page in her notebook, she didn't
glance up as he reached her side and nudged her son out
of the way.

At the open door to the library, Eamon Sadler looked
back at Phoebe once. Then, grinning, he darted inside. He
went straight to the nearest bookcase and began perusing
titles.

As Phoebe gave a running commentary on the linenfold
paneling, the coffered ceiling, and carved woodwork
around the bookcases, the group spread out to examine
whatever interested them: the books, the mantelpiece, the
views outside the windows. In fact, this latter detail appeared to have most captured the children's interest, and
Phoebe wondered if she should rather have arranged a garden tour for them. She would consider that for the next
time a classroom visited.

Suddenly something struck her as not quite right, and a
quick count revealed a couple of children missing. She almost asked Miss Carmichael to search for the errant pair,
but, on better advisement, whispered her request to
Amelia. With an alarmed look her sister hurried out.

Phoebe returned her attention to the group. Mrs. Bell seemed particularly interested in a framed photograph on the small table beside Grampapa's favorite wingback chair, the one where he would set his brandy in the evenings after dinner when he settled in to read.

What could possibly hold the woman's attention about a photograph of her great-grandparents on their wedding day? The historical aspect of their clothing? Or, perhaps, the fact of its being an calotype, the process of coating paper with silver chloride that had begun to replace the older daguerreotypes. Meanwhile, her son merely hovered, sometimes raising his chin to study the ceiling, sometimes staring unseeing out the French doors to the terrace.

The Hawkhursts made a circuit of the room, with Mrs. Hawkhurst scanning the furnishings with a critical eye. "Rather pedestrian," she murmured under her breath. "Entirely predictable. Good heavens, that wingback. It's positively shabby." As earlier, her husband nodded his agreement.

Phoebe's back stiffened. How dare this woman disparage Grampapa's favorite chair, the one he found such comfort in after a busy day of reviewing estate revenues?

Time to move on, she decided, as quickly as possible. "Please follow me, and we'll proceed into the withdrawing room. We don't use that room much anymore, but in the old days the ladies would retire there after dinner, while the men lingered in the dining room with their brandy and cigars. Then everyone would reassemble in the drawing room."

Amelia met them in the Great Hall. She had a pair of boys in tow, both of them looking decidedly pleased with themselves, although their expressions quickly melted into ones of feigned innocence when their teacher once more took charge of them. It was then Phoebe realized one of the adults was missing. Had someone lingered in the library? Slipped off in another direction? This time she sent Eva to search.

After the withdrawing room Phoebe led them into the music room and then the dining room, where she dispersed the visitors around the mahogany table to make room for everyone. She spoke of the herringbone flooring, partially covered by the ruby-and-sapphire tones of a Safavid dynasty Persian rug; the carved plaster medallion around the Waterford Crystal chandelier; the Italian sideboard; and the matching, marble-topped Second Empire ormolu buffets.

From there, they entered the long expanse of the drawing room. "It's filled with furniture now," she told her audience, "but in past decades it would have been cleared out, but for seating along the walls, the rugs taken up, and used as a ballroom."

Several more times, as she explained the origins of the room's design and furnishings, Phoebe appealed silently to Eva or Amelia to hunt down laggers and wanderers. By the time they reached the opposite end of the house and arrived in the Petit Salon, which had been cleared and tidied following breakfast, she estimated she had had more than a half-dozen such mutinies.

Near the end of the tour she sent the children outside with Miss Carmichael and Eva before escorting the adults into the little-used garden room. Not quite a conservatory, yet not quite a proper room, Grams had years ago declared it chill and damp most of the year and likely to cause any number of maladies. If the family wished to enjoy the outdoors, she had ruled, they could very well go outdoors. Yet Phoebe included it today because if its mid-nineteenth-century mosaic-tile floor and ceilings depicting the Greek creation mythologies of Gaia and Eros, both of whom sported rather scanty clothing—which Phoebe had always suspected influenced Grams's decision to shun the room.

Speaking of shunning . . . once again, they were a person short. Or was that two? Good heavens, the way the guests were milling about made it hard to tell who might be missing. Phoebe shook her head and reassured herself that in a mere few minutes the tour would be over.

"Here, along this wall, below these windows," she pointed out, "you see the Greek god Hermes and the goddess Hegemone in marble relief. This continuation of the nature theme represents the heralding of springtime, apropos in a room that would have been brimming with plants in my great-grandfather's time. And here—"

A gasp drew her up short. Had she miscalculated yet again and shocked her visitors with the artwork here? Yet as she looked around, she could see no trace of offense in the faces of the others—until her gaze landed on Amelia. Odd. Amelia had been in this room enough times to know it as well as Phoebe did, and she had years ago stopped giggling at the images. There was no mirth now in her sister's wide eyes or in how her teeth caught at the corner of her lips.

Inviting the guests to feel free to take closer looks around the room, she hastened to her sister. "What on earth has come over you?"

She pulled Phoebe farther into the corner and raised a shaky hand to point, albeit discreetly. "There. Him. Phoebe, he has a gun under his coat."

CHAPTER 3

"A gun?" Phoebe turned to look, but Amelia elbowed her in the ribs.

"Don't be obvious. We need to get these people out of here." She gasped again. "No, we have to warn them. They could be in danger. We must telephone the police."

"Sh! Don't do a thing. Let me handle it."

As he had in the other rooms, the young man who had accompanied Arvina Bell showed only a cursory interest in his surroundings. Phoebe meandered over to him, speaking a few words to some of the others along the way so he wouldn't realize she had him in her sights. "Have you enjoyed the tour?" she asked when she sidled up beside him.

"Oh, um . . . yes, very much. Thank you."

Phoebe couldn't help grinning at his barefaced lie. "I'd say you were bored to tears for most of it."

"No, that isn't true . . ."

"It's all right, I've a feeling you only came to accompany your . . . mother, is it?"

His entire bearing relaxed as he smiled down at her. "Yes, you're right. Mrs. Bell—Arvina Bell—is my mother.

I'm Hayden Bell. Do you know she's writing a book? That's what brought her here today."

"About the great houses of the Cotswolds. Yes, I was informed when the group booked the tour. Quite an undertaking on her part."

He nodded. "Between you and me, I'm not entirely sure she knew what she was getting herself into when she proposed writing the book, but a publisher called her bluff and now I'm wondering if she's up to the challenge."

His assessment elicited a laugh from Phoebe, who found herself enjoying his candor—despite Amelia having spotted a gun beneath his coat. Could she have been mistaken? "I'm sure she'll rise to the occasion. But please do tell her that if I can be of any assistance when it comes to the section about Foxwood Hall, she must telephone over. I'd be pleased to answer any questions or supply additional information." Her gaze fell to young Mr. Bell's coat, which, though unbuttoned, had fallen closed to conceal whether or not a weapon lurked beneath. She raised her eyes just as quickly, but he must have noticed, for he casually raised a hand to refasten the buttons.

"I'll relay your offer to my mother, thank you, Lady Phoebe."

"Tell me, have you been in the area long?" Phoebe asked him. "You and your mother are both unfamiliar to me, and I thought I knew every soul in and around Little Barlow."

"I grew up in Gloucester, and after my father died two years ago, my mother arranged to move here for a quieter life. She grew up in the area, you see, and only left when she married. I, on the other hand, have been away from Gloucester until recently. First the war, then London. But I'm in Cirencester now."

"A lovely town, Cirencester, but then, aren't *all* our Cotswold towns and villages lovely? If you'll excuse me, Mr. Bell, I'll be concluding things now."

Without looking hurried, she returned to Amelia. "I think he's all right. We had a very nice conversation."

"Nice conversation?" Amelia gawped as if witnessing the very flight of Phoebe's good sense. "Are you daft? He has a *gun.*"

Phoebe placed a hand on her sister's arm. "He fought in the war, Amellie. It's probably his old sidearm or something he picked up in a field somewhere. A lot of soldiers brought them home with them, even if they shouldn't have. After four harrowing years in the trenches and never knowing if you'll live or die in the next moment, it probably offers him a sense of comfort, of control."

"What about the ones who can't control the impulse to lash out?"

"I don't believe he's one of them. He's an amiable young man and we're not going to assume the worst. Let's start ushering everyone outside." She glanced around the room. "Now, where did Mr. Sadler go? And Miss Chapman. And speaking of Arvina Bell . . ."

Phoebe hoped they'd already gone outside to convene by the motorcars. What a morning. She couldn't remember ever being quite so happy to walk through the front door and down the steps to the drive.

Before bidding the children good-bye, Phoebe answered several more questions, which, she suspected, had been suggested to them by their teacher. Then they filed back onto their motor bus. Miss Carmichael thanked her heartily and apologized for any ill behavior on the part of her students.

"Nonsense." Phoebe waved away her concerns. "But I believe in future we'll arrange garden tours for children instead. Perhaps our head groundskeeper, Mr. Peele, would lead them, and we could even arrange for each child to plant something in a pot to take home. What do you think?"

"That's a splendid idea, Lady Phoebe. Do let us know if you decide to put it in action." With that, the woman boarded the motor bus, and they went on their way. Phoebe turned back to the historical society members, still mingling near their motorcars. Ah, there was Mr. Sadler. He must have left the garden room early to come outside. Oh, and Miss Chapman was snapping a few pictures of the roofline.

Phoebe walked over to the group to bid them a good day. "Thank you all so much for coming. I hope you enjoyed yourselves. Are there any final questions?"

"Has anyone seen my mother?" Mr. Bell sported a worried frown as he scanned the forecourt and the sweep of lawn on either side. "I appear to have lost track of her. Again."

"When did you see her last?" Phoebe asked him, ready to send Eva and Amelia searching.

He wrinkled his nose in thought. "To be honest, I'm not entirely sure. Certainly, in the drawing room. And, I believe, in the Petit Salon . . ." He reached up, slipping his fingers beneath the lock of hair that fell over his brow and rubbing back and forth. "I thought she was beside me as we entered the garden room. Did anyone see where she went?" he asked the society members.

Miss Chapman walked over, her stylish handbag slapping against her thigh. "I can't say I remember her being in the garden room."

"Nor I," Lady Primrose remarked. Her eyes narrowed as she apparently attempted to imagine the room with everyone in it.

"I lost track of her, too." Dr. Bishop smoothed the long handlebars of his mustache. He looked vaguely disappointed at having been given the slip. "She must have needed to make a notation about one of the other rooms."

"Probably waited behind and sneaked back into the garden room to study those lewd designs." Mrs. Hawkhurst sniffed and raised an eyebrow. "Goodness, Abel, have you *ever*?"

"Never, my dear," her husband said as if by rote, with little feeling behind the words.

"I thought they were artistic and really quite lovely," Lady Primrose remarked.

Mrs. Hawkhurst glared at her, and Lady Primrose's smile wilted.

"I'll go in and look for her." Amelia started for the front steps, but Phoebe stopped her. She couldn't have explained what prompted her to halt her sister in her tracks, only that an uneasy sensation had crept over her.

"Eva, would you go, please?"

"Of course." Eva hurried inside.

Several minutes passed before Eva reappeared. She stood framed in the front doorway several moments, looking lost, almost as if she stood poised before an unfamiliar scene. That ominous sensation closed around Phoebe. She set her feet in motion and met Eva at the bottom of the steps.

"My lady . . . something . . . has happened."

For a moment Phoebe had trouble finding her voice. She cleared her throat. "Did you find her?"

Eva nodded. "In the library. My lady . . ."

Phoebe needed no further explanation to understand something dreadful had happened. Without another word she hurried up the steps and made short work of the Great Hall. The relative dimness of the library made her strain to make out anything while her vision adjusted. At first, she saw nothing amiss. Then a pair of legs and the hem of a dark blue skirt took shape in the alcove of the large French window. One side of the curtains hung loose, concealing the rest of what—no, *who*—lay behind it. But those sensible Oxfords and sturdy ankles told her all she needed to know about the identity of the individual.

Eva came up beside her. "It's her. It's Mrs. Bell."

"Did you . . . look?"

"The tieback, my lady. It's around her neck."

"Here we are once again, Miss Huntford." Chief Inspector Perkins, who had for many years manned Little Barlow's tiny police station, let go a long-suffering sigh, as if he held Eva personally responsible for Arvina Bell's death, which, thankfully, he did not, despite her having found the body. "It's becoming a regular thing, isn't it?"

"Yes," she said, and sealed her lips, unwilling to respond to what had been, obviously, sarcasm on his part. He had already interviewed most of the family and all the members of the Little Barlow Chapter of the Greater Cotswold Historical Society, and combed through the library for evidence.

"Conducting tours, eh?" He cocked his head at her. She failed to see how the question would help lead him to the person who strangled Arvina Bell, so she didn't bother to unseal her lips. She could do this all day; as a lady's maid it was part of her job to keep opinions and observations to herself, hidden behind a placid expression. Not that she ever had to resort to such pretense with her ladies, but sometimes, when there were visitors at Foxwood Hall, or when they traveled to other estates, such skills had served her well. "All right, then, Miss Huntford. Can you account for the whereabouts of each historical society member at all times?"

It was her turn to let out a sigh. "Actually, I can't."

He studied her a long moment, his lips pinched, then signaled to his constable sitting off to the side with a pencil and notepad. "Brannock, bring the other two in here. Maybe we'll get to the bottom of things quicker questioning them all at once." The chief inspector's tone implied he had better things to do with his time, leading Eva to wonder what those things could possibly be.

Miles Brannock apparently wondered as well, for there was no mistaking his puzzled look as he rose and left the Petit Salon. Nor did Eva mistake the meaning of the slight lift of the corners of his mouth as he passed her, a tiny smile for her alone.

Miles, as she called him during their private time together, returned presently, escorting Phoebe and Amelia into the room. Mr. Perkins had them state their names, as if they weren't all well acquainted with one another. Then he repeated the same question he had asked Eva.

"There were so many of them," Lady Phoebe said, looking at a loss, an expression mirrored by Amelia. "I don't think we realized how difficult it would be keeping everyone together."

"No, we most certainly didn't realize." Lady Amelia plucked at the topmost tier of her skirt. "Our mistake seems to have been in inviting both the historical society and the children from the village school."

"Bit off more than you could chew, eh?" Mr. Perkins gave a dismissive snort.

"They simply kept slipping away," Lady Phoebe explained. "The children, the adults. Sometimes alone, other times in pairs. Often they would lag behind, poring over something that particularly interested them, once the rest of us had moved on. And the house *is* rather large, you see—"

"I am perfectly familiar with the size of the house, Lady Phoebe," the chief inspector snapped. "I'm not an idiot. All right, then. Brannock, make a note of the fact that these three"—he encompassed them all with a sweep of his sausagelike fingers, a gesture that made Eva wish to slap his hand—"had no notion of what they were doing. When we dusted the library for fingerprints and compared them to the ones we took of the tour guests, we found that *all* of them had touched *something*. Including the children, mind you. Is this what you had intended?"

"Well, no." Lady Phoebe brushed at imaginary wrinkles in her sleeve. "Of course not."

"Yet you invited a host of strangers into the house, then failed to keep track of them. Resulting in a woman's death."

"Sir?" Miles rarely interrupted during an interrogation, as Eva had learned over the past several years. His job, as constable, was to sit and take notes, not make observations. Yet make them he always did; he just didn't typically express them to his superior.

"A question, Brannock?" It wasn't an invitation for Miles to make an inquiry, but rather a sharp reprimand obviously intended to silence him. It didn't work.

"Yes, sir. Don't you think it's rather a far stretch to say opening Foxwood Hall to a tour resulted in Arvina Bell's death?" he asked in his light Irish brogue.

"They did open the house to a tour, didn't they?"

"Yes, sir, they did."

"And a woman is dead, isn't she?"

"True enough, sir. However, the one didn't necessarily lead to the other. Whoever killed Mrs. Bell in all likelihood would have done so at the first opportunity, whether here or elsewhere. Tossing the blame at the feet of Miss Huntford and Ladies Phoebe and Amelia is not only harsh, it's unfair, sir."

Chief Inspector Perkins turned an angry shade of scarlet, except for his nose, which always tended toward violet no matter his mood. Eva bit down on the insides of her cheeks, fearing Miles's career was about to screech to a jarring halt. Miles merely gazed placidly back at his superior, his bright blue eyes calm as if he hadn't a care in the world. The chief inspector's mouth opened, then closed and flattened, and he turned his attention back to Eva and the sisters.

"Did anything about any of these people strike you as unusual?"

All three shook their heads.

"Suspicious?"

Eva and Lady Phoebe again shook their heads. Lady Amelia, however, worried her bottom lip and peeked at the chief inspector from beneath her golden lashes.

"Lady Amelia? Did you see something suspicious? If you did, you had better speak up."

Lady Amelia turned to her sister, her eyes large and worried. "I don't *wish* to mention it, Phoebe," she whispered, "but mustn't I?"

Lady Phoebe blew out a breath. "I suppose you must. Go ahead, Amellie."

Eva had no idea what they were talking about and watched the youngest Renshaw sister fidget while she gathered her thoughts. Then, "The young gentleman. The victim's son. He had . . . well . . . a gun on him."

"What? Why wasn't I informed of this sooner? Brannock, go get him. Bring him to me this instant." To Eva and the sisters, the chief inspector said, "That's all for now. You may go."

"Chief inspector," Lady Phoebe said in a rush as Eva and Lady Amelia came to their feet, "I spoke with the gentleman in question. Nothing about him seemed at all dangerous. He had no interest in the house that I could see; he only came to accompany his mother. And . . . he fought in the war," she added, as if that explained everything.

That may have been so, Eva silently reasoned, but the effects of battle and the horror of the trenches had been known to severely cripple a man's mind, as well as his body, and prompt him to violent and irrational acts. Not in most cases, of course, but it had been known to happen. Could such have been the case today?

"No interest in the house," the chief inspected countered, his eyes going narrow and mean, "except perhaps to murder his mother here."

"It's not as if she was shot, though," Lady Phoebe tried again. "His gun is neither here nor there."

"His gun, Lady Phoebe, is about to be in my possession, and this man in my custody, unless he can account for his whereabouts at the precise moment his mother expired in your library."

Eva led the way out, with Lady Phoebe and Lady Amelia dragging their feet behind her. She could all but feel Lady Phoebe's effort to hold further arguments in check. In the Great Hall the rest of the family stood together: Lord and Lady Wroxly; Lady Julia, who held little Charles in her arms, and Hetta hovering close behind them; and their brother, Fox. They formed a small but formidable battalion at the base of the stairs.

Eva lingered nearer to the Petit Salon as her ladies went to speak with their family. Miles returned with Mr. Bell in tow. The young man traversed the Great Hall with his head down, his brow furrowed, his arms folded protectively across his chest. He didn't look up or acknowledge Eva as he passed her. His coat was buttoned and she saw no sign of the pistol. Miles gestured for him to enter the salon, while he himself lingered outside the doorway.

"I'm sorry Perkins spoke to the three of you that way, Eva. None of you is to blame."

She allowed herself the luxury of tracing his features with her gaze—the curve of his brow, the straight line of his nose, the unexpected lushness of his lips against his pale Irish complexion. From the high-placed windows opposite the first-floor gallery, sunlight streamed in and burnished his hair to a deep, rich russet. She longed to brush her fingers through it. Instead she placed her hand in his offered one and threaded her fingers through his. "I suppose it's his job to be impertinent."

"No, it isn't. He's in a particularly bad humor because he didn't like being called away from home today. I think he was a bit off his trolley last night. You know how he likes to cuddle up with his whiskey." This bit of information came in an undertone spoken close to her ear. His breath tickled her skin, and she longed to be elsewhere with him. They had been stepping out together these last few years. She knew him and she trusted him implicitly. If anyone could solve this case, it was Miles.

With a little help from Eva and Lady Phoebe, of course.

"Did you find any fingerprints in the alcove?" she asked.

"Nothing even faintly conclusive. A lot of people have looked out those windows since the last time the maids dusted. The family, the guests, the children, as evidenced by the small prints we found. And as for the cord itself, for our purposes it's impossible to obtain prints from braided silk. Besides, the killer might have worn gloves. Do you remember anyone doing so?"

Eva tried to think back. "Some of the ladies, initially, as ladies do."

"Not much help in that, I'm afraid."

"No." She pointed into the Petit Salon. "Will you tell me what's discussed in there?"

"Do you have to ask?"

"Brannock!" came an impatient call from inside.

"Duty calls." Miles gave her hand a squeeze and ducked his head lower to meet her gaze evenly; once again, the smile he showed her was for her alone. He didn't lean in to kiss her, but she felt kissed all the same. Then he released her and disappeared inside.

CHAPTER 4

"Do go ahead and say it, Grams." Phoebe could barely meet her grandmother's eye as she reached the huddle of her family at the foot of the Grand Staircase. Beyond them came the subdued murmurs of the historical society members in the drawing room, asked to remain until the chief inspector said otherwise. Amelia had gone straight into Grampapa's arms. She turned to regard Phoebe with a sorrowful look as Phoebe admitted to her grandmother, "You were right, and we were wrong. You told us so."

To her surprise, Grams shook her head and embraced her briefly. "I intend saying no such thing. No one could have foreseen what happened. I didn't like the idea, true, but I never thought anything more than an inconvenience would come of it. Certainly, nothing of this sort."

A bit of the weight lifted from Phoebe's chest. "Thank you, Grams."

"What happens now?" Julia shifted Charles higher in her arms, which prompted Hetta to lean in and offer to take the child.

"If Madame's arms grow tired, I take him," the maid said in her heavily accented English. From Switzerland,

Hetta had spoken very little English when she had first come to serve Julia more than a year ago.

Julia passed him over. "See if you can put him down, thank you, Hetta." She turned back to Phoebe. "I thought I stayed away long enough this morning for the house to have settled back to normal. Had I known I'd walk into a crime scene, I'd have gotten myself a nice suite of rooms somewhere—anywhere—for the evening."

"Now, now, my dear." Grampapa placed a hand on Julia's shoulder. "It's not Phoebe's fault. Your sister meant well, and it was a sound idea, but for what happened."

The door of the Petit Salon opened abruptly. Chief Inspector Perkins strode out and continued across the hall to them. "We'll be going presently. I believe we have our killer."

"You mean Mr. Bell?" Had Phoebe been wrong about the young man? He had seemed so amiable. So temperate in his manners. Appearances could be deceiving, of course, and he *did* have a gun. "Has he confessed?"

"Confess? Don't be ridiculous." The man's comment prompted a loud clearing of Grampapa's throat, which, in turn, caused the chief inspector to duck his head in deference. "Forgive my cheek, sir. But, no, Lady Phoebe, he's denying it with all the fervor of a barefaced liar."

She wasn't about to be dismissed by this man. "What did he have to say about the gun?"

"It's a Luger. German. Says he picked it up in a field at the end of the war and brought it home."

Grams's eyes went wide with indignation. "Why on earth would he bring a gun here?"

"He claims, Lady Wroxly, that he was the victim of a cutpurse in London some months ago. A nasty one, according to him. Bloke beat him soundly when he resisted. P'haps it's true, p'haps not. Doesn't much matter. I've dealt with his kind before. Sons and mothers, indeed. I can tell you, I've seen no shortage of resentment between young men and their aging mothers. Especially when the mother holds the purse strings."

"Does she?" Julia asked; for no particular reason, Phoebe thought, than to satisfy her curiosity.

"He admitted that he stands to inherit her house and a modest savings to go with it. He clerks for an accountant in Cirencester, so, frankly, he likely could use extra cash coming in."

"But it makes no sense that he would murder her here," Phoebe insisted. "Why not in her own home, where he might have made it look like a break-in?"

"Who knows?" Mr. Perkins rubbed his nose. "If there was any logic at work here, he wouldn't have murdered her at all."

Phoebe believed differently. A murderer always believed he or she acted logically, twisted though their justifications might seem to everyone else.

Down the hall, Constable Brannock led Mr. Bell out of the Petit Salon. The young man put up no resistance at all; he seemed dazed and perhaps not entirely aware of what was happening. Constable Brannock didn't at all look as though he relished his present task, and even hastened to steady his prisoner with a hand at his upper arm when Mr. Bell nearly tripped on the hall runner.

Constable Brannock didn't stop as he passed Phoebe and the others, but kept Mr. Bell walking to the front door. Phoebe stepped forward. Was the man guilty? Did he somehow snap in the library, grab the nearest article to use as a weapon—a drapery cord—and rid himself of a mother who had become overbearing and impossible to live with? Had she said something to set him off? Had there been animosity building between them, perhaps since he came home from the war? Perhaps he didn't measure up in her eyes, and she had stolen every opportunity to let him know it. In a way Chief Inspector Perkins had spoken true, not just about mothers and sons, but any family members. Add to that the effects of the war on a man's psyche, and one could find oneself in a volatile situation.

But surely Mr. Perkins had made his judgment far too quickly, based on one simple fact: Hayden Bell had carried a gun under his coat.

"Mr. Bell," she said as he and Constable Brannock paused before the front door. Phoebe crossed to them. "Is there anyone we can contact for you?"

"Thank you, Lady Phoebe, but no. I'll contact the office I work for. I clerk for a group of solicitors, you see. I'll . . . er . . . let them know I won't be at work tomorrow morning."

She nodded, and Constable Brannock took him out. Behind her, she heard her grandparents speaking with Chief Inspector Perkins.

"Through the dining room?" Grams asked him to clarify. Curious, Phoebe returned to them, taking the hand Amelia reached out to her and holding it tight.

"Indeed, Lady Wroxly. It looks like he let himself out through the French doors in the library, and back in through the dining room."

"I thought the dining-room doors were locked," Grampapa commented. "They usually are this time of day."

"Broken window," the chief inspector informed him. "He was able to reach in and unlock the door."

"Heavens, so easily?" Grams shuddered. "It's getting so we'll have to post guards throughout the house night and day. Such things never happened when we were young. The thought of our peace being disturbed in such a way never entered our minds years ago, before the war. Isn't that right, Archibald?"

Grampapa agreed with a nod. "Not here, in the country. In London perhaps, but never here." He shook his head sadly.

Raising an eyebrow, Julia cocked her head to the chief inspector. "I suppose you inquired where everyone was at the time of the crime?"

"The problem, Lady Annondale, is that the exact time of the crime cannot be accurately pinned down. And your sisters here . . . Well."

"Well, what?" Julia raised the other eyebrow and turned her inquiries toward Phoebe and Amelia. "What does that mean?"

"It means we couldn't keep track of everyone at all times." Phoebe slid her gaze away from her eldest sister, having no desire to see the censure in Julia's countenance.

"Seems they were in all manner of places at different times." Mr. Perkins reached into his coat pocket as if looking for a pad of paper, but came up empty. He tapped his chin instead. "Let's see now . . . Mr. and Mrs. Hawkhurst at one point were in the drawing room gazing out at the gardens. Lady Primrose said she lingered in the dining room, returned to the music room, and ended up in the Petit Salon after the others had left it. Ophelia Chapman sneaked belowstairs for a peek at the kitchen and such. Said she wanted details for some articles she's writing. And Eamon Sadler hurried up the stairs for a quick look at the portraits hanging in your gallery."

"Can anyone corroborate any of this?" Phoebe asked.

The chief inspector shrugged. "The servants did see Miss Chapman belowstairs, so her story checks out. As for the rest . . ." He shrugged. "What does it matter? Each of them is an upstanding member of the community. Are you going to tell me Lady Primrose Scott, the wife of an MP, committed murder? Or either of the Hawkhursts? Really now." He chugged a condescending laugh.

"What about Mr. Bell?" she persisted. "Did he say how he and his mother became separated?" That was one detail that niggled at her, and probably wasn't in Hayden Bell's favor.

"He claims his mother dallied more than once, and he'd had to backtrack to find her. The last time?" The chief inspector shrugged. "If you ask me, a house full of itinerant visitors gave him the perfect opportunity to rid himself of a mother who had become a nuisance. It's my job now to extract a confession out of him. If you'll excuse me, I'll say good day. Lord and Lady Wroxly." He nodded in deference and set his bowler on his thinning hair.

"It's your job to find the truth of the matter," Phoebe murmured to his retreating back. The low hum of voices in the drawing room reminded her that the rest of their visitors were still in the house. She turned to her grandparents. "I'll go tell them all they can leave now. The chief inspector apparently forgot to."

"I'll come with you." Amelia was still holding fast to Phoebe's hand. Together they entered the drawing room, where all eyes instantly fixed upon them. Fairfax, apparently playing host to the group, trotted over from where he had been nosing Mr. and Mrs. Hawkhurst's hands, eliciting a sour look from the latter.

"Hayden Bell has been arrested," Phoebe announced, seeing little reason to prevaricate. "Or, at least, he's been taken in on suspicion of murdering his mother."

"Good heavens." Vesta Hawkhurst surged to her feet. "This is appalling. What a harrowing day. Who could have imagined . . ." She broke off and wiped a hand against her side. She then lifted her handbag, snapped it open, and dug inside. Whatever she found was too small for Phoebe to make out, but she held it between her thumb and forefinger and slipped it between her lips.

Her husband rose beside her. "It's all right, my dear. Don't upset yourself any further." To Phoebe, he said, "I take it we're permitted to leave, then?"

"Yes, that's what I came in to tell you. You may all go. And you have our deepest apologies for . . . well . . . for how things turned out today."

Lady Primrose also rose from an armchair near the terrace doors. "In light of what did happen, Lady Phoebe, might one assume the society will be reimbursed for the entrance fees?"

Eva made her way along the garden path to the hothouses. As the wooden framework with myriad glass panels rose against the sky, she remembered another of Lady Phoebe's ideas for putting the estate to better use. Expand the hothouses and the kitchen garden to grow enough produce to be sold at market, as they had done during the war. Once again, the countess had been appalled. Now, during peacetime, that was the job of the tenant farms, she had insisted; her husband was no gentleman farmer, nor would he be made to be one. In truth, Eva didn't believe the earl would have objected, had his wife been amenable to the notion. But Lady Wroxly had dismissed it with even more vehemence than she had the house tours, and that had been that.

The countess couldn't be blamed, not entirely. As Phoebe often pointed out, Lady Wroxly feared the changing times, which had snowballed during the war and now catapulted ahead at breakneck speed. The old, ordered ways would never return, and everything familiar and comfortable to the countess seemed in danger of disappearing forever.

At the hothouse that supplied the manor with flowers year-round, she turned in and gently closed the door behind her. She scanned the rows stretching before her. "Lady Phoebe?"

A reddish gold halo of upswept hair popped out from behind a stand of potted mandarin trees, each teeming with tiny white blossoms. "Over here."

Eva set out toward her, pleased as ever her lady hadn't chosen to bob her hair as so many women were doing. The Renshaw sisters had such lovely hair, all in different shades of gold, thick and wavy but not untamable, a joy for Eva to arrange with pins, combs, and the like.

Lady Phoebe held a pair of clippers, a basket filled with fragrant blossoms at her feet. When Eva reached her, Lady Phoebe cast a circumspect glance out the nearest glass panel. "Did anyone follow you?"

"No, there was no one in the service yard when I came out." She shoved her hands into the pockets of her cardigan. Despite it being May, the air had taken on a sharpness, or had today's events simply sapped her body of warmth?

"Good. Neither Mrs. Sanders nor Mrs. Ellison should send anyone out here for another hour at least, so we have time to speak privately."

The housekeeper and cook, respectively, would each be sending out an assistant for flowers for the dining-room table and anything needed for the preparation of dinner. For now, Eva and Phoebe could count on being left alone.

Lady Phoebe gestured toward her basket. "Grams loves the fragrance of mandarin blossoms and I thought these would lift her spirits. She's having a lie-down before dinner. What happened today has left her shaken, to be sure. And Grams is not shaken by much."

"I'm sure they'll help cheer her."

"I had to try something."

"Finding the killer would do," Eva suggested. "Assuming it isn't Hayden Bell."

"I honestly don't know if he did it or not. I can't decide. When Trent Mercer was accused of murdering his father last autumn, I *knew* in my very bones he didn't do it. I might have had smidgeons of doubt once or twice, but overall I knew Trent would be proven innocent." Phoebe set the clippers aside. "What I *do* know is the chief inspector made his judgment hastily, based on the scantiest of circumstantial evidence. If Mr. Bell *is* guilty, it would be difficult for a jury to convict him and he could be let go. Or, if he *isn't* guilty, he could hang for something he didn't do."

"I agree. Mr. Perkins has made a shoddy job of it. Again."

"Then let's go over what we know."

Side by side, they began a slow stroll of the aisles, working their way up and down past stands of flowering plants ranging from those found locally to the farthest reaches of the British Isles, to exotic places such as the Orient and South America. Rich, sweet fragrances filled the air, from tiny blossoms in soft hues to vibrant blooms so large they would fill Eva's hand.

Lady Phoebe held up one finger and began by saying, "Arvina Bell was strangled in the library with a thickly braided drapery cord, and nowhere on the body, the cord, or elsewhere in the room are there fingerprints that point specifically to her murderer."

"And nothing was stolen from the library," Eva went on, "or from Mrs. Bell's person. She still wore the mourning brooch I'd noticed on her lapel this morning. And her handbag was on the floor near her, her purse still inside, the money apparently untouched. It almost reminds me of . . ." She trailed off, thinking of a night last autumn, when, in their efforts to clear Trent Mercer's name, they had found themselves victims of a cutpurse. Lady Phoebe's bag had been snatched, only to be dropped nearby by the escaping culprit, the money all there.

"Yes," Lady Phoebe agreed, "I noticed the parallel, too. No, I would venture to rule out money as a motivator."

"Unless, as Mr. Perkins suspects, Hayden Bell was motivated to inherit his mother's property."

Lady Phoebe acknowledged the possibility by inclining her head. "Let's move on for the moment. Whoever murdered Mrs. Bell appears to have exited the room through the French doors onto the terrace."

"And let him or herself back into the house through the dining room. Have you had a chance to look at the broken windowpane?"

"I did that right before I came here. It was a neat break."

"Neat? How so, my lady?"

Lady Phoebe help up two hands to simulate a small windowpane. "There were no marks on the frame around it, no chips or scratches, so whatever was used must have been small enough to break only the glass."

"A rock, perhaps."

Lady Phoebe frowned. "Perhaps."

"Or a fist."

"There would have been blood."

"Not if the killer wore gloves, which would account for a lack of distinguishing fingerprints." They turned into the next aisle, and Eva brushed the fronds of a palm tree aside. "There isn't a lot to go on."

"Not in physical evidence, no." Lady Phoebe's eyebrows drew tightly inward. "A lack of fingerprints, the possibility of the killer wearing gloves. It certainly suggests some amount of premeditation, doesn't it? Not necessarily having to do with the murder itself; that might have been a last-minute necessity. But someone might have come to Foxwood Hall with a certain plan in mind."

"To what end, though, if nothing was stolen?" Eva folded her hands at her waist as they continued walking, threading her fingers as if to weave together strands of logic. "Perhaps we should focus on the society members themselves, rather than the evidence. They are all quite different from one another. Different walks of life, different circumstances. I'd say the only thing most have in common is their involvement with the historical society."

"Hayden Bell isn't a member. He was exceedingly quiet during the tour, almost as if he didn't wish to bring attention to himself." Lady Phoebe gently fingered a bloom on the stand of orchids they passed. "That in itself could be seen as suspicious."

"You said he wasn't particularly interested in seeing the house, that he'd just accompanied his mother." Eva thought back. "I wonder if he was helping her with the book she was writing."

"If he had taken an interest in the project, it doesn't seem likely he'd kill her in the middle of it. But what about the others? Mr. and Mrs. Hawkhurst are sheer poison. Did you hear their comments about the house?"

"I did, my lady. They were horribly rude. Made me wonder why they bothered coming at all. Dr. Bishop, on the other hand, was courteous and rather quiet, like Hayden Bell, except when he was attempting to catch up with Mrs. Bell. But he did show an interest in everything you spoke about. Mr. Sadler too."

"Yes, Eamon Sadler. A rather stodgy fellow for someone his age. He was particularly interested in the library. Couldn't wait to get inside. His eagerness might almost make one suspect him." Lady Phoebe shrugged. "Then again, why *wouldn't* a bookseller be interested in seeing a library?"

"There then were Miss Chapman, the magazine writer, and Lady Primrose, both politely interested, both attentive," Eva said.

"And both of whom wandered off alone, at least once

each, during the tour." Lady Phoebe came to a halt in front of a dwarf Victoria plum tree, according to the placard stuck into the pot. "Going back to the Hawkhursts, they appeared in accord with each other, although I did notice that Mrs. Hawkhurst's opinions took precedence, with her husband readily agreeing with whatever she said."

"I noticed that, too, my lady. We can tell who's in charge in that marriage."

"Did you also notice the friction between the Hawkhursts and Lady Primrose? I wonder what it's about." Lady Phoebe plucked a violet blossom and handed it to Eva. She held it beneath her nose and inhaled the light scent.

"Historical society business, I would imagine," Eva said. "Lady Primrose is the treasurer, is she not?"

"She is. Do you think there could be some chicanery with the finances?"

"Possibly, but I'm not sure how that would have involved Mrs. Bell," Eva mused.

Lady Phoebe shrugged. "She might have discovered the theft and threatened to expose the culprit."

"I don't know about either Hawkhurst, but I cannot imagine Primrose Scott harming a fly." Eva almost laughed at the thought.

Lady Phoebe did, then laughed again as she said, "Or Vesta Hawkhurst, for that matter. She might dirty her hands or break a nail, and that would never do. Come, we'd better get back before someone comes looking for us."

"One thing we can be sure of, my lady." Eva reached for Lady Phoebe's hand and gave it a reassuring squeeze. "Miles won't let things rest until the truth comes out. If Hayden Bell is innocent of his mother's murder, he'll find a friend in Miles Brannock. Miles won't be deterred by Chief Inspector Perkins wishing to have done with this case."

CHAPTER 5

Phoebe and Eva parted ways at the gate in the privet hedge. Eva continued to the service entrance, and Phoebe went through the gate into the formal gardens and up the terrace steps. Fox met her in the drawing room, Fairfax at his side. Phoebe bent to greet the animal rather than face her brother's disapproving frown.

"Where the devil have you been?"

Her first instinct, as she straightened, was to inform him her whereabouts were none of his business. But the urgency lurking beneath his irritation changed her mind. "Why? What's happened?"

"Grampapa discovered something missing, that's what. Come along, he's in the library." He pivoted on his heel.

"Something missing from the library?" Phoebe hurried to keep up with him. Fairfax trotted along beside her, seeming eager to join in on this latest development. "But we looked the room over more than once. There was nothing—"

"Apparently, there is." Fox's heels clunked rapidly across the marble flooring of the Great Hall, each step echoing against the vaulted ceiling two stories above them.

Phoebe decided not to question him further. She would have her answer momentarily.

Their grandparents were in the library. That was, Grampapa was in the library, while Grams hovered on the threshold. Amelia and Julia stood off to one side, their faces mirroring Phoebe's own puzzlement. Fox came up behind Grams and placed a hand on the center of her back. "We're here, Grams," he said gently. "I found Phoebe."

Despite the terse way he'd greeted Phoebe in the drawing room, she now felt a smidgeon of pride in him for the solicitous manner he showed Grams. It was a significant change from his indifferent arrogance of only two or three years ago. Fox had matured in the past year, and while he sometimes fell back on his old ways, especially with his sisters, she had begun to see the future earl taking shape within the boy.

Phoebe went to the threshold and put an arm around Grams's shoulders, relieved when she didn't stiffen or, worse, pull away. True, Grams had earlier absolved Phoebe of all responsibility for what happened, and she never uttered a word she didn't mean, but until this moment Phoebe hadn't realized how much guilt she carried for a murder occurring here, in their home. The very fact that only Grampapa had ventured past the doorway, while the others lingered in the hall, spoke of a long time passing before the shock and horror of this day would begin to fade.

Phoebe kissed her grandmother's cheek and stepped around her, leaving the Staffordshire bull pup at Grams's side to offer her what comfort he could. She went to her grandfather's side. "Fox says something was stolen. What is it, Grampapa?"

He had been making another sweep of the room, poring over the bookshelves and examining the surface of every table and cupboard. Even looking inside.

"Grampapa, we did this already. The police searched, too. Please, what was taken?"

He returned to her and raised a hand to her cheek. "It's nothing of value. I don't understand it at all. But the photograph of my parents that has sat there these many years"— he pointed to the small marquetry side table beside his wing chair—"is gone. I've sent below for Mrs. Sanders. She should be here any moment."

"I remember it being there during the tour." She also remembered Arvina Bell's apparent fascination with it. The photo had been a favorite of Phoebe's as a child. She had loved to hold it close by its gilded frame and stare at her great-grandmother's beautiful wedding dress. Her great-grandparents had been married in 1840, after Queen Victoria had popularized bridal gowns of pure white lace and satin and long flowing veils. Phoebe had thought Great-Granny Eloise had looked like a princess, and she had yearned to someday wear that very dress at her own wedding.

Footsteps broke into her memories as Mrs. Sanders, Foxwood Hall's housekeeper, came into the room. She entered calmly enough, her hands folded at her waist, her peppered hair pulled neatly back in a bun at her nape, and her dark clothing crisp and wrinkle free. Yet her gray eyes held wariness, as if she feared she had done something to jeopardize her position. And here they were in the very room where someone had died that very morning. Did poor Mrs. Sanders believe she would somehow be blamed?

"My lord, you sent for me?" Her voice held the dignified cordiality with which she always addressed any member of the family. Yes, Mrs. Sanders saved that steely-edged tone for the lower servants. Still, Phoebe heard a note of caution.

She understood Mrs. Sanders's trepidation. The housekeeper was never, never sent for in the middle of the day, not to this part of the house. She tried to catch the woman's eye so she could offer a smile of reassurance, but Mrs. Sanders's gaze never wavered from Grampapa's.

"Thank you for coming, Mrs. Sanders."

The woman bobbed her head. Grampapa walked past her and came to stand by the wingback chair. He gestured at the table. "Mrs. Sanders, has the photo of my parents been taken belowstairs for any reason? Perhaps to polish the frame?"

The housekeeper had begun shaking her head before he'd finished speaking. "No, my lord. I can assure you it has not. It was polished only last week, and though it is dusted daily, it isn't due for another polishing for another week."

"And have you ever known any of the servants to take an interest in it?"

"No, my lord. I can't think of any reason why any of them would take more than a passing interest in such an item."

"Please inquire with them just the same, Mrs. Sanders."

"I will, my lord. Will that be all?"

"Yes, thank you, Mrs. Sanders."

Once the woman had made her retreat, Phoebe repeated what she had already told her grandfather. "I remember the photo being there during the tour. One of the visitors . . . well . . . it was Mrs. Bell herself . . . seemed fascinated by it. I can't begin to imagine why, other than it being part of the history of the house. Perhaps she was interested in learning about our ancestors for her book?"

"Perhaps." Grampapa looked about him, as if expecting to find the missing photo. "But that doesn't explain where it went. Poor Mrs. Bell didn't take it, but perhaps whoever killed her did. What could an old wedding photo possibly mean to anyone outside this family?"

An uneasiness crawled through Phoebe, but she waited

until the family had dispersed and she was able to speak with Grampapa alone. She found him in the billiard room at the top of the Grand Staircase.

Before she entered, she could hear the halfhearted taps and clinks of the balls, a sign her grandfather was putting little effort into his solitary game. Bending for his next shot, he looked up as she came in, appearing mildly surprised as she went to the rack on the wall and selected a cue stick.

"Mind if I have a go?"

He gestured at the table. "Be my guest, please. You girls don't often join me here."

Phoebe couldn't help grinning at the irony of that. "We were rarely encouraged to."

"No, I suppose you're right. Your grandmother doesn't consider billiards a proper pastime for young ladies. Perhaps I should have sneaked you in."

Phoebe hit the cue ball, resulting in the three-ball rolling into a corner pocket. Grampapa's eyebrows went up.

"It appears I didn't need to sneak you in. You took care of that yourself."

Phoebe sent another ball rolling across the felt, this time into a side pocket. She felt her grandfather's eyes upon her as she straightened.

"Why don't you tell me what's on your mind, my dear. I can tell it's something more than the fact of Mrs. Bell's death, though I would venture to guess it's related."

He had always been able to read her moods. She laid the cue stick across the table. "I've been thinking. Please don't take this the wrong way."

"I won't know how to take it until you tell me what it is." He set his own cue stick down beside hers. Taking her hand, he brought her to the long leather sofa beneath the bank of windows overlooking the formal gardens. He handed her down onto the cushions in gentlemanly fashion and settled beside her. "Now, then . . ."

Phoebe drew a breath to steel herself for an unsavory subject. "I began thinking about the possibility that Mrs. Bell wished to learn more about our ancestors."

"That isn't so unusual, given the nature of the book she was writing."

"Yes, but with the photo apparently stolen, I believe it might have meant more to her, and to whoever murdered her, than simply the history of our family."

"I'm afraid I'm not following you, my dear. What else *could* it mean?"

Phoebe needed another deep breath before going on. "Grampapa, are we all that remains of the Renshaw family? I'm talking about direct descendants of your parents."

"I know of no others . . ." He trailed off, his lips remaining parted as he studied her features. "Are you insinuating what I think you're insinuating?"

He had spoken sternly, and more bluntly than he typically did to Phoebe and her sisters. She didn't reply, and his complexion darkened.

"Where on earth could you have gotten a notion such as that?" He started to rise.

Phoebe stilled him with a hand on his forearm. "Don't be angry, Grampapa. It's not uncommon, you know. There could be—"

"Illegitimate Renshaws running about? Again, what put such a notion into your head? It's no proper subject for a gently bred young lady."

"Grampapa, please. I'm not a child anymore, and such things neither shock me nor . . ." She paused to find the right words. When she struck upon them, she concluded more confidently, "Nor negate the values you and Grams, and my parents before you, instilled in me. I assure you,

I'm merely trying to understand what happened here today."

After a lengthy pause, he relaxed beside her. "Yes. I apologize, my dear. I clearly overreacted. It's just that you're accusing my father of a dreadful betrayal of my mother."

"Not *accusing*. Only suggesting a possibility. Will you at least allow me to do a little searching, here in the house?"

"You're speaking of their diaries and other personal effects, aren't you?" When Phoebe didn't answer, he patted her knee. "You'll find what you need in a storeroom on the second floor. Mrs. Sanders can let you in. But say nothing of this to your grandmother, please."

Eva entered Lady Phoebe's bedroom to find her and Amelia sitting on the floor near the hearth, several photograph albums spread out on the rug around them. "Have you found anything?"

Both young ladies shook their heads, and Lady Phoebe said, "Not yet. But we're not giving up hope. Grampapa is certain there's a duplicate wedding photo in one of these albums." She turned to the next page, each of thick, heavy cardboard. "He and Grams had the albums made years later, so they're familiar with their contents."

She closed the one she'd been perusing, then patted its wooden cover decorated in faded scarlet velvet and rose-pink ribbon. "I thought for sure it would be in this one. There are pictures of Great-Granny Eloise and her sisters taken in their family home before they left for the church. Then some in front of the church itself, and then here, in front of the house, and on the terrace. The one we're searching for was taken in the library itself."

"It must have been dreadfully expensive to have so many pictures taken in those days," Eva observed, gazing down over Lady Phoebe's shoulder. "My parents have only two photos from their wedding, and that was many years later when photography wasn't nearly as expensive."

"I suppose Great-Grandpapa and Great-Granny hadn't had those concerns." Phoebe opened another album and added absently, "Not then, anyway."

Perhaps not, Eva thought, but by the end of the century, it had become clear the old ways could not continue indefinitely. The economy had shifted from farming to industry, while at the same time crop prices had dropped, leaving the great estates cash poor and scrambling to find solutions. Hence the sudden flood of American heiresses who now held English titles. Such solutions had proved temporary at best, but who could have foreseen the Great War and the devastating blow it would deal, not only to the country's finances, but traditional ways of thinking?

Eva went to stand over Lady Amelia, still turning pages in the album open in her lap. "Anything there?"

"The photos in this one appear to be later." She pointed without looking up. "A shame they didn't date them. Oh, goodness. Phoebe, do come and see. I believe this is Grampapa as a baby."

Lady Phoebe scooted across the rug, while Eva crouched beside Lady Amelia for a better view. She smiled at the image. A woman, her wide belled skirts arranged around her, held a babe of no more than a year on her lap, the child swathed in what appeared to be a gown of airy lawn. Wisps of pale hair curled around his forehead, and long lashes shadowed cherubic cheeks and a tiny mouth set in a pout.

Eva looked closer. "He appears to be sleeping."

"No doubt," Phoebe said with a chuckle. "In those days, how else to entice a baby to sit still long enough for the photographer to capture the image?"

After they had looked their fill, Lady Amelia set that

album aside and turned to another. Lady Phoebe went back to the one she had been looking through, and Eva picked up another. Although she had glimpsed the photograph in question, she wasn't nearly as familiar with it as her two ladies. Still, if she came across any wedding photos, she would bring them to their attention. The albums themselves were works of art, the thick page bordering each photograph decorated with flowering vines, birds, and butterflies. The minutes ticked by in quiet companionship. It might almost have been a pleasant afternoon.

And then Lady Phoebe's hand came down with a thwack. "This is it!"

She instantly came to her feet and brought the album to the dressing table. There she worked the photograph carefully out through the slot through which it had been slipped into the framework of the page. Beckoning to Eva and Lady Amelia, she carried it to the window to study it in what little sunlight the overcast sky offered.

"What is it about this photo?" she murmured. "What's so special here?" She pushed the photo at Eva. "You look. Maybe I'm too close to it."

Eva took the photograph, mindful of the edges of the old paper, however thick it was. The previous Lord and Lady Wroxly were standing side by side, her arm linked through his. In her other hand she held a bouquet of lilies and baby's breath. They both wore serious, almost solemn, expressions, but she knew that to be common in photographs from the period, as it took several minutes for the image to be processed onto the paper in the camera.

"The background is quite fuzzy." Eva looked across at her ladies. "I can't make out any distinct details."

"What about their clothing?" Lady Amelia came to peer over Eva's shoulder. "Is there anything significant about what they're wearing?" She bent closer to the photograph, her finger tracing little circles in the air near the image.

"Grams has those earrings now. And the brooch. Oh, and the ropes of pearls, of course, though she rarely wears them anymore." She wrinkled her nose and glanced up at Phoebe. "One supposes all that jewelry is worth a fortune. Could that be it?"

"You mean that someone wanted a record of the kind of jewelry to be found here?" Eva thought a moment. "It's possible, although why steal the photograph? A thief would deduce that there is a lot more than this to be found, although the lion's share is locked away in the silver vault, isn't it?"

"It is, and someone would either need to be an expert safecracker or come armed with a stick of dynamite." Lady Phoebe joined them near the bed. "But I believe you're right, Eva. No one needs an old photograph to tell them there has been valuable jewelry passed down through the generations. Like the estate itself, Grams and Grampapa say we're merely the custodians of such things until we hand them on to the next generation." She stared hard at the photo. "Honestly, I would never wear much of it. The smaller items that have sentimental value, perhaps, but those pearls, for instance? Amelia, can you imagine?"

Lady Amelia chuckled. "You could tie a person up with ropes so long. But, no, I'm in agreement with you, Phoebe. So much good could be done if we were to . . ." Phoebe nodded thoughtfully and Amelia compressed her lips, frowning. "But if we're merely the custodians, have we the right to sell any of it?"

Lady Phoebe replied by slipping an arm around her sister, then returned her attention to the photograph. She reached to take it from Eva. "You're right about the background being too blurry for us to make out anything important. Yet something in this photo *is* important, but we're missing it."

Eva considered the events of the morning. "Mrs. Bell

was killed in the library. This photo was taken in the library. Perhaps the answer is there, in that very room. But if so, again, why steal the photograph?"

"Let's not forget the two events occurred some eighty years apart," Lady Amelia reminded her. "How can what happened so long ago be related to Mrs. Bell's death?"

Lady Phoebe darted a gaze at her sister, and Eva caught the uncertainty in her expression. But then Lady Phoebe seemed to come to a decision and her expression cleared. "I've actually been mulling that over. And wondering . . . Perhaps there are descendants we didn't know about. Ones who now wish to make their claim on what they see as their inheritance."

"Phoebe, don't be silly. How can we have relatives we're unaware of?" Lady Amelia eyed her sister askance, before the realization apparently dawned on her. "You mean . . . ones from the wrong side of the sheets?"

Eva bit down on the inside of her lip to prevent herself from grinning. Lady Amelia had matured into a lovely young woman, yet she retained a certain naivete and ingenuousness. Eva hoped she never entirely lost them.

"Yes," Lady Phoebe replied calmly. "And perhaps the photo is symbolic to the individual."

Her sister's cheeks glowed with chagrin. "Then Great-Grandpapa would have . . ."

"Studying this picture convinces me that such might be the case. There is nothing else here, no other clues to go on." Lady Phoebe handed the photo back to Eva. "Grampapa has given me permission to search through our great-grandparents' personal documents. They're in the attic. I'm going to get started tomorrow."

"I'll help you," Lady Amelia offered, but faintly, as if her heart wouldn't be in it.

Lady Phoebe smiled kindly at her sister. "You needn't. Eva and I can manage. Right, Eva?"

"Of course. But while we pore through old records looking for indications of . . . well . . . of secret relatives . . . we also need to consider, quite carefully, each and every member of the historical society. Because if there *is* an unknown descendant of your great-grandfather's coming for their perceived share of the Renshaw legacy, it must be one of them, mustn't it?"

CHAPTER 6

Phoebe awoke the next morning to the sounds of commotion in the corridor. Gray light seeped through a gap in her curtains, and the clock on her bedside table confirmed the earliness of the hour. Quickly donning her wrapper, she opened her door to discover a trunk and several valises being carried out of Julia's bedroom. Her grandmother stood nearby, her face gripped by sadness.

"Grams, what's going on?"

Before Grams could answer, Julia called out from inside the room. "I'm leaving, that's what's going on."

Phoebe waited until Douglas, one of the footmen, came through the doorway with a valise in one hand and a leather case tucked under the other arm, and then went into Julia's room. "Leaving? Now? At seven in the morning?"

"I want an early start. I can't stay here right now, Phoebe, not with Charles. It's too dangerous. I'm taking him to Lyndale Park."

"I understand your fears, of course." Phoebe watched as Julia checked through some of the drawers in the clothes press, then strode into her dressing room, apparently making sure she hadn't forgotten anything important. "But is Lyndale Park a good idea? With the baby? What about Ernie?"

She referred to Ernest Shelton, second cousin to Julia's deceased husband, Gilbert Townsend. Before Charles's birth, Ernie had been Gil's heir and had set all his hopes, not to mention ambitions, on eventually inheriting the estate, fortune, and business concerns, along with the title of Viscount Annondale. To put it mildly, Ernie had not been pleased with the birth of Julia's son, nor had he taken pains to conceal his ill will toward the child, and toward Julia.

Julia dismissed Phoebe's concerns with a shrug of one shoulder as she came back into the room holding a cashmere shawl. "Ernie's not currently at Lyndale Park. After sulking the rest of the winter after the news of Charles's birth, he packed himself into his motorcar at the first hint of spring, and no one has seen or heard from him since."

"Good heavens, not at all? Maybe something happened to him."

"I doubt it. Ernie is nothing if not thoroughly resilient. He's probably in London, or maybe even Brighton, spending his inheritance. It's not as if Gil left him destitute. One would think Ernie might show a smidgeon of gratitude. Ah, Hetta, there you are."

The Swiss woman filled the doorway, her arms secure around baby Charles, who stuck out his hand to wave at his mother and Phoebe. Hetta came in, followed by Grams.

"Let me hold him for a moment, Hetta." Grams's entire manner transformed as Hetta transferred Charles into her arms. Known for a demeanor bordering on stern, Grams beamed at her great-grandson while a steady stream of nonsensical words tripped off her tongue. The baby laughed at her and attempted to slip his fingers into her mouth. Grams almost allowed it, but at the last moment she echoed his laughter and turned her head to the side. Then she buried her face in his chubby neck and made the most undignified, un-Grams-like sound Phoebe had ever heard. Charles burst into high-pitched guffaws.

Even Julia laughed soundly at their antics. Still grinning, she handed the shawl to Hetta. "Here, take this to wrap him in. It'll be chilly yet."

Grams cupped Charles's wispy head—so like that of Grampapa in the picture they had found yesterday—and gazed over at Julia. "I suppose you must take him?" She immediately shook her head. "Of course you must. He must be kept safe. Douglas will drive you?"

"As long as you can spare him here," Julia replied. Douglas served in the house as a footman, but whenever needed he served as a chauffeur, using the family's touring car. That left their official driver, Fenton, free to drive Grams and Grampapa in their Rolls Royce wherever they needed to go. "And Hetta will be with us. Isn't that right, Hetta?"

The woman drew herself up like a soldier coming to attention, one with blond braids wrapped around his head instead of a helmet. "I let nothing happen to Madame and baby."

Phoebe didn't doubt her word. Neither did Grams, apparently. She kissed the top of Charles's head and handed him back to Julia's maid. "Very well."

"It's not as though we'll be gone forever," Julia said. "Just until . . . matters here are cleared up."

"Take Amelia with you."

Both Phoebe and Julia reacted with surprise to Grams's decree. Julia said, "She's not even up yet. I really want to set out straightaway."

Grams remained undeterred. "I'd insist Phoebe go as well, but I know she won't be budged. And Fox returns to school tomorrow." Grams turned to Hetta. "Would you please wake up Lady Amelia? I'll hold Charles again."

Hetta held the baby fast. "He'll help young lady wake faster."

"Quite right." Grams turned briskly back to Julia. "There, it's settled. If I know Amelia, she'll be ready shortly."

"All right." Julia sighed. "In the meantime I'll explain things to Grampapa. Is he up yet?"

"In his study," Grams replied.

"I'll go talk to him now, then. Hetta, bring Charles to my grandfather's study once Amelia is up. He'll want to see his great-grandson before we leave." On her way out, Julia paused before Phoebe, surprising her by reaching up and placing her palm against her cheek. "Do what you do so well, do it quickly, and be careful. You and Eva both."

It was all Phoebe could do to keep the tears from falling during breakfast. Not so much because she wouldn't be seeing her nephew for the foreseeable future; she knew he'd be just fine with Julia, Amelia, and Hetta doting on him. But Julia's parting message had been so uncharacteristic of her—so *out* of keeping with their usual struggle simply to remain civil with each other—that those words of caution had unraveled her. Motherhood had changed Julia for the better, no mistake about it. No, not *changed*. Motherhood had brought back more of the old Julia, before the war and their father's death had caused her to erect those prickly walls around herself.

Amelia, on the other hand, was all smiles as she consumed her breakfast, though Phoebe heard the forced cheer in her voice. She might be going to Lyndale Park, but her fears would remain here at Foxwood Hall. Still, she apparently had taken it upon herself to keep everyone's spirits up.

"Truly, Grampapa, it's good for Charles to have such a

jolly adventure, isn't it? His first. I know his aunts Veronica and Mildred will spoil him ridiculously."

"Veronica Townsend spoiling a baby?" Fox scoffed down at his plate. "That old prune?"

"Fox." Grampapa used the severe tone he only ever took with his heir. "That isn't kind, nor is it accurate. Veronica Townsend hasn't had an easy life. But when push came to shove last autumn, she proved a friend to you and your sisters."

"Actually, Julia proved a friend to *her*," Fox contradicted him, no doubt remembering how Veronica had predicted Julia would send her packing from Lyndale Park once the baby was born, but Julia had surprised her by assuring her Lyndale Park would be her home for as long as she wished. At a frown from Grampapa, Fox lowered his gaze. "Sorry, sir. But, yes, I'm sure Charles will be just fine there."

"Is it true Ernie's no longer there?" asked Amelia. "Do you suppose he'll return once he hears we're there with the baby?"

"According to Julia, he left months ago and hasn't contacted anyone since. So I don't see how he'll know if you and Julia are there or not." Phoebe glanced over at Grams. "Just as well, if you ask me. He wasn't very nice to Julia last autumn, nor at the wedding last spring, for that matter. It's best he stays away. Perhaps he'll finally make a life elsewhere."

"Yes, well, Lyndale Park technically belongs to Charles now, doesn't it?" Grams lifted her teacup from its saucer. As she tipped it for a sip, the backstamp declaring the item made by Crown Lily Potteries in Staffordshire served as another reminder of their adventures last fall. "I agree that Julia should make her son's claim perfectly clear to the others living there. I only wish she were doing it for better reasons."

After breakfast and seeing Julia, Amelia, and Charles off on their trip, Phoebe and Eva met on the back staircase and climbed to the second floor. Mrs. Sanders met them on the landing, her heavy set of keys dangling from her hand. She brought them to a door, opened it, and gestured for Phoebe to precede her through. They entered a forbidden section of the second floor, at least forbidden to the women of the household. Only Mrs. Sanders had the authority to unlock that door and lead them down the hallway they currently traversed. This was the men's side of the servants' quarters, strictly separated from the women's section.

It also led to another set of stairs that opened onto a level of the attic used for storage. Visits to this part of the house were few. Most of what accumulated here over the years was never looked at again. Mrs. Sanders chose another key on her ring and opened a door.

"This is where your great-grandparents' things were brought." She reached up to turn a switch on the wall. A light overheard flickered and came on. "Should two hours do, or shall I give you more time than that?"

It wasn't lost on Phoebe that the housekeeper didn't offer to leave the key with them so she and Eva could lock up when they were finished. Mrs. Sanders took her job seriously; she never broke a rule, not unless Grampapa himself ordered her to do so.

"That should be ample time, Mrs. Sanders. Thank you."

The woman walked away, leaving them alone. Together Phoebe and Eva faced a room filled with trunks and boxes. Two wardrobes occupied opposite corners.

"A lifetime's worth of memories reduced to this." Phoebe sighed.

"Only the items that couldn't be used by others, my lady. Everything of value was passed on to your grandparents, and then to you, your sisters, and Fox."

"I wonder . . ." Phoebe picked her way to one of the armoires and swung the doors open. She flipped through several gowns, all of silk and satin in various colors. The skirts and even the sleeves were voluminous. Turning, she grinned ruefully. "I was hoping there might be clothing here that could be given away through the RCVF. But it's all positively Victorian."

"As they should be." Eva went to the other armoire and opened its doors. "These look like they belonged to your great-grandfather." She took a suit coat down from the bar and held it up in front of her. The frock coat with satin lapels reached below her knees. "Also quite Victorian. They'd make wonderful costumes for a fancy-dress ball." She slid the coat back between the others hanging from the bar. "I very much doubt you'll find what you're looking for in either of these, but a quick peek onto the shelves and into the drawers is in order."

Phoebe agreed and did the same, finding no diaries or letters secreted away among the decades-old clothing. It was difficult to prevent herself from examining each article, however, as the workmanship and fabrics were exquisite. Much heavier than anything she was used to, but lovely and luxurious.

They turned their attention to the rest of the room. Two trunks yielded the kinds of records Phoebe had hoped to find: an estate diary in several volumes, numerous stacks of letters, and a family memoir her great-grandfather had begun writing, though he had never finished.

"He died young, relatively speaking," Phoebe observed, examining the homemade cover of the memoir. "Only fifty-seven at the time. A riding accident. Shocked everyone."

"Yes, I remember learning about it." Eva smiled and gave a shrug. "Foxwood Hall's history is a subject at the local school, you realize."

"What an odd thought, that a family's private history

should be part of the schoolroom curriculum. Well, let's gather what we have and bring it all downstairs. We've both got quite a lot of reading to do."

The next morning Eva was in the middle of scanning through a particularly mundane winter of 1862 in the previous Lord Wroxly's estate diaries when she learned she had a visitor. She and Lady Phoebe had divided up the stacks of records from the attic and taken them to their respective rooms. They knew better than to expect an indiscretion on the previous earl's part to have been recorded anywhere in these tomes, but there might be a clue, such as a maid hired and unexpectedly sacked not long after.

Eva had stolen upstairs to her room beneath the eaves only minutes ago for another read, in between readying Lady Phoebe for her day and helping her sort through another donation of goods for the Relief and Comfort of Veterans and Their Families, the charity also known as the RCVF.

Now she laid the diary she'd been flipping through aside and came to her feet. Connie, the housemaid who'd alerted her to her visitor, had already hurried away without bothering to tell her who it was. Eva was both delighted and apprehensive to find Miles waiting for her in the servants' hall belowstairs.

He was standing near the corner of the table, staring up out of the windows set at ground level. A single glimpse told her he wasn't looking at anything in particular, but rather had fallen deep into his private thoughts. As Eva came through the doorway, however, he turned and quickly approached, stopping just short of taking her in his arms and kissing her. That was something they did only rarely here in this house, and never in the servants' hall, where anyone might walk in.

She took a quick moment to silently admire his stature

within the policeman's black uniform. His helmet sat on the table. "Why do I have the feeling this isn't strictly a social call?"

"You're right, it isn't. I wanted to catch you up on the latest at the station." He pulled out a chair for her, then sat beside her, leaning close to speak quietly. "We've discovered Hayden Bell has something of a record. Theft and assault, all committed in his youth. Seems he fell in with a bad lot at school and got himself into trouble."

A cold sensation slithered through Eva. Had Lady Phoebe been wrong in her assessment of Hayden Bell's character? "He was arrested?"

"Several times, spent some months in reform school."

"Assault." Eva sat back. "Then he does have violent tendencies."

"He *did*. But after his last arrest, the one that resulted in his being sent away, he's kept a clean record. Nary a toe out of place. Distinguished himself bravely during the war. Fought at the Somme, saved the lives of two comrades who'd been wounded."

The conflicting reports left Eva's mind swimming. "So, then, what does this all mean? I suppose given Mr. Bell's childhood record, Chief Inspector Perkins is more convinced than ever he's guilty."

"He is. However, circumstances have forced him to release Bell for now. There simply isn't enough evidence linking him to his mother's death. No more so than any of the other society members who wandered off during the tour. He's been told to remain close, though, so he'll be staying at his mother's cottage."

"If only we had kept better track of everyone." Eva made a fist and brought it down on the tabletop, albeit lightly. "What gooses we were, thinking we could do this with no experience whatsoever. If—"

Miles took her chin between his fingers and turned her

to face him. "Don't go blaming yourself. Lady Phoebe either. It was a simple enough prospect, conducting a tour of this old pile. Who could have guessed a killer lurked among a passel of schoolchildren and the studious members of a historical society?"

"Thank goodness the children left when they did."

He released her chin to grasp her hand; he raised it to his lips and pressed a kiss against her knuckles. Then he pushed to his feet and helped her to hers. "I've got to get back. I just wanted to fill you in."

"Is there anything we can do? To help, I mean."

His smile held both amusement and teasing accusation. "Aren't you already helping?"

"I suppose we might be, in a small way." Her cheeks warmed despite her attempt to be coy. He knew quite well she and Lady Phoebe would not be content to let matters lie if they feared the wrong individual had been accused. "Actually, we're going over estate records and letters from the time of the last earl." She told him about Lady Phoebe's theory. He listened carefully, frowning in thought.

"Interesting. If there is any truth to this, then one of the society members might be the earl's by-blow."

She winced slightly at his use of the indelicate term. Yet there was nothing delicate about producing illegitimate children. "Given when the earl died, we're probably talking about the child of the . . . er . . . by-blow."

"Let me know if you unearth anything."

"Of course."

He picked up his helmet, cradling it in the crook of his arm as he hesitated. "If the opportunity arises—*without* endangering yourselves—see if you can talk to some of the historical society members. Perhaps one might let slip something about his or her background. But do *not* ask them about Mrs. Bell's death. Understood?"

"Understood." She ran her fingertips over his woolen

sleeve, and he stole the opportunity to lean in and peck her on the cheek.

"Good. I'll see you soon."

He let himself out, and Eva stood smiling another minute before smoothing her dress and leaving the servants' hall. In the corridor another woman dressed similarly to her, in black cotton that covered her arms and hung to below her calves, stepped into her path.

"Entertaining gentlemen, are we?" A woman in her midfifties, with severe black hair and a pointed chin, Fiona Shea served as lady's maid to the Countess of Wroxly. As such, she enjoyed an elevated status among the servants. Unfortunately, Miss Shea often took that privilege to heart by casting judgment on the actions of others and giving them grief.

"Constable Brannock was here on official business, Miss Shea."

"A likely story. What would Mrs. Sanders have to say about it?"

"I presume Mrs. Sanders already knows. She sent Connie upstairs to let me know the constable wished to speak with me."

"The *constable*. How formal we are."

"Miss Shea, is there something I can assist you with? Because if not, I have other matters to attend to."

Eva started to walk around her, but Miss Shea once again blocked her path. "Lady Phoebe is far too lenient with you. It doesn't set a good example for the others. Obviously, you were far too young for this position. The Renshaws should have known better. You should learn your place, Miss Huntford. Or perhaps you're ready to move on from service, with your *constable*?"

Several retorts came to mind, all of them meant to cut the other woman off at the knees. Yet Eva voiced none of them. Instead she compressed her lips, slipped past, and wondered what could have made Fiona Shea so bitter she felt compelled to take her frustrations out on others.

Eva had neither the time nor the inclination to allow herself to be baited. Who might the chief inspector turn his suspicions on next? Or would he continue to pursue evidence that led him back to Hayden Bell, whether he was guilty or not? As she made her way to the laundry facilities, she contemplated each member of the historical society.

Of all of them, only the Hawkhursts had been truly unpleasant. They had angered Eva, airing their criticisms of the house so openly. Their hostility toward Lady Primrose had been thoroughly uncalled for. As with Miss Shea, their bitterness seemed deeply rooted, as if some past misfortune or injustice colored their every experience.

There was no denying the Hawkhursts were snobs. Or that they were grumpy. But did that make them potential killers? No, no more so than it did Miss Shea. And, after all, they hadn't turned their ill humor on Mrs. Bell, at least not that Eva had noticed. Of the nine adults, including Miss Carmichael, who visited Foxwood Hall yesterday— goodness, was it only yesterday?—there were seven seemingly ordinary individuals who might harbor a dark and violent nature.

Which one . . . which one?

After collecting an armful of clothing, pressed and folded, to be returned to her ladies' rooms, she hurried up the service stairs. Lady Phoebe would wish to know that Hayden Bell had been released.

CHAPTER 7

The Rolls-Royce stopped outside a two-story cottage with purple periwinkles and golden honeysuckle spilling from the window boxes on either side of the front door. A thatched roof presided over Cotswolds' honey-golden stone construction, the property framed by rolling hills and the faint outlines of the rooftops of Little Barlow in the distance, making this as picturesque a setting as one could hope for.

Fenton, the chauffeur, hopped out of the driver's seat and opened the rear door. He handed Phoebe out and then extended the courtesy to Eva. Fox, however, slid out on his own. His presence today is why they had come in the Rolls Royce, as Phoebe's Vauxhall made a tight fit for three.

"So this is where she lived," Fox observed, scanning the cottage's façade. "Nice little place. Seems a shame."

Phoebe traded an ironic glance with Eva. Yes, Arvina Bell had made her home here in recent years, along with a town house she still kept in Gloucester, apparently. Her son would be staying here for the foreseeable future, until Chief Inspector Perkins made his arrest, whether it be Hayden Bell himself or another member of the historical society. Mr. Bell was the reason they were here now. He had telephoned Foxwood Hall and asked Phoebe to come. He had significant news to tell her. Or to *show* her, he had said.

Phoebe didn't bother to comment on her brother's vast understatement in terming someone's murder a shame. All she did say was "Let Eva and me do the talking. He's expecting all three of us, so we won't be taking him by surprise. I told him I wouldn't come alone."

"Should have let me bring one of Grampapa's rifles."

"Don't be ridiculous. You're still a child." She couldn't help a quick roll of her eyes. Another glance at Eva confirmed that she shared Phoebe's sentiments, though she forewent making any obvious gestures.

"Not too much of a child for you to bring me along for protection," he pointed out with a haughty tilt of his chin.

"Granted, you *are* looking more the part these days." Indeed, if Fox grew any taller, his feet would hang over the end of his bed and he would have to duck his way through doorways. His shoulders, too, had begun to broaden, though he retained a young man's reedy figure. She had brought him, not so much because she expected him to physically protect her, but because there was safety in numbers. It wasn't likely Hayden Bell would try anything with all three of them there.

"I'll knock," Eva said, and walked up to the front door.

Phoebe turned to Fenton. "Wait here for us, please."

His eyebrows went up in a show of indignation. "I'm not going anywhere, my lady."

Yes, she knew if need be—if he detected any signs of danger—Fenton would come storming into the house to help them.

Hayden Bell opened the door even before Eva knocked. The breeze took that moment to graze the front of the house, ruffling his shirt and lifting the dark hair from his brow. As Eva had mentioned to her yesterday, a jagged scar marred his left temple from eyebrow to hairline. She noticed also that the hand holding the door latch trembled slightly.

"Lady Phoebe," he said, eyeing Eva and Fox quizzically, "thank you for coming."

"I told you I wouldn't come alone," she replied. "You already know Miss Huntford. And this is my brother."

If he took issue with Phoebe bringing protectors, so to speak, he gave no indication of it, but rather accepted Eva's and Fox's presence as a matter of fact. After their initial greetings they entered the cottage through a small vestibule that opened onto a narrow hallway. To either side, doorways opened onto a dining room and parlor, respectively. A staircase led to the first floor. He escorted them into the parlor.

"My mother's maid will bring tea, if you wish."

"Please don't bother, Mr. Bell." Phoebe remained standing, though he gestured toward the settee. "We're very curious as to why you asked us here."

He nodded, not pointing out that he hadn't asked *them,* only Phoebe. "Then come with me."

He preceded them back into the hallway and up the stairs. At the landing he went into a room on the left. Phoebe followed to discover very little furniture other than a desk, a cupboard, and some bookcases. Eva came to stand beside her. Fox remained on the threshold.

"This was my mother's office," Hayden Bell explained. He beckoned them closer. "And this is her manuscript about the Cotswolds' great country estates. At least, all of it I can find." Phoebe frowned as he held up a stack of paper far too thin to be called a manuscript. "It is—or was—due in six months, according to her contract with her publisher. Since early this morning I've turned this room upside down and inside out. I can find nothing else but this—an introduction, chapter one, and several other chapter outlines. That's all."

"I don't understand." Phoebe glanced around the room, as if answers might be sitting on a shelf. "Did you search in her bedroom? Perhaps she worked on it there as well."

"I looked. There's nothing. Only this." He tossed the manuscript onto the desk with a light plop.

Fox cleared his throat for attention as he moved into the room. "Are you sure you've been home long enough to have searched everywhere? You *were* in jail until when? This morning?"

"Fox," Phoebe murmured in admonition.

But Hayden Bell took the comment in stride. "Last night, actually. Rather late, but I came straight here, had dinner, and got some sleep. I was up early and went right to work looking through my mother's things." He paused, raising his right hand to his temple, where perhaps the skin itched from the jagged scar. Once again, Phoebe noticed the slight tremor in his fingers. Perhaps sensing her scrutiny, he shoved the hand in his trouser pocket. "This is all I found, and it troubles me deeply. I believe her lack of progress could be related to her death."

"If this troubles you," Eva said, "why did you telephone Lady Phoebe? Why not the police?"

He made a little flourish with his left hand, taking in the papers he'd dropped back onto the desk. "What is there to tell the police? That my mother had been lagging in her work? That she hadn't been writing as diligently as she should? I should think they would consider that neither here nor there. And as for her fellow society members . . ." He trailed off, hesitating.

"Yes? What about them?" Phoebe prompted.

"Lady Phoebe, of everyone present during the tour, you and Miss Huntford are the only ones I'm certain didn't murder my mother. And the schoolchildren, of course."

"What about their teacher?" Fox piped up.

Phoebe whirled on her brother. "Are you determined to make me regret asking you to come?"

"Sorry, I thought it worth mentioning." His mouth quirked with impatience.

"It isn't," she retorted. "Miss Carmichael had her hands full, as it was, keeping an eye on her charges."

"Well, I don't see what's significant about Mrs. Bell's manuscript, or lack of it," Fox persisted.

"Then why don't we let Mr. Bell finish explaining." Phoebe turned back to Hayden Bell to find that his green eyes had remained on her while he waited out her tiff with Fox.

Now he said, "My question is this. If she hadn't been writing about Foxwood Hall or any other house, for that matter, why was she on the tour?"

"For inspiration, one would suppose," Eva suggested. "Perhaps she didn't know where to begin, and she hoped the tour would help point her in the right direction, literally speaking."

"Perhaps," he said with a nod, "but why begin with Foxwood Hall, then? Her outline suggests the house would have been somewhere in the middle of the manuscript. Why would she not have requested to see, perhaps, Sudeley Castle or Hidcote Manor, which were to occur earlier in her book?"

"Perhaps she decided to reorder the chapters," Phoebe said.

"Actually, why join the tour at all?" Eva moved closer to the desk, glancing down at the manuscript. "Why see the house with so many others in tow, when she could have telephoned over from the post office, explained her purpose, and asked to see the house alone?" She turned around, speaking now to Phoebe. "I'm sure your grandparents would have permitted Mrs. Sanders or Mr. Giles to show her round."

Phoebe nodded her agreement. "You're right. She would have learned more on her own and been able to ask more questions without being interrupted. Without all the distractions."

"Then why *was* she on the tour?" Fox asked.

"Exactly," Hayden Bell said. "Whatever the reason, it may have led to her death."

Eva had promised Miles she wouldn't delve into Arvina Bell's death with the members of the historical society. She feared she was about to break that promise. But at least she would do so in a public place, where she could come to no harm.

Later that day, after switching the Rolls Royce for the Vauxhall, Lady Phoebe had dropped her outside the Calcott Inn, a Georgian mansion of stone and slate that had been converted to a hotel and restaurant at the end of the last century. Lady Phoebe had driven back to the village proper, while Eva went inside for a prearranged appointment. She entered the dining room and spotted Ophelia Chapman immediately. The young woman wore another fashionable ensemble, this time in rose pink, the belted tunic and skirt trimmed in taffeta. A wide-brimmed hat beribboned in matching taffeta completed her look, straight out of a recent page of *La Mode,* although Eva suspected that, once again, Miss Chapman's clothes were less expensive versions of the originals.

"Thank you for seeing me," Eva said as she slipped onto the chair opposite the journalist.

"You're welcome. Your telephone call left me intensely curious." Miss Chapman tipped her head down while at the same time peeking coyly out from beneath her hat brim.

"I assume this has something to do with Arvina Bell's death?"

"In a way, yes. How well did you know her?"

"Not well at all, I'm afraid."

"What about the other members of the historical society?"

Before Miss Chapman could answer, the waiter came with their menus. Eva didn't bother to glance at the one he offered her. "Oolong tea and an apricot scone, please." To Miss Chapman, she said, "The scones are excellent here."

"Make that two." Once the waiter walked away, Miss Chapman leaned forward. "I truly don't know any of the members well, Miss Huntford. As I explained when we met, I don't reside in the area. I'm really only a member by association."

"I don't understand."

"I pay my dues in order to make use of the society's records and any information they come upon in the areas I write about. I belong to historical societies all over England, although usually only for a year or so. Once I've moved on to explore another region for the magazine, I don't tend to keep up my membership."

"I see. Then how long have you been a member of the Little Barlow Chapter of the Greater Costwald Historical Society?"

"Only for the past few months. Three or four, I believe. They've been a tremendous help, really. And, of course, as a magazine writer it's far easier for me to gain entry to a great house like Foxwood Hall as part of a larger organization. Toffs tend to be a bit squirrelly when it comes to allowing journalists into their homes." She gave a pretty shrug, fluttering the ruffles along her neckline. "I suppose one can't blame them. But I mean no harm. The public has a hunger for such places. With so many families moving to the cities nowadays, there's a growing nostalgia for the countryside. They enjoy seeing the pictures and reading the descriptions even if they don't wish to return to the old feudal way of life."

Eva couldn't help chuckling at Miss Chapman's use of the word *feudal* when referring to traditional farming on the outskirts of a great estate. But Miss Chapman had unknowingly opened a door to another line of questioning. Eva hoped to learn more about the woman's background. Could she secretly be a Renshaw? "I trust you live in one of the cities, then? London?"

They fell silent as the waiter returned with their tea and scones. Eva poured for Miss Chapman, and then for herself. They each helped themselves to the jam and clotted cream that came with their repast. Then Eva repeated her question.

The woman smiled and nodded. "All my life. Even throughout the war, despite the zeppelins and the Gotha bombers."

The reminder sent chills through Eva. Though Little Barlow lay far from London and the other strategic places that had been bombed by the Germans, the threat—and the fear—had hovered over all of England during those years. "Were you working as a journalist then, too?"

"I joined *Country Heritage* in '17. We did a lot of morale pieces. In fact, I believe we ran something on Little Barlow back then, about the efforts to collect and deliver supplies for the soldiers. I didn't write that one, though."

"Oh, yes, I believe I remember it. Foxwood Hall was the center of those efforts. The ground floor practically became a warehouse. So tell me, how did you come by your career? I'm sure there weren't many women in the field in '17."

"Still aren't, other than the society columns. But, true, there were even fewer then." Miss Chapman broke off a piece of scone and chewed with an appreciative expression. "If you must know, *Country Heritage* is owned by my uncle. The *wealthy* one." She made a disparaging roll of the eyes. "It's merely a hobby for him, but it meant the world to me when I finally wore him down enough that he allowed me on board, even if, at the time, it was only to proofread others' work."

"But you worked your way up to being a writer."

"I did." Her pride was evident even in those two simple words. "And I'll go further still. I don't intend writing about houses and the countryside forever, you know. The *Times.* That's my eventual goal. But until then, I'll produce the best articles I can for whoever will pay me to do so."

"Did you get all you need for your descriptions of Fox-wood Hall? And what about your photos of the front of the house? Did they come out well?"

"They haven't been developed yet. I'd actually hoped to take some of the back of the house, and the gardens as well." She stared down into her tea, then raised the cup for a sip. "After what happened, of course, I couldn't ask."

"It might be possible for you to return. How many more days do you intend staying in Little Barlow?"

"Oh, I've still lots more to do here. *Country Heritage* isn't only interested in manor houses. The village, its church and school, some of the farms . . . They all add to the charm of my articles."

"I'll see what I can arrange, then, and let you know." Eva took another bite of her scone, relishing the blend of jam, cream, and the bits of apricot inside. Then she sat back and regarded Miss Chapman, deciding it was time to return to her earlier questions. "Are you quite certain you haven't observed anything unusual among the historical society members? Tensions, resentments, that sort of thing?"

"Are you a policewoman in addition to a lady's maid, Miss Huntford?" Miss Chapman gave a little laugh.

"I'm protective of the family I serve." If she sounded

defensive, so be it. "We allowed people into the house and look what happened. It was almost certainly one of them."

"I thought the police made an arrest. Mrs. Bell's own son."

"He's been released for now, for lack of evidence."

"I see." A shudder passed across Miss Chapman's shoulders. "That means a killer is most certainly still at large."

"Yes, so if you remember anything useful, please don't keep it to yourself."

"I'm sorry, I really can't think of a thing. For the most part everyone has been professional and quite dedicated to the society's purpose, at least that I've observed." Miss Chapman drained her teacup, then frowned. "What you just said, about the killer being almost certainly one of *them*. What you meant to say, I should think, is one of *you*. Myself included, no? Am I a suspect, Miss Huntford?"

Eva managed to take her leave of Ophelia Chapman some minutes later without quite answering her question. Did Eva consider her a likely suspect? On the whole, no. As Miss Chapman herself had pointed out, she didn't reside in Little Barlow or even the Cotswolds, and so had little knowledge of her fellow society members, and few opportunities to garner hostilities toward them. For her, they were a means to an end; she was not invested in the organization the way the others were and would likely let her membership lapse once she had completed her research.

And yet . . . Miss Chapman had wandered away from the group at least once that Eva remembered. That meant she might have had opportunity, if not an obvious motive. She could not be entirely ruled out.

There was also the little white lie she had told. She

claimed she hadn't witnessed any hostilities among her fellow members. But the rancor between the Hawkhursts and Lady Primrose had been plain for all to see during the tour. Eva had winced over it more than once. So had Ladies Phoebe and Amelia. Could Ophelia Chapman truly be as oblivious as all that?

Hardly. The woman was, after all, a journalist. Then why had she pleaded ignorance?

CHAPTER 8

After collecting Eva at the Calcott Inn, Phoebe planned to drop her at her parents' farm for a visit with her mother. Eva nixed that idea the moment she slipped into the two-seater Vauxhall and shut the door.

"I'm going with you to see the Hawkhursts."

"But we decided we would divide the society members between us according to their social standing." They had done it before, with Phoebe looking into the lives and secrets of those who were more on a par with her family, people who would never deign to answer the questions of a lady's maid. Meanwhile, Eva would converse with fellow servants and working people, who often became tongue-tied around people of Phoebe's background. The system had served them well in the past.

"I'm thoroughly content to let you do all the talking," Eva replied, "but I insist on being there with you. Miss Chapman reminded me that at some point we will come face-to-face with Arvina Bell's killer. We won't know when that will happen. It could even be upon our arrival at the Hawkhursts' estate."

Phoebe thought this over as she changed gears and maneuvered the Vauxhall through the gates of Sunderly, a manor house built in the Palladian style. From the road the place projected an image of authority and permanence, as estates were meant to do, as if it had always existed within its wide vale, nestled between two hillsides and surrounded by lush trees. Yet as they drove closer, Phoebe detected faint signs of neglect that sparked a memory. Overgrown hedges, flowerbeds slowly going to weed, grime clinging to the corners of the house's many mullioned windows. "Something here isn't right."

"Your cousin Regina's house," Eva said as if reading her mind.

Phoebe nodded, held almost transfixed by the similarity between Sunderly and High Head Lodge, which she and Julia—and Eva—had visited in the summer of '19. Regina had bought the house and planned to completely remodel the inside, discarding the Victorian furnishings in favor of the new and modern. When they had visited, Regina had only just moved in and hadn't yet hired on a full staff, so the place had presented a rather disregarded air.

The Hawkhursts, she knew, had not recently moved into Sunderly.

Phoebe had not bothered to telephone ahead. When a maid admitted them, she asked them to wait in a receiving parlor off the entrance hall while she went to inquire whether Mr. and Mrs. Hawkhurst were "in." Phoebe guessed they were, although whether they wished to receive company was another matter.

She and Eva remained standing, examining their surroundings and finding evidence that conditions outside extended inside the house as well. Little accumulations of dust, an edge of a rug needing repair, a shelf that seemed oddly empty of whatever ornamentation had been meant to be displayed there.

"Something odd is certainly going on," Phoebe said in the faintest of whispers.

"Yes. And allowing a housemaid to answer the door?" Eva ran her forefinger along the surface of a side table, then held it up and blew off the dust. "What on earth are the footmen doing? Or the butler?"

"If there are any."

A moment later the maid reappeared. "Please follow me." She brought them to a drawing room with elaborate plasterwork climbing the walls. A multibranched chandelier dripping with crystal hung from within a center medallion. Several of its bulbs were dark, while others illuminated strands of cobwebs.

"Please make yourselves at home," the maid said. "Mr. and Mrs. Hawkhurst will be with you presently."

Phoebe took a seat on a silk upholstered armchair near the hearth. Eva took up a less prominent position by perching on a small side chair beside a French window. A faint mustiness tickled Phoebe's nose. A few minutes later the couple entered the room looking far from pleased to have company. Phoebe came to her feet and shook their hands. She smiled. They did not.

When they had taken their seats, Mr. Hawkhurst looked her over and then darted a glance at Eva. He made no comment on Eva's presence as he placed a hand over his paunch and asked, "To what do we owe the pleasure, Lady Phoebe?"

"Please forgive my intruding on you this way. I wished to see how you both were doing."

They traded puzzled glances. With a frown Mrs. Hawkhurst repeated, "How we are doing?"

"Yes. Something dreadful happened at Foxwood Hall yesterday, and I cannot help but feel partly responsible for the distress you must be experiencing as a result."

"We can assure you, Lady Phoebe," the husband said, "we're perfectly fine."

"Are you?" She allowed herself to sound astonished—which was not a far stretch from the truth. "But how can you be, when an acquaintance of yours lies dead?"

"What my husband means to say is that yes, we are distressed over poor Arvina's fate, and quite shocked by the circumstances. Naturally. But we certainly don't hold you at all responsible. You or your family."

"Thank goodness. That certainly sets my mind at ease. Was she a very close friend?" Phoebe injected sympathy and commiseration into her tone. Once again, the pair looked puzzled, but only briefly.

"We can't say that she was, not really," Mrs. Hawkhurst replied. She fingered the strand of pearls around her neck. "Our backgrounds were so very different, you understand. Oh, she was pleasant enough and a valued member of the historical society, but it wasn't as if we socialized. It wouldn't have been quite the proper thing, would it? Despite everything being so topsy-turvy because of the war, one needs to maintain certain standards, doesn't one?" She turned to her husband. "Isn't that right, dear?"

"Quite right, my dear."

Phoebe didn't dare turn her gaze in Eva's direction, for fear they would both double over laughing. What colossal snobs the Hawkhursts were. How they must have lamented their lack of title, but they certainly put a good deal of stock in being landed gentry. Phoebe wondered where the money had gone.

"But surely you would have been aware if Mrs. Bell had been having any personal difficulties." Again, Phoebe kept her tone sympathetic and at the same time inquisitive, that of a bored young woman keen on hearing all the sordid details. It seemed to be working, judging by the eager glint that entered Mrs. Hawkhurst's eye. "One wonders why on earth someone would wish to kill her."

"One certainly does," the woman agreed emphatically.

"Surely, she must have mentioned something to you. An argument with a fellow member, or with her son?"

"Why, no." Mrs. Hawkhurst looked to her husband for consensus. He raised his eyebrows and shook his head. "She seemed to get on well enough with everyone, but we simply didn't invite that sort of familiarity, did we? Not from any of our fellow members."

"We know better than that, Lady Phoebe." Her husband draped one leg over the other and rested his elbow on the arm of his chair. Quite the master of the manor, Phoebe thought with an inner chuckle. "But it seems you're insinuating that one of the members murdered her. Is that what the police think? Now that Mr. Bell has been released, that is."

"You've heard, then."

"We have. Chief Inspector Perkins telephoned us this morning." Mrs. Hawkhurst reached across the small distance to place a hand over her husband's. "Abel—that is, Mr. Hawkhurst—requested the chief inspector keep us informed. He is only too happy to do so. But I do worry that he has allowed a murderer to walk free."

"He might come to rue his decision," her husband put in. "As might we all."

"But I understand there isn't enough evidence to hold him. So perhaps he's innocent, after all."

"Let's hope so, for the chief inspector's sake." Mr. Hawkhurst gave a sniff.

"For all our sakes," his wife added.

Phoebe came to her feet and extended her hand. "Thank you for seeing me. I'm so relieved to learn you're both doing so well after the tragedy at Foxwood Hall."

She cocked her head. "Had that been your first outing since returning home?"

The Hawkhursts stood as well. Each shook her hand, while gazing blankly back at her. Mrs. Hawkhurst said, *"Since returning home?"*

"Yes. Well, I just assumed." Smiling, she made a point of looking up at the chandelier with its garlands of crystal and cobwebs in nearly equal measure, her meaning being that the house must have been shut down and only recently reopened. Hence the disarray. "It must have been lovely to get away for a time. But not the most auspicious homecoming, not by any means. Well . . ."

She signaled to Eva, who had stood when she had. Phoebe traced a path to the hall, Eva trailing a few feet behind her, as a proper lady's maid should do. But the moment they were back in the Vauxhall, Phoebe turned to her.

"Did you see how their color drained when I let them know I'd noticed the inadequate condition of their home?"

"I most certainly did. That, and other reactions they had to your questions. They certainly like to confer silently with one another, don't they?"

"They do." Phoebe shook her head. "To think, they had the gall to criticize Foxwood Hall." Phoebe put the car in gear and started down the drive.

"It's always been my experience that those who fail to measure up to their own standards are quick to disapprove of others. But that's not all." Eva clutched the edges of the seat as Phoebe turned onto the main road. "It's also been my experience that whenever one person in a marriage does all the talking, with the other simply agreeing with everything their spouse says, that couple is hiding something."

"I believe you're right. But whether that something has

to do with Arvina Bell's death or not remains to be seen. On to Lady Primrose?"

Eva pointed straight ahead and down the road. "Onward."

Unlike the Hawkhursts, the Scotts lived in a modest Georgian dwelling several miles outside of Little Barlow, in the middle of pastureland dotted with sheep. Tidy stone walls lined the front of the property on either side of the drive, and several pretty outbuildings stood where the land rose behind the house.

"A gentleman's farm," Lady Phoebe commented as she brought the Vauxhall to a stop behind a sturdy and rather expensive-looking motorcar.

"That looks brand-new, or nearly so." Eva studied the vehicle, a sleek model in sapphire blue with a black roof, the highly polished chrome headlights and running boards glinting with sunlight. "It's no farm lorry, is it?"

"No, indeed. The Scotts might not live in a mansion, but they're certainly not short on cash."

"Not living in a mansion could be the very reason they're not short on cash," Eva replied, knowing those great houses, Foxwood Hall included, were often a drain on a family's resources. As had certainly appeared to be the case with the Hawkhursts.

A housekeeper opened the door to them. They entered through a foyer papered in a floral pattern on a hunter-green background, and from there into a well-appointed parlor with soft-golden walls, a polished stone fireplace, and conservative, upper-middle-class furnishings. Correct, respectable, and tasteful. Again, this was no farmhouse, nothing like Eva's parents' cottage on the outskirts of the village. Their single-story dwelling consisted of a parlor, a large kitchen, and three bedrooms, and had been built with economy in mind, allowing it to be heated inexpensively in winter and maintained with as few repairs each year as possible.

This house, though modest compared to Foxwood Hall or the Hawkhursts' Sunderly, nonetheless made a statement about its owners. Again, the words *conservative* and *respectable* popped into Eva's mind, along with *unobjectionable* and *uncontroversial*. Exactly the message a member of Parliament and his wife would want to send to their neighbors and prospective voters. The Scotts were neither trying to compete with their betters nor intimidate their less-well-off neighbors.

So clearly did that intent come across, the room almost felt staged.

"Please have a seat while I tell Lady Primrose you're here." The housekeeper curtsied and hurried out of the room. Moments later they heard the brisk clacking of footsteps in the hall.

"Goodness, Lady Phoebe. And Miss Huntford. I wish I had known you were coming. I've sent Esther to make tea. You'll stay for tea, won't you? I'm afraid I must look a fright. I wasn't expecting company, you understand. Not that it's any inconvenience, mind you . . ." Lady Primrose trailed off, looking perplexed and ill at ease. She did not, however, look a fright, but wore a lace-trimmed shirtwaist and pleated skirt with a silk cardigan thrown over her shoulders.

The woman rubbed her hands together. "Please have a seat. As I said, Esther should be in with tea any moment." She darted a glance over her shoulder.

"We didn't mean to disrupt your day," Lady Phoebe hastened to say. "Do let us sit and I'll explain why we've come."

She gave Lady Primrose the same story she had told the Hawkhursts, about holding herself to blame for putting them through the distress of Arvina Bell's death. While she did, Eva took further stock of the room. It obviously served as both parlor and library, as floor-to-ceiling shelves lined the wall to either side of the fireplace, crammed tight with both leather- and cloth-bound volumes. This room spanned the width of the house from front to back, with light pouring in from both directions. A wide bay window overlooked the front garden. A parlor grand piano took up the greater portion of a rear corner, placed just so, to the right of the French doors that gave out onto a ground-level terrace. Wisteria climbed an arbor and poured over the garden wall.

Eva returned her attention to the room. The mantelpiece boasted a few framed photographs of Lady Primrose, her husband, and their two sons, and a couple of photos of the sons alone, both of them nearly young men. If Eva remembered correctly, neither had been old enough to go to war. Probably off at school, then. Interspersed among the pictures were a few porcelain knickknacks, a couple of pieces of silver, and, holding court over all the rest, an ivory-inlaid mantel clock. Once again, it all seemed correct, expected—almost to the point of being clichéd—as did the vase of flowers on the sofa table and the wing chair off in a corner of its own. Where Mr. Scott read the evening newspaper, undoubtedly.

What continued to be *un*expected was Lady Primrose's shrill voice in Eva's ears, at times jarring, at other times almost tremulous. "You mustn't worry a jot about me. It was dreadful, yes, but in all honesty Arvina and I weren't particularly close."

"You're not the first member of the historical society to tell me that," Lady Phoebe said, echoing Eva's very thoughts. The Hawkhursts hadn't been broken up about Mrs. Bell's death, either.

"No?" Lady Primrose seemed distressed by that pronouncement. "She was quite a nice person, mind you, it's just that we hadn't much opportunity to socialize outside of the organization. I'm sure she enjoyed a close circle of friends and acquaintances."

Had she? Eva wondered. They should have asked her son about her social life. She made a mental note to do so at the next opportunity.

The housekeeper came through the doorway with the refreshments. As she neared the sofa table, Lady Primrose started to jump up, then appeared to think better of it and sank back on her seat. Instead she moved the vase of flowers out of the way to allow the housekeeper to set down the tray.

"Thank you, Esther, that will be all." Lady Primrose reached for the teapot, but stopped when Lady Phoebe spoke.

"Then you've no idea who might have wished to harm her?"

"*Harm her?*" she repeated, sounding scandalized. "None whatsoever, other than perhaps her son." She hefted the teapot. "But I understand the police have released him."

"This morning," Lady Phoebe informed her.

"There wasn't enough evidence to continue holding him," Eva put in, "for now at least. The police are investigating all avenues."

"*All avenues?*" Lady Primrose looked up from pouring. "Who else could possibly have done it? Oh, I don't expect you to answer that." She waved a hand at them and continued pouring.

"Has your husband returned from London?" Lady Phoebe asked, changing subjects as Lady Primrose handed her a cup and saucer.

"*My husband?*" The questioned seemed to startle the woman. "Uh, no. No, he'll be detained another week at least. He offered to come home directly. But I told him no, he's got important business to tend to in London and I wouldn't hear of him dropping everything to run down here and hold my hand."

Lady Phoebe dropped a lump of sugar into her cup. No sooner had she passed the bowl to Eva than Lady Primrose practically shoved the creamer into her hands. "So, then you're alone here?" Lady Phoebe said.

"*Alone?*" The woman gave another anxious reaction, like a skittish fawn who starts at every stir of the wind as it grazes through someone's flowerbed. "No, not completely alone. Goodness no. There is Esther, and Jessie, the girl who cleans for us. She comes and goes each day. And Arthur, our gardener, who also drives when I need him to. And then there are the boys who come to tend the sheep, although they stay out in the fields. There's no need for them to come into the house." Her expression turned somber. "Why? Do you believe I'm in danger? Surely, you're not suggesting that because someone murdered Arvina that . . . that all of us at the historical society might be . . . ?

"I'm not suggesting that at all, Lady Primrose." Lady Phoebe sipped her tea. "But until the police have wrapped up this case, it might do to make sure the house is locked up tight at night."

The woman's dark eyes sparked with fear. "Yes, yes, that does make sense."

"Tell me, you've been the society's treasurer for how long now?" Lady Phoebe asked the question lightly, as if it were merely idle curiosity.

"Only the past year. The former treasurer moved away."

"Any problems with the finances?"

"Not since I've been doing the books." Her lips parted in an eager smile. "I was always top of my class in mathematics. Oh, goodness." She lifted the platter of cakes and thrust it toward Lady Phoebe so forcefully some of the petit fours slid perilously toward the edge. "Esther baked them. They're delicious."

Lady Phoebe plucked up one of the colorful treats between her fingers. "I noticed a bit of tension between you and the Hawkhursts. I couldn't help but wonder why. Have you known them a long time?" She took a bite and watched Lady Primrose intently.

"*A long time?*" She had reverted to repetition again. "Yes—or, rather, no. A few years. No more than that."

Lady Phoebe smiled. "So whatever animosity exists between you is a recent development?"

"There is *no* animosity. None at all. Funny you should think that." Lady Primrose leaned to set her teacup on the low table between them, then came to her feet, signaling an abrupt end to the conversation. "It was so lovely of you to stop by." Her gaze darted to Eva. "Both of you. But as you can see, I'm quite all right. And quite well taken care of."

Eva and Lady Phoebe set their teacups aside and stood as well. Outside, Lady Phoebe turned to Eva. "She was as jumpy as a fox in hunting season."

"I pictured a fawn. Not merely nervous, mind you, but frightened."

"I agree. But of what? The murderer? The Hawkhursts? Her husband, who she insisted must remain in London?"

"Did you notice the state of the parlor?"

They ducked into the Vauxhall, and Lady Phoebe turned to Eva with a frown. "What do you mean? It seemed perfectly in order."

"Rather too much so. I kept thinking how predictable it all was, how staged, as if . . ."

"What?"

Eva thought it over, searching for the correct words to

describe the impression the parlor had left on her. "As if the room, the entire house, in fact, was a kind of disguise the Scotts are wearing to . . . I don't know . . . perhaps to protect themselves."

"Isn't that what all politicians do? Masquerade at being whatever their constituents wish them to be?"

"But in the privacy of their home?" Eva shook her head, still attempting to grasp the sensation that lingered inside her. "Are they also trying to deceive themselves? Each other?"

"*Each other,*" Lady Phoebe repeated. "Perhaps you're on to something there. I'm not sure exactly what, but something. Lady Primrose is of an aristocratic background, the daughter of the Earl of Lychester. She'd have been well educated to take her place in society and assume the responsibilities of someone of her station. She might not have married a man with a title, but she is certainly the correct sort of wife for an MP."

"There is that word again: *correct.* I thought it while we were inside, about the furnishings. Even the family photos on the mantel were carefully posed, the expressions just so."

Lady Phoebe was watching her closely. "I'm tempted to point out that a lot of homes are as you describe, as are a lot of family photographs. But I trust your instincts. And there is no denying the woman was a nervous wreck. She couldn't get us out quickly enough, even before I asked her those pointed questions about finances and the Hawkhursts. She practically tossed the cream at me, not to mention the petit fours."

"That's another thing. It was obvious she didn't want us there, yet she prolonged our stay by offering us tea. Not because she wished to be hospitable, in my opinion, but simply because playing the hostess is the done thing for a woman of her position."

"She was keeping up appearances."

Eva nodded. "Raising the question, what lurks behind the façade?"

With no immediate answers when it came to the Hawkhursts, Lady Primrose, or Ophelia Chapman, Phoebe decided they had time to visit one more member of the historical society before night fell, and Grams and Grampapa began to worry about their whereabouts.

"Dr. Bishop or Eamon Sadler?" she asked Eva, once they reached the main road.

"Well, I don't believe either of us has been to Mr. Sadler's shop."

Phoebe squinted against the late-afternoon sun as she turned the motorcar toward Old Gloucester Road. "I had no idea it existed until the historical society requested their tour of Foxwood Hall and provided me with the list of members who would be attending."

Eva tugged her hat brim lower to shade her eyes from the oncoming rays. "I realize it hasn't been in operation long, but how very odd that neither of us knew of it."

"Odd, indeed. You would think he'd have shouted his presence from the rooftops to attract business. But I was excited to learn of it and I admit I'm rather keen to browse his stock."

"To Sadler's shop, then."

The directions Phoebe had gotten from the historical society brought them some seven miles outside the village, to the northwest. This location, too, struck Phoebe as odd. A bend in the road revealed a cottage she had driven by a number of times in the past on her way to more distant locales. Now, however, rather than being a private residence, a sign swinging from a bracket above the door pronounced: SADLER'S RARE BOOKS EMPORIUM. "I suppose the rent is considerably less expensive than in the village, and it looks as though he lives here as well."

"I believe a family called the Kentons resided here previously." Eva turned her head to study the façade as Phoebe brought the Vauxhall up alongside the cottage. "They came into the village on market days to sell vegetables."

"I believe you're right." Phoebe took in the structure as well. It was a typical two-story Cotswold cottage of honey-gold stone and a thatched roof. It was situated close to the road, with property on either side and a garden in the back. The remnants of a barn, henhouse, and a shed attested to the small farm the Kentons had maintained. Phoebe remembered that not only one of their sons, but a daughter as well, had died in France, he an infantryman and she a nurse. That must be why the parents had left, to start anew elsewhere, away from the memories.

She opened her door and stepped out. Despite her melancholy musings, she also experienced both the excitement of entering a new bookshop and the apprehension of questioning a possible murder suspect. "People who love books are in a category all their own, don't you think?"

"Perhaps. But if you're thinking he can't have murdered Mrs. Bell simply because of his love of the written word, I fear you could be mistaken."

"Quite right. He had been eager to see the library at home, the very room where you found Mrs. Bell. At the time I didn't think it at all unusual for a bookseller to wish to examine a private library, but now we must consider that whatever drew Mrs. Bell back into that room also could have drawn Mr. Sadler there." Could that something have been the photograph of her great-grandparents?

Eva went to the front door of the cottage, which served as the entrance to the shop. When she opened the door to allow Phoebe to precede her inside, a bell jangled above their heads. They stepped into a large room that spanned the house from side to side, which must have been both parlor and dining room for the Kentons. Now shelves of books lined the walls, with several lower cases dispersed throughout, along with two library tables.

When a head popped out from behind a counter, Phoebe recognized Eamon Sadler by his dusty brown hair with its untamable cowlick and the slight hunch that marked him a man who spent much of his time poring over books. His spectacles caught the glow of sunset through the front-facing windows.

"I'll be with you momentarily," he said in a casual way, as if he hadn't recognized who had entered the shop.

Indeed, he probably hadn't. Phoebe realized that with the afternoon light pouring in through the room's two front windows, all he could see of them were their outlines.

"Mr. Sadler." She went to the counter. "It's Phoebe Renshaw and Eva Huntford, from Foxwood Hall."

"Goodness, so it is." He peered at her through his spectacles. She saw that he had been studying a notebook that lay open in front of him. He swung the cover closed, opening a drawer on his side of the counter. He dropped the notebook in and quickly shut the drawer with a bang. "Lady Phoebe, to what do I owe the pleasure?"

"I hope we aren't disturbing you. It looks as though we caught you in the middle of settling your books for the day." She gestured to where the notebook had been.

"Nonsense, it's no interruption at all. What can I do for you?"

She once again explained her visit, as she had to the Hawkhursts and Lady Primrose. She and Eva had come to see to the state of his well-being after the tragedy at Fox-wood Hall.

"Yes, it was most horrid. Unimaginable, even for some-one who reads as much as I do. Do you read much, Lady Phoebe?"

The sudden change in the conversation took her aback. But then, the others had been just as eager to avoid the topic. She couldn't blame them.

Meanwhile, Eva had begun a circuit of the shop, perus-ing titles along the shelves. Every so often she slid a book from its place and examined its cover and the edges of its pages. Whatever had caught her interest, she would ex-plain later.

Phoebe turned back to Mr. Sadler, just in time to catch the anxious look in his eyes as he, too, followed Eva's progress through the shop. "Were you well acquainted with Mrs. Bell?"

"*Mrs. Bell?*" He said it as though they hadn't a moment ago been discussing the woman. Phoebe had ignored his question about reading. Was he annoyed that she had cir-cled back to her original questions? "No, not well, I'm afraid. A pity. Poor woman. Any leads on who did it? I understand they released her son."

The news had indeed gotten around quickly. "Yes, which means the killer is still at large, Mr. Sadler. I hope you're able to lock up tightly here at night."

He gaped at her. "Do you mean I might be next? Is someone targeting the members of our little historical so-ciety? Why would they? We're no threat to anyone."

"I merely meant that it pays to be cautious. Especially since the police haven't yet established a motive for Mrs. Bell's murder." Phoebe placed her hands on the countertop and leaned slightly over it. "*Could* there be anything about the society's activities that have angered someone? Or has them worried about something?"

"Worried about what?"

Phoebe straightened. "A historical society digs into the past. There could be something someone doesn't want unearthed. Can you think of any controversial or scandalous family secrets the society has discovered lately?"

The man looked shocked. "My dear Lady Phoebe, we are a scholarly organization. Our purpose is to preserve the history of our little piece of the Cotswolds, and document its architecture and traditions. Nothing more. People's private lives are exactly that, as far as we're concerned."

"Still."

Ridges formed between his eyes as he regarded her. He removed his spectacles and pinched the bridge of his nose. When he replaced them, his gaze darted to Eva as she once more took a book from a shelf, leafed through, and placed it back. Phoebe heard her footsteps suddenly pick up speed, and she glanced over her shoulder as Eva turned into a little hallway that undoubtedly led to what had been the kitchen, and perhaps still was. What would she want there? It wasn't like Eva to venture where guests, or in this case shoppers, weren't welcome.

Mr. Sadler hurried out from behind his counter. "Ah, Miss Huntford, please stop. Miss Huntford!"

CHAPTER 9

"It's just that you might not wish to . . . Those are . . ."

Phoebe crossed the room, coming up behind Mr. Sadler to glimpse a gallery of framed photographs hanging on both walls of the small corridor. Why had he reacted so strongly to Eva seeing them?

"How fascinating," Eva exclaimed, and leaned closer to view one in particular. Phoebe moved around Mr. Sadler.

He raised a hand as if to stop her. "Lady Phoebe, truly, you shouldn't . . ."

The hallway was dusky, but she could still make out what held Eva's fascination. In each picture a different, strikingly beautiful young woman stood or sat in various poses, scantily clad in ruffles and flounces adorned with feathers, ribbons, and bows. Their décolletages plunged and their arms and legs were bared.

Quite bare.

"Good heavens." She wasn't scandalized, exactly, but the images did bring a wave of heat to her face. "They're cabaret dancers, aren't they?"

"Er . . . they are." She heard the chagrin in Mr. Sadler's voice.

"From the turn of the century, I should think." Eva moved from one photograph to the next. "Can you switch on a light?"

"Miss Huntford, I hardly think—"

"Here we are." Phoebe tugged the chain on the overhead fixture. Mr. Sadler flinched in the light now flooding the little hallway, leaving Phoebe thoroughly aware of his embarrassment. As Eva had said, the photos were fascinating. "Yes, they do appear to be at least a couple of decades old. Are they Parisian, Mr. Sadler?"

"Yes, French dancers. All of them famous in their time." He moved beside Eva. "If you'll notice, they're all signed. That's why I have them. For their historic value. I don't sell one often, but they do fetch a fair price if a collector happens by. Gentleman clients all, of course."

"Of course," Phoebe agreed, biting back a grin at his continued discomfiture.

There were about fifteen photographs in all. Each woman smiled boldly for the camera, her hair a mass of curls piled high on her head, her face glowing from the application of cosmetics. Not that Phoebe could see the colors, but the shadows on their eyelids and beneath their cheekbones, along with the contrast between their plumped lips and smooth skin, made it apparent.

"How did you come by them?" Eva asked as she turned, causing Mr. Sadler to take a startled step backward.

"I've a colleague in Paris, another antiquarian. We often trade books . . . and other items . . ." He gestured at the photographs. "But come. Perhaps I might interest you in a book on Victorian fashion. *Ladies'* fashion, that is. I have periodicals and catalogues from the last century you might find interesting . . ."

He herded them out of the corridor. In the main room he hovered over the stacks, looking for whatever he deemed suitable for an earl's granddaughter and her maid. He assembled a short pile on one of the library tables. There were the fashion guides he had mentioned, along with a charming book on Victorian etiquette, an illustrated volume of poetry, and a tome on local birds. Phoebe took the latter two, and Eva, something of a fashion expert in her own right—as it was part of a lady's maid's job to be—chose one of the catalogues.

They paid for their purchases and took their leave, only to be surprised by the sight of Abel Hawkhurst coming up the walk. He stopped when he saw them and gawked.

"Why . . . er . . . Lady Phoebe. Miss Huntford. Didn't expect to see you two again today. That is to say . . . er . . . what a pleasant surprise." He looked Phoebe up and down. "What are you doing here?"

"The same as when I visited you and your wife, Mr. Hawkhurst. Seeing how Mr. Sadler is faring. Also taking the opportunity to have a look at his shop. What an interesting place. Wouldn't you agree, Eva?"

"Quite interesting, yes." Eva's eyes twinkled, as she no doubt thought again of those exotic photographs.

"Yes, well. I'm here to browse the selection, myself. Looking for something on Cotswold regiments from past wars. It's a great interest of mine. Didn't fight in the Great War—too old, more's the pity. Saw some fighting in the Second Boer War, though. Yes, a great interest of mine, military history. Especially when it includes our Cotswold men. Brave lads, here in the Cotswolds." He touched the brim of his bowler hat. "Good day to you both, then."

After he fumbled with the front door and went inside, Phoebe murmured in Eva's ear. "Did you notice it?"

She didn't need to explain. "You mean that he gave us

that long-winded explanation of why he was here when, in fact, you hadn't asked him?"

"Precisely. I suspect he's here to peek at those photos." They shared a laugh and went on their way. They hadn't gone far along the road when Eva made another observation.

"The books in the shop—they're dusty, as though no one ever touches them."

"So that's why you were pulling books off the shelves, but not bothering to open most of them." Phoebe changed gears and pressed the accelerator. "Mr. Sadler probably doesn't get much business this far out of the village."

"It would appear not." Eva gazed with unseeing eyes out the windscreen, obviously distracted by her own thoughts. "One would suppose he'd take a feather duster to them at least occasionally, but that doesn't appear to be the case. I find it very strange, indeed, that a bookseller, who couldn't wait to see the library at Foxwood Hall, would allow his own inventory to fall to ruin that way." She turned to face Phoebe full on. "Why would a man who claims to love books do that?"

Phoebe had no answer for her.

That evening Julia telephoned and spoke to Grams. She, Amelia, and the baby had arrived safely at Lyndale Park after waiting out a rainstorm in the dining room of an inn north of Worcester. At breakfast the following morning Grams fluttered about the buffet table, picking up serving spoons, only to place them back down without filling her plate. She finally settled on a soft-boiled egg and a bit of smoked salmon. When she took her place at the table, she sighed listlessly and showed little inclination to eat.

"Grams, what's wrong?" Phoebe asked. "Besides the obvious, of course."

Grams lifted her teacup and held it between both hands as if to warm them. "I'm not quite sure. Something in Julia's voice last night. It has left me . . . unsettled and a trifle worried."

Phoebe didn't understand. A glance down the table told her Grams's declaration had puzzled Grampapa as well. "They arrived at Lyndale Park unscathed, didn't they? Did you speak to Amelia?"

"No. Julia said Amelia had a light dinner sent up to her room and went straight to bed. A headache, she said."

"I'm sure she'll be fine today," Grampapa tried to reassure her. "Amelia's a strong girl. She always rallies quickly."

Grams shook her head impatiently. "That isn't it. It was Julia. It was . . . something she wasn't saying. And it made me fear something wasn't quite right."

"But if she wasn't saying it," Phoebe said, snatching at a logic she didn't quite believe in, "then it couldn't be anything important."

And yet . . . her own experiences with her elder sister had taught her that often, in the face of some difficulty or other, Julia distanced herself from the rest of the family and drew inward. If only Eva was with her now. Julia had always confided in Eva, even after Eva ceased attending her as a lady's maid. To be sure, Eva never betrayed Julia's or anyone else's confidence, but she could be depended upon to offer sound and encouraging advice. Phoebe wondered if Hetta, as devoted as she was, would be quite up to the challenge.

Before they could debate the circumstances any further, Mr. Giles came into the dining room and whispered in Grampapa's ear. Phoebe's stomach took a sudden twist. She thought she heard . . .

"Ernest Shelton, did you say?" Her grandfather looked

for clarification at the butler, who nodded. "Good heavens, this is a surprise. Show him in."

Phoebe felt her guard go up. What would Ernie Shelton be doing here in Little Barlow, especially since he hadn't so much as sent a card of congratulations upon the birth of Julia's baby? They all knew how he felt; he had made it abundantly clear all along that there would be no love lost between himself and his infant cousin, or between himself and Julia, for that matter.

Ernie appeared in the doorway, his hat in his hand, as if he thought he might need to make a quick getaway and hadn't wished to relinquish his tweed trilby to the cloak closet. "Good morning, everyone. I do hope I'm not intruding?"

From beneath the table, in the vicinity of Grams's satin-slippered feet, came a *woof,* a brief thudding across the rug, and then Fairfax stuck his snout out from beneath the table linen. His nose worked as his soft brown gaze found Ernie. He gave another *woof,* but not a very enthusiastic one.

"Mr. Fairfax, come." Grams gave a light tap of her foot. The dog retreated under the table and returned to her side. "Of course you're not intruding, Ernest. Have you had breakfast?"

Grampapa came to his feet and went to shake the younger man's hand. "Good to see you, Ernest. How have you been?"

"Fine, thank you, Lord Wroxly." Looking over at Grams, he added, "I ate at the hotel, thank you, but I'll happily take a cup of coffee." Ernie waited while Vernon, the head footman, placed another chair at the table beside Fox. He also brought another cup and saucer. Ernie helped himself to the coffeepot already sitting on the table.

"Are you staying at the Calcott Inn?" Phoebe asked,

still thoroughly baffled by his arrival. "Have you been here long?"

"Yes," he replied, "and no. Only got here last night."

"Why?" This blunt query came from Fox, his expression tight, his eyes brimming with suspicion. Whatever friendship Phoebe and her siblings had felt toward Ernie Shelton had long since been eroded by his erratic behavior.

Even so, Grampapa shot a quelling look across the table. "Fox."

Fox ducked his head and mumbled a less-than-sincere "Sorry."

"I came to see Julia, actually," Ernie replied rather too brightly. "And the baby, of course. Is she not down yet? Or exercising a lady's prerogative of breakfasting in her room?"

"She isn't here," Phoebe told him. "She and Amelia have gone to Lyndale Park. You must have crossed paths with them, without knowing it."

"Perhaps we would have done"—Ernie took a sip of his coffee, wrinkled his nose, and reached for the sugar bowl—"but I haven't come from Lyndale Park, actually. I've been traveling. Spent a few days in Newquay recently, enjoying the seaside. Nothing like the seaside for calming one's nerves, I find." He glanced around the room. "Are you sure Julia's not here, and it isn't that she doesn't wish to see me? Because if that's the case—"

Did he think he'd find Julia crouching in a corner of the dining room, trying to keep out of sight?

"Good gracious, Ernest." Grams straightened on her chair, bringing her considerable height up another inch or two. Fairfax, noticing the change in her demeanor, let out a whine. Phoebe believed only she noticed the bit of smoked salmon Grams slipped him without ever taking her gaze off Ernie. "You're not suggesting we're *lying* to you, are you?"

"Of course not, Lady Wroxly. But . . . she really isn't here, then?"

Ernie found himself the recipient of four incredulous stares from around the table. Make that five, as Fairfax trotted out, came around, and stared up at him as if he couldn't quite decide what manner of creature he was.

"So Julia and Amelia fled with the baby." When they all nodded, Ernie continued with an odd, almost accusatory, skepticism, "And yet the rest of you stayed."

"This is our home," Grams asserted. "We shan't be driven out, shall we, Archibald?"

Grampapa's hesitation led Phoebe to suspect that perhaps he did wish they had left along with Julia. But he said, "No, indeed, my dear. We are quite safe now, for we are all of us, the servants included, on the alert."

"And how do you know one of your servants didn't commit the deed?" Ernie's eyebrows rose as he sipped his coffee.

This time Grampapa did not hesitate. "Because they are part of this family. We know them and trust them."

"You sound awfully sure of yourself."

Phoebe's anger simmered, but Grampapa remained calm. "I am."

"So then, will you return to Lyndale Hall now?" Grams looked and sounded eager, eliciting a chuckle from Phoebe.

Ernie shot her a glance and replied, "We'll see. I haven't decided yet."

Whatever could he mean by that? Phoebe hurried through the rest of her breakfast and went to use the in-house telephone. She intended to ask that the Vauxhall be brought round from the carriage house, but on second thought she replaced the earpiece on the cradle and went upstairs to collect her hat and handbag.

* * *

"If you don't mind, I'd prefer to walk to the carriage house," Lady Phoebe informed Eva when they met in the corridor belowstairs. They let themselves out the service entrance and took the road skirting the property to the carriage house. "I have a bit of angry energy to work off."

She filled Eva in, first on Grams's uneasiness concerning Julia—which Eva believed could be chalked up to the confines of a long ride to Staffordshire—and then Ernie's visit, leaving her shaking her head at the audacity of the man. Although, she shouldn't be surprised, not after the events of last spring and autumn. "The cheek of that man. I almost wish I could have been a fly on the wall. Imagine anyone in his right might accusing your grandmother of a falsehood. Good heavens."

"Grams took it rather well, considering. And Grampapa was a veritable saint, when what he could have done was order Ernie out. It's a good thing I hadn't been alone with him. As it was, I managed to hold my tongue, but only just."

"Admirable, my lady."

They continued along the road, not graveled and raked like the drive leading from the main road to the forecourt, but a dirt lane pitted from the weather and lined with Cotswolds' natural foliage. The warm air vibrated with a low buzzing as bees collected pollen from the bright golden agrimony, white snowdrop, and purple thistle tumbling along the verges on either side. No, the road might not be manicured, but in some ways Eva preferred the unpretentious, unaffected beauty of a country lane to the artificial perfection of the most-cared-for estate park. Rather like the difference between flopping comfortably down on the sagging settee in her parents' cottage as opposed to perching on the edge of a silk-covered chair in the Renshaws' drawing room.

Some twenty minutes later Lady Phoebe brought the Vauxhall to a stop outside a modest house a few miles outside the village, partway between Little Barlow and the even tinier hamlet of Redvale.

When George Bishop answered their knock, he showed the same surprise as the other members of the historical society had. Lady Phoebe quickly gave him the same explanation she had given the others.

"Isn't that kind of you, Lady Phoebe. And you, too, Miss Huntford. How lovely of you to have called." If their unexpected visit left him at all perturbed, he showed no sign of it. He invited them in and shook their hands. "Yes, yes, righto, I'm fine, if shocked and dismayed. Our dear, *dear* Arvina. And they've no idea who might have done it?"

A faint odor of antiseptic drifted across the oak-floored entryway. To the right a door stood open and Eva caught a glimpse of the doctor's surgery, sparsely furnished with an examination table, a chair, and a glass-fronted cabinet holding a sparse number of supplies. Well, she didn't imagine he got very many patients this far outside of both villages. She was reminded of Eamon Sadler's bookshop. Perhaps the good doctor had moved to the area to enjoy semiretirement, tending to the occasional dyspepsia, sore throat, or fractured limb when local folk either hadn't the time or the funds to seek out their regular physician.

Dr. Bishop led them into a parlor across the hall from the surgery. The room revealed the age of the cottage, with its low ceiling and hewn oak beams, an uneven floor, and a massive stone fireplace. The space held a comfortable array of furniture framed in oak, with a few mementos scattered around the surfaces. What one might expect of a semiretired country doctor, especially a bachelor.

"They do believe it could have been one of the historical

society members," Lady Phoebe said as they filed into the room.

His complexion ruddied and he let out a nervous laugh. "I hope you don't think I did it."

"Certainly not," Lady Phoebe replied without hesitation. "Of all the members you are the only one who can be accounted for during the entire tour. You never left our sight, did you?"

"I suppose I didn't, at that." He pulled a cord beside the hearth. "Just ringing for tea," he told them, and took a seat across from them. "But I cannot imagine any of the others capable of such violence. Nor can I imagine a reason."

"Sometimes the reasons are right in front of our eyes, but we fail to see them because we don't wish to," Eva said. Although she often deferred to Lady Phoebe when it came to speaking up when they were together, something about Dr. Bishop's modest home and easy demeanor put her at ease. "How well did you know Mrs. Bell?"

"Not well enough, I'm afraid." A gravelly sigh escaped him. "Not as well as I should have liked."

Yes. Eva and Lady Phoebe had both noticed and later remarked on the doctor's efforts to draw Arvina Bell's attention. She had had none of it, but that might have been because she had been far more intent on recording every detail she could about Foxwood Hall. And yet, her son had discovered a manuscript that for the most part had gone unwritten.

Curious.

"I'm sorry," Lady Phoebe said simply.

"I'm a widower, you see. These ten years. Arvina seemed like the sort of woman who . . . Well, that is neither here nor there now, is it?"

"You're new to our area, aren't you, Doctor?" Eva paused when the parlor door opened and the housekeeper brought in tea. She smiled at them all, set down the tray, and began pouring. With her task soon achieved, she smiled again and left them alone.

"What were we saying?" Dr. Bishop fixed his tea and sat back, holding his cup and saucer on his thigh. "Oh, yes, how long have I been here. Only these past several months. Finally grew weary of London and tending to patient after patient. Thought country life would be just the thing. Quiet, peaceful, uneventful. Yes, yes, that's what a man my age comes to value. Nice people hereabouts. And then, of course, there is the historical society. It's a splendid way to get to know a place. And other people. That's how I met Arvina . . ."

Seeing him about to fall into morose thoughts, Eva quickly moved the subject along. "Did she talk much about the book she was writing?"

"Oh, indeed, yes. All the time." He held his cup and saucer aloft as he stretched out his legs and crossed his ankles. "She was most excited by the project. Very eager to see your Foxwood Hall." He looked away.

"Did she say how far along she had gotten on the manuscript?" Lady Phoebe asked.

"I believe she said about halfway through."

Eva and Lady Phoebe traded fleeting glances. So Arvina Bell lied about her progress. Eva asked, "Do you know if she had been collaborating with anyone?"

"Collaborating? Oh, you mean with someone like Miss Chapman? Not to my knowledge, although she and Miss Chapman seemed friendly enough." His eyebrows shot up. "My word, you don't think Miss Chapman did it? Some kind of literary rivalry perhaps?"

Eva held up a hand to stave off his sudden suspicion. "We're not insinuating anything of the sort."

"We're merely trying to understand what happened," Lady Phoebe put in. "It was in *our* home, after all."

"Ah, yes, just so. Well, if you ladies wish to know what I believe . . ." He sipped his tea and then smoothed his fingers over his mustache. "The police had their man and let him go. That son of hers. I don't know what he was like before the war, but I believe the battlefield left its mark on him. He doesn't seem quite right to me. Doesn't seem all there."

"The battlefield left its mark on a great number of men," Lady Phoebe said, "but they don't murder their mothers."

Eva agreed, but in their experience some men—and one in particular—did commit violence, and even murder, as a result of the trauma they'd experienced in the trenches.

"It simply couldn't have been another member of the society, I tell you." Dr. Bishop's voice turned stern, almost angry. "Either one of the servants did it—"

"They didn't," Eva and Lady Phoebe said at once. Lady Phoebe set down her tea and crossed her arms in front of her as if ready to stand her ground.

"Or someone entered the house without anyone's knowledge, or Arvina's own son is guilty."

"But, Doctor, how can you be so certain when, as you said, you've only been living here a few months," Eva calmly pointed out. "Can you really say you know your fellow members well enough to rule each of them out?"

"Yes, I *certainly* can. They are each of them an upstanding individual. Each of sterling character. Why, I'd trust any one of them with my very life."

Eva couldn't help thinking the gentleman protested too much. And that, of course, raised her suspicions. Not that he himself had dispatched Mrs. Bell. They knew of a certainty he had not. But did he have knowledge of the killer? Did he fear for his life, should the truth come out?

Another question popped unbidden into Eva's mind. Had Dr. Bishop conspired with the murderer? Had his overtures toward Mrs. Bell been more fervent than his behavior at Foxwood Hall suggested? Perhaps she had done more than ignore him; perhaps she had scorned him. And he, in anger and disappointment, retaliated . . .

No, she was being silly. The man had a perfect alibi, staying right before her very eyes during every moment of the tour. And if he was overzealous in defending his fellow members, that only made him a loyal and unwavering friend.

She hoped.

CHAPTER 10

❦

Fox left early that evening, driven by Fenton to the train station for his return to Eton. After dinner Phoebe sat up with her grandparents in the Rosalind sitting room, named for her great-great-grandmother. She and Grampapa played a halfhearted game of chess, while Grams flipped through the pages of several magazines. At her feet Fairfax snoozed with his head on his paws. How small their household had become. How large and echoing the house seemed.

They turned in early, but Phoebe didn't sleep long. Her eyes fluttered open, and in the next instant she found herself entirely awake. She couldn't say what had roused her, but a sense of unease rippled through her.

A voice rose, muffled by distance and her closed door. The sound carried a desperate note through the house. *Grams.* It brought Phoebe out of bed and to her feet. She crammed them into her house slippers and, not bothering to snatch up her wrapper, ran to the door. Her heart pounded in her throat.

Another door swung open and Grampapa came stumbling out of the bedroom he and Grams shared, his wrapper half on and half swinging limply. Fairfax streaked out behind him. Despite Grampapa calling to her to stop, to let him go first, Phoebe reached the staircase first. She grabbed the bannister and ran down in a half-blind panic. Grams's voice filled her ears again—Grams, who never raised her voice, never caused a fuss, never asked for help. She was asking now, over and over again.

As Phoebe neared the bottom of the stairs, a shadow sped by her. Footsteps thudded across the Great Hall, the noise caught against the vaulted ceiling and ricocheted back down at them. She couldn't make out whom those footsteps belonged to, and at the moment she almost didn't care. What she did see, what sped both her pulse and her own steps, was her grandmother sitting on the floor in a pool of moonlight cast through the high clerestory windows. Her nightcap trailed down her back on its strings, her braid had come partially undone, and her wrapper had twisted around her legs.

Phoebe fell at Grams's side, her body shuddering with fear. "Grams, are you hurt?"

Grams gripped Phoebe's arm and hung on tight. Fairfax lumbered over to them, his nose working furiously. Grampapa reached them and sank to his haunches, reaching his arms around Grams. "My dear, are you all right?"

"Yes, I . . . I think so." She gave her head a shake and blinked several times. Phoebe wished she could do the same and awaken from what must surely be a nightmare.

At the sound of a door opening, she looked beyond the staircase to the stream of servants pouring out from behind the baize door. Mr. Giles led them as they filed across the hall. "My lord, my lady, we heard such a ruckus."

"Giles, summon the police," Grampapa ordered. Then, "Mrs. Sanders, help me bring my wife into the drawing room. Vernon," he addressed the head footman, "bring in glasses and brandy. The rest of you men, spread out. There is an intruder in the house."

Phoebe didn't think so, at least not anymore. She believed the footsteps she'd heard had been the intruder making his escape. He'd be a fool to linger with the entire household awakened. One of the maids went around the hall switching on lights. On the floor, near where she had found Grams, lay a two-branched candelabra, one thin curl of filigreed silver bent at an awkward angle. Phoebe leaned down closer and detected a smidgeon of crimson on that particular branch, along with a smear on the marble flooring. Grams apparently had wounded the intruder.

Good for you, Grams.

And there, Phoebe saw when she straightened, beyond the staircase where the hall narrowed to the corridor leading to the Petit Salon and the garden room, lay the scattered shards of a Meissen vase that had been knocked from the eighteenth-century console table upon which it had perched.

That immediately sparked a memory. The vase had been removed earlier for the house tour, as had several other treasured pieces that sat within reach, to prevent just such an occurrence. Their culprit, Phoebe reasoned, had not known the vase would be there, and had therefore not used caution in that part of the corridor.

"Where is Stevens?" she wondered aloud. The servants all traded blank glances. She referred to a footman, one of the newer ones. For these past three nights Grampapa had instituted a schedule of night watches, and Stevens, she remembered, had the first watch tonight. A glance at the long case clock, which read twenty past midnight, confirmed that Stevens should be here. He should have heard. If Phoebe had been awakened from all the way upstairs, not to mention servants from below stairs and the second floor, surely the night footman should have been alerted.

She had a sudden misgiving about the young man's welfare.

A hand reached for her from behind. "My lady—Phoebe, is your grandmother all right?"

"Eva." Phoebe turned and reached for her maid—and friend—and embraced her. "Grams was attacked. Someone was here, in the house. I must go to her. She's in the drawing room. Please see what you can find out for us."

"Oh, good heavens. Yes, I'll see what I can learn."

Phoebe hurried away, finding her grandparents and Fairfax near the hearth, along with Grams's maid, Miss Shea. In a house robe and slippers, her braided hair hanging over one shoulder, Miss Shea stood several feet behind Grams's chair, her hands folded at her waist, silent but ready to intervene on behalf of her mistress if necessary. But what a small group they made now, with Julia and Amelia at Lyndale Park, and Fox having returned to Eton.

Grampapa crouched before Grams's chair and pressed a snifter into her hands. "Drink a little, my dear. It will steady you."

"I *am* steady, Archibald. As steady as I can be under the circumstances." Despite the claim, her hands shook, sending ripples through the brandy in the glass she held, and an ashen pallor had settled over her face. Grampapa nudged the glass to her lips and she took a sip. It worked, and a bit of color infused her cheeks. Fairfax rested his stout chin on her knee, and she absently stroked his head.

Phoebe took the armchair opposite Grams and moved it a few feet closer before lowering herself into it. "Can you tell us what happened?"

Grams hesitated, took another sip of brandy, and drew in a breath. "I couldn't sleep, what with worrying about Julia on top of everything else."

Phoebe and Grampapa nodded. Phoebe herself had spoken briefly with Julia earlier that evening, had even tossed out a couple of leading questions, to which Julia had responded cheerfully. Amelia hadn't added any portentous information, either, but had seemed content to be at Lyndale Park. Still, through the years Phoebe had learned to trust her grandmother's instincts. She had an uncanny ability to see through multiple layers of deceit, as each of the Renshaw siblings, in turn, had discovered.

"I decided to come down for a spot of sherry," Grams went on. "I sat in this very chair, trying to calm my thoughts. I didn't even bother switching on a lamp, as I found the darkness and the moonlight against the windows soothing. And then I heard a noise from out in the hall. At first, I assumed it was Stevens making his rounds, so I didn't think a thing of it, until I heard a smash. With a certainty I knew that sound could not have been Stevens. None of our people would move so clumsily about this house, not even a new servant."

The shattered Meissen vase.

"I also realized that I was essentially cut off from everyone else in the house, for if I tried to make my way back upstairs, the intruder might intercept me in the hall. I looked around for anything I could use as a weapon and snatched up the first thing that came into my sight—the candelabra that sits there." She pointed to a table. "I was still holding my sherry, and when I leaned to set it down, someone tried to grab me from behind."

They all turned their heads toward the hearth, and Phoebe saw the slivers and small puddle of liquid that had been Grams's glass of sherry. Grampapa, who had sat back on his heels during Grams's narration, rocked forward to put his hands at either side of her waist. "Dear heavens above, Maude. You might have been killed. How did you end up in the hall?"

"Yes, well, I swung backward, over my head, with the candelabra. I felt an *oomph* and heard a grunt from my assailant . . . and then I ran, still clutching the candelabra. He came after me, caught up about where you found me. I swung at him again and again, even as he knocked me down. I shouted for help . . . and then . . . and then he simply ran off. I heard Phoebe's voice, and then yours, Archibald, and I knew I was safe. Thank goodness. Thank you for coming to my rescue."

Phoebe sprang up from her chair and went to her grandmother. "Oh, Grams. I've never been so frightened as when I heard you shouting for help." Hot tears threatened to spill over. "I don't know what I would have done . . . what any of us would have done if . . ."

Grampapa rose and set a hand on Phoebe's shoulder. "Don't, my girl. We needn't imagine the worst that might have happened. But perhaps Fox was right about something he said before he left for school earlier."

"What was that, Grampapa?"

"He suggested opening the gun cabinet in my study and arming ourselves."

The notion sent a start through Phoebe. "He did?"

"He did?" Grams echoed. Where Phoebe might have expected shock, she heard only curiosity from her grandmother, as if she were only now realizing that Fox was no longer a little boy.

"Yes, but I told him no. That we would not descend into barbarity." Grampapa paused and shook his head. "Now I wonder. Perhaps there is no other way to protect ourselves."

"If I might make a suggestion . . ." Miss Shea, who had maintained a silent and nearly invisible presence, now came forward from behind Grams's chair. "Perhaps the dog should be let loose to roam the house at night, as a security measure."

"No," Grams said with a decisive shake of her head. Her hand covered Fairfax's head as if in a benediction. "Mr. Fairfax stays with us at night, where he's safe."

Phoebe's heart warmed at her decree.

"And as for guns," Grams went on, "Archibald, you were right in your first assessment. We must not become what we fear. Besides, next time it *could* be a footman knocking something over. Or one of us. I will not have bullets flying through this house."

"Then we must keep our bedroom doors locked at night," Grampapa said, "and stay put until morning."

As Grams nodded to this, Phoebe couldn't help thinking that until the killer had been caught, they'd be prisoners in their own home. But she kept the thought to herself. Before she could muse further, Eva came quietly into the room.

"Excuse me, my lord, my lady. Stevens has been found."

Once Eva made it clear that Stevens was in no condition to walk to the drawing room, Lord and Lady Wroxly asked her to return to the garden room—where the footman had been found—and learn as much as she could from him. Lord Wroxly had forbidden Lady Wroxly from rising from her chair, and he refused to leave her side. Even Lady Phoebe had opted to remain in the drawing room. Even so, Eva didn't miss the imperative look Lady Phoebe had sent her. She would want all the details later.

In the garden room Stevens had been moved off the mosaic-tile floor, where Eva had last seen him, and onto a wrought-iron-framed chair. He sat hunched over, elbows on the arms of the chair, his forehead resting on his palms. Eva had been glad the family hadn't asked many questions, for she wouldn't have liked to tell them Stevens had been found prone on his back, mouth open, snoring, and reeking of spirits. Gin, if she had her guess.

Vernon had pulled up another chair to face the younger footman's. Mr. Giles was in the room, along with Mrs. Sanders, looking on with stern expressions. The others, apparently, had been dismissed, probably sent back to their beds. She could only imagine the speculating presently among roommates, and the flagrant gossip that would grip the staff tomorrow, despite Mrs. Sanders's rules.

Vernon folded his hands and let them dangle between his knees as he leaned toward Stevens. "Where did you get the alcohol?"

"I don't know . . ." The words came out slurry, as one might expect from someone who was inebriated to the point of passing out.

"What do you mean, you don't know? Damn your eyes, Stevens . . ."

Eva came up behind the head footman and set a hand on his shoulder. "Vernon. Perhaps that's not the way."

He craned his neck to look up at her. She saw the anger and frustration simmering in his eyes. "Would you like to try?"

"If you'll allow me to, yes."

With a huff he vacated the seat, and Eva settled herself onto it. "Stevens, do you remember what happened tonight?"

He took several moments before answering, drawing deep breaths into his lungs. Then he shook his head. "It's all so foggy."

"Everything is always foggy to a drunk."

Eva waved a hand to shush Vernon. "Think. You were making your rounds, yes?"

"Yes. I started my shift at ten o'clock. Room to room, like the earl instructed me. Checked all the windows and doors along the way."

Connie came in then, carrying a tray with a coffeepot and an earthenware mug. She placed it on a table and poured, then brought the mug to Stevens. He thanked her, holding the cup below his nose, seeming to breathe in the curling steam.

"Thank you, Connie," Mrs. Sanders said. "That will be all. You may go to bed."

After the girl left, Eva started again. "How did you come to be in this room?"

He gazed around him, and it was obvious he couldn't quite focus on his surroundings. After a sip of coffee he said, "I suppose I was here checking the door, like everywhere else."

"But you don't specifically remember?"

"I remember the other side of the house. The dining room, drawing room, even the library. I didn't like going in there, not after what happened, but I did it because it was my job."

"Did you go into the Petit Salon?"

"There is a broken window in the Petit Salon," Mr. Giles put in. "It must be where the perpetrator entered the house."

Stevens frowned. "I must have done. Or perhaps I saved it until after this room. I don't rightly remember, Miss Huntford, nor do I remember a broken window. I'm sorry. I wish I did, but I don't." His eyes fell closed a moment. He groaned and placed his forehead in his free hand. Eva sat ready to snatch his mug, should he appear to lose his grip on it. Or to lurch back out of the way, should he become ill. Neither happened, but she remained wary.

She decided to be direct. "Do you remember breaking into Lord Wroxly's drinks cabinet?"

"No, Miss Huntford, I don't."

"Did you steal liquor from belowstairs?"

"I don't remember having done."

"Have you ever imbibed on the job before?"

"Never. I swear, Miss Huntford."

Vernon stepped forward, looming imperiously over the younger man. "How do you know if you can't remember anything?"

"I . . . I think I'd know if I was in the habit of drinking on the job."

"Or maybe you're not in the habit of admitting to it," Vernon charged.

"Vernon, please." Eva caught his gaze and held it. She didn't have to say another word as knowledge of the events of two Christmases ago passed between them. Vernon dropped his gaze. He had also been accused, that Christmas, had been interrogated by the police, while his superiors made assumptions. Eventually he had been proven innocent to his own and everyone's vast relief. He could not now but admit that Stevens could be proven innocent as well.

If not for the gin vapors wafting off him . . .

But there could be an explanation for that.

The sound of the front-door knocker echoing through the hall startled them all. Mr. Giles wasted no time in going to see who it was, while Eva nearly sagged in relief. The police had been summoned, so that would be Miles— and Chief Inspector Perkins, of course. The latter wouldn't be pleased about having been awakened in the middle of the night, to be sure.

Yet she felt sorry to hand Stevens over to them, even to the conscientious and fair-minded Miles Brannock. The chief inspector and his constable had a job to do, and the next hour or so would be difficult for Stevens under their interrogation. Still, Eva hadn't gotten anywhere with him, really. Perhaps Miles would manage to jog his memory. Perhaps more coffee might do the trick.

Mr. Giles returned to the garden room alone. The policemen had gone into the drawing room first to speak with the countess. Eva made her way there to find Lady Wroxly retelling the details of her ordeal.

Suddenly her ladyship stopped and gasped. "I remember something about my attacker. Or, at least, I remember seeing something most curious—dots glowing in the air in front of me."

"*Dots,* Lady Wroxly?" Chief Inspector Perkins compressed his lips, but not before Eva caught the hint of a grin. "Perhaps it was stars you were seeing, after being knocked to the floor, my lady."

"Don't be ridiculous," she snapped in reply. "These were greenish, glowing dots . . ."

"An airman's watch," Eva said, then bit down on her bottom lip. Speaking up that way in front of her employers wasn't the done thing for a lady's maid, but she wouldn't allow Lady Wroxly to be ridiculed by the chief inspector.

"That's probably correct." Miles held up his left arm and tugged back his sleeve to show the aviator's watch that encircled his wrist. During the war Miles had flown bombing missions over Germany, and this watch, with radium applied to the dial, had allowed him to coordinate the time, even at night, without lifting his hands from the controls. He held up his arm and displayed the watch calmly, as if it were of no account at all.

Eva knew better; she knew how he had vowed never to step foot in an aeroplane again, certainly not as its pilot. Those missions haunted him. He had admitted as much to her once, and once only, and never spoke of them again after telling her he continued to wear that watch, with its harrowing memories, its guilt and accusations, as a reminder of what a man is capable of, despite every better intention he might harbor. He wasn't proud of his war service. Despite being assured he had been doing his duty, helping defeat the enemy, he had learned that sometimes the enemy whose lives were shattered by the blasts were families with children and grandparents who had never done anyone a bad turn.

She shook away those thoughts—Miles's ghosts that she felt powerless to help him overcome.

"So this individual wore an aviator's watch," the chief inspector was saying. "Then we can safely assume he flew aeroplanes in the war. All we need is a list of airmen and where they reside, and we can narrow down our suspects."

"Perhaps, but not necessarily," Miles corrected him. "Those watches are available nowadays and anyone might have come by it. My guess is he wore it to keep track of how much time he spent here in the house. Probably wished to stick to a strict schedule—get in, find whatever it was he was after—and get out, all under a certain amount of time. Less chance of being caught."

"I foiled his plans, then, didn't I," the countess said with grim humor.

Lord Wroxly, who sat beside his wife and never let go of her hand, said, "Could this have anything to do with the photograph that was stolen from the library?"

The chief inspector shrugged. "One supposes it could, my lord. But as you yourself said, there was nothing in that photo that suggested anything of value. It could merely have been taken as a kind of souvenir of the murder."

"A *souvenir?*" Grams's mouth dropped open. "Like purchasing trinkets and collecting shells on one's holiday at the shore? What a ghoulish notion."

"There are culprits, unbalanced individuals, who think this way, my lady," the chief inspector explained.

"But even if it hasn't to do with the photograph exactly, surely it's connected to Mrs. Bell's death," Lady Phoebe said.

"In all likelihood, yes," Mr. Perkins agreed. The group

fell silent, until the chief inspector cleared his throat. "*Ahem*. If you can think of nothing to add at the moment, Lady Wroxly, we'll go and speak with your footman, as well as determine the point of entry. I suggest you all remain here for now."

Eva waited until the two policemen had left the drawing room, then told the family, "Mr. Giles said he discovered a broken window in the Petit Salon. It's fairly certain, then, that the chief inspector will tell you the intruder came in through that room."

Lady Phoebe shuddered. "I hate to think it. I've always loved that room. Now it will remind me how vulnerable we are here. The Petit Salon, the library . . . the house feels tainted. Almost cursed."

"Now, now." The earl looked as close to cross as Eva had ever seen him when not chiding Fox for some perceived wrongdoing. "We can't have that kind of talk, Phoebe. This is still our home, the ancestral seat of the Renshaws, and we must not cower in the face of adversity."

No one seemed to have a reply for that, and a tense silence fell, until footsteps heralded the return of Miles and Chief Inspector Perkins.

"It looks as though the assailant came in through the Petit Salon," Mr. Perkins confirmed. "As your butler pointed out to me, a window had been broken, the lock easily opened. It looks as though our suspect exited the same way, although we'll be able to tell more in the morning. I've instructed Mr. Giles to keep the servants out of that room. Yourselves as well, Lord Wroxly. We'll be back in daylight to dust for fingerprints."

Eva saw them out, her hand connecting briefly with Miles's, once the chief inspector had cleared the threshold. "I doubt he'll be back tonight, but keep to your rooms," he murmured to her. "Lock your doors. I'll be back early."

She acknowledged him with a nod and a weak smile, and returned to the drawing room. Phoebe and her grandparents came to their feet, and Eva followed them upstairs. Lady Phoebe appeared too restless to sleep, a notion confirmed when she gestured to Eva to come and sit by the hearth in her bedroom.

"The Petit Salon," Lady Phoebe reiterated. "Do you remember who claimed to have become lost and ended up there alone?"

"Indeed, I do. Lady Primrose. Do you think she returned to the room during the tour to judge whether it might make an easy entrance for a break-in?"

"It makes one wonder, doesn't it? Using that room doesn't appear to be random. The windows *are* among the oldest in the house."

"And she's no frail old woman, is she?"

"No, she is not. My guess is she could climb in through a window if need be."

"Or strangle another woman?" Even as Eva said it, the possibility seemed outlandish. The daughter of an earl? The wife of an MP? Crawling through windows in the dead of night and attacking elderly ladies? But then she remembered the woman's house and the air of pretense that had hovered over the parlor. "For certain she's hiding something. Something rather momentous."

Lady Phoebe nodded. "Something that perhaps brought her here tonight in her effort to keep it from being discovered. I fear Grams kept her—or whoever it was—from doing that. Which can only mean one thing."

"Yes." Eva drew a deep breath and let it out on a sigh. "Whoever it was will be back."

CHAPTER 11

Phoebe stood in the library, arms crossed in front of her as she scanned the shelves, walls, and tabletops. She had switched on all the lamps to augment the morning sunlight. Surely, the missing picture had something to do with Arvina's death *and* the break-in last night. Was anything else missing? Had the intruder gotten this far before being sidetracked by Grams?

She even forced herself to examine the alcove where Mrs. Bell had met her death. The act of standing even near the spot sent chills through her and made her feel rather wobbly, but she looked nonetheless. But nothing now seemed out of the ordinary. Even the curtains and tiebacks—new ones—had been put in place as if nothing had ever happened.

She walked along the far wall of bookcases, her gaze searching and analyzing. She thought of Eamon Sadler, who had practically sprinted into the library to pore over the collection. Had there been something of extreme value here, something the family had been unaware of, that he had wished to steal? Had Arvina Bell caught him in the act? Phoebe ran her fingers along the spines, hoping something unusual might jump out at her, or she'd find an empty space where a book had been.

"My lady, Miles says the dusting revealed nothing." Eva came into the room. The constable and the chief inspector had returned soon after breakfast, the former examining the Petit Salon and dusting for fingerprints, the latter interviewing both Grams and Stevens again.

"Gloves," Phoebe concluded.

"Again, yes. Just as in Arvina Bell's death. Which makes it look as though the murderer and intruder are one in the same."

"I never believed them to be anything but." Phoebe blew out a breath that stirred the finger curls Eva had arranged to frame her face. "I haven't an inkling of what I'm searching for, but I'm going to keep at it."

"I'll help you."

As they moved from room to room—library, withdrawing room, dining room, etc.—they essentially retraced the steps of the house tour. In the drawing room all traces of last night's struggle had been cleared away, the spilled sherry and crystal fragments gone. Phoebe almost wished they hadn't been, though she suspected they would have revealed little about Grams's attacker and much more about the courage and sheer stubbornness with which Grams had fought back. But Phoebe didn't need physical evidence to tell her that.

In the doorway Miles Brannock cleared his throat for their attention. "Lady Phoebe."

"Yes, Constable. Please come in. Eva and I were just, well, looking for clues."

He flashed a smile. "Find anything?"

"No," Eva told him. "We're all but certain her ladyship interrupted the crime before it happened."

"I believe so, too," he concurred. "We've found nothing particularly helpful in the other rooms, nor learned anything significant from the footman. Will he get the sack, do you think?"

"I'm honestly not sure," Phoebe said. "My grandfather tends to give everyone the benefit of the doubt, and he likes to believe the best of people until proven wrong. But this was my grandmother attacked last night." She didn't add that for a marriage that had taken place in the previous century, when so many were arranged out of convenience, Grams and Grampapa had been a love match from the start, and still were. If Grampapa deemed Stevens responsible for what happened, Stevens would go. "What do you think about him?" Phoebe asked the constable. "Was he simply drunk, or could there be another explanation for his being incapacitated last night?"

"I can't say for certain, at least not yet." Constable Brannock came farther into the room and leaned his hands against the carved back of an armchair. "But it's awfully coincidental that he chose last night to become stone cold drunk when he was supposed to be making his rounds. Now, is this something he does every night, after hours and in the privacy of his bedroom? Perhaps. I understand the man he shares with is away from Little Barlow at the moment?"

"That's right," Eva said. "Douglas drove Ladies Annondale and Amelia to Staffordshire."

The constable nodded. "That's what Stevens told us. We'll need to get in touch with him, just to corroborate whether or not Stevens has been drinking on the sly." He regarded Phoebe. "Can you contact your sister for us, please?"

"I'll put in a call to Staffordshire today."

"Thank you. When you talk to Lady Annondale, please let me know."

"I will, Constable."

As he left, Mr. Giles came into the room. "Lady Phoebe,

there is a Mr. Bell here to see you. And Miss Huntford, too." The butler sounded mildly disapproving as he mentioned Eva's name, and Phoebe had little doubt he *did* disapprove of someone coming to the front door and asking to speak with one of the staff. It must have been rather confusing for him that Mr. Bell also asked to speak with Phoebe herself, as if she and Eva had mutual acquaintances. Which they did. A longtime butler like Mr. Giles would find that highly irregular.

But what had induced Hayden Bell to return to the very house where his mother met her end? She exchanged a glance with Eva, whose expression mirrored Phoebe's own thoughts—the matter that brought him must be pressing, indeed.

"Please show him into the . . ." Phoebe hesitated, considering. If they stayed in the drawing room, they might be interrupted by other members of the family while they discussed whatever Mr. Bell had come to talk about. She couldn't meet with him in the library—not in the very room where his mother was murdered. Finally she hit upon it. "Please bring him to the garden room. Eva and I shall be there presently."

When Mr. Giles left them, Eva came to Phoebe's side. "Are you certain we should see him? For all we know, it could have been him last night. Remember, the intruder wore an aviator's watch. Hayden Bell fought in the war."

"So did a lot of other men. Besides, he was an infantryman, not an airman."

"That doesn't mean he didn't come by the watch somewhere—in a trench, on another man . . ." Phoebe winced at the implication, and Eva took her hand and gave it a gentle squeeze. "I'm only suggesting that we must be careful. Exceedingly careful."

"And we will be. This isn't the middle of the night. There are people about and we'll be quite safe." She could see that Eva wasn't entirely convinced, but she suspected her qualms had more to do with her usual protectiveness than any real fear of Hayden Bell. "Come. Let's see what he has to say."

In the garden room Mr. Bell stood before one of the large windows, gazing out at the slightly foggy distance. He clutched a leather folder, tied closed with a thong. He turned as he heard them come in. "Lady Phoebe, Miss Huntford, thank you for seeing me. Especially under the circumstances." He gave a halfhearted, awkward smile. "Some people think the police released me prematurely, but I assure you, I'm no murderer."

Phoebe stole a peek at Eva, and it was plain neither of them knew how to respond to that. She merely gestured toward the wrought-iron table and chairs nestled between a potted ficus, whose twisting branches were looking sparse, and an equally spindly olive tree. From the ceiling the Greek goddess Persephone gazed down at them, looking as curious as Phoebe herself felt.

"What can we do for you, Mr. Bell?"

He placed the portfolio on his knees and opened it. "I discovered something curious. No, that's an understatement. I've discovered something that might explain quite a lot. I've continued going through my mother's things." Here he stopped and met their gazes. "Despite her being . . . gone . . . it feels rather wrong, rifling through her belongings. It fills me with a strange sense of trespassing, and an irrational fear of being caught in the act." He laughed weakly. "Does that make any sense?"

"It does, Mr. Bell," Phoebe assured him. "You've hardly had time to process your mother's passing. Some families don't sort through their loved one's belongings until years after the fact."

"Yes, well." He glanced down at the papers in the folder on his lap. He took the topmost one and passed it to

Phoebe. Eva leaned closer to see what it was as Phoebe began reading. Mr. Bell explained, "I believe my mother's true purpose in coming to Foxwood Hall was to search for something. You see there a reference to an old rumor of a fortune secreted away somewhere in this house."

Phoebe studied the page. "That's impossible. I've never heard a whisper about this. Nothing. Grampapa has surely never mentioned it. And he should know, shouldn't he?"

"Not necessarily." Mr. Bell pointed at the paper in her hands. "My mother learned of this secret from John Willikins."

"The butler before Mr. Giles," Eva murmured.

"Yes, they were friendly, you see. They'd known each other since before my mother married. I believe they even might have courted for a short time."

"He must have been much older than she was," Eva pointed out.

Mr. Bell nodded. "And I believe he told her about this fortune right before he died, which was less than a year ago. He achieved a very old age, you know, although according to Mother, he'd entered his dotage quite some years ago, poor man."

"I'm sorry," Eva said, "but if Mr. Willikins was senile, why would your mother put any stock in such a claim?"

"Because after the last time she saw him, right before he died, she said she found him remarkably lucid. Said he spoke of the past as if it were yesterday. And he remembered her vividly, although there had been other occasions when he treated her as though she were a kindly stranger come to look in on him."

Phoebe narrowed her eyes as she tried to make sense of this development. "She told you nothing of this supposed hidden fortune?"

"Not a word."

Phoebe wasn't entirely sure she believed him. He wasn't

a member of the historical society and had come, he claimed, merely to keep his mother company. It could have been the other way around, with him having learned of this fortune and using his mother to gain entry to the house.

"But there is more in her notes," he said, oblivious to her suspicions, "about clues as to where the fortune had been hidden. She makes mention of a photograph."

Phoebe managed to stifle a gasp. "That photograph has gone missing, Mr. Bell. It was in our library. Perhaps you remember seeing it?"

"I'm sorry, no, I didn't pay attention the way the rest of the group did."

She started to hand him back the page of notes, but he waved it away. "I think you should keep that. Along with the rest." He closed the folder and passed it to her. "I'm hoping this might lead to the person who killed my mother and ultimately clear my name. I'm still a suspect, you realize. And I've brought it to you, rather than the police, because if anyone can discover if there is any truth to this rumor, or if my mother died while on a fool's errand, it's someone who lives in this house."

"You're right, Mr. Bell. I intend to start asking questions immediately."

Eva knocked softly on the open door of the butler's pantry. "Mr. Giles, do you have a few minutes, sir?"

He looked at her and frowned, not in annoyance, but in puzzlement. Then his expression cleared. "Miss Huntford, it's you. Yes, yes, of course. Do come in." He rose to take a wooden chair away from the wall and set it beside his desk so Eva could sit. "What can I do for you? I do hope nothing is amiss."

"Thank you, sir. And no, there's nothing wrong. Well, that is to say, there is. After all, a woman died above stairs only two days ago."

"A bad business, that." He might as well have been discussing a minor tussle over a dart game at the local pub.

"Sir, you've been at Foxwood Hall since the former earl was alive, yes?"

"Indeed, I have been, Miss Huntford. In fact, the former Lord Wroxly's butler trained me."

"John Willikins?"

He sat back, smiling. "You know your Foxwood Hall history, Miss Huntford. Yes, that's correct. John Willikins taught me everything I know. A good man, John. Of course in those days I'd never have dared call him by his Christian name. No, it was always Mr. Willikins, until much later when we became friends."

"I'm sure, sir." She joined him in chuckling over such a preposterous notion. Then, sobering, she leaned closer and propped an arm on the desktop. "Sir, do you remember Mr. Willikins ever speaking about a fortune hidden here at Foxwood Hall?"

She very well expected him to chuckle over that notion, or perhaps laugh outright. He shocked her by tapping the side of his chin and nodding. "I do, at that, Miss Huntford. Not while John was still here as butler. No, it was many years later when I visited him at his . . . Oh, where was that?"

"His niece's house, near Gloucester?"

"Right again, Miss Huntford. Yes, he and I kept in touch over the years, and when I heard he'd taken poorly, I went to visit him." He heaved a doleful sigh. "Poor man, to lose his wits the way he did, and he being one of the most sensible individuals I've ever had the privilege to meet. Broke my heart to see him that way."

"I can imagine, sir."

"Although he was lucky in that his great-niece was able to take him in and see him properly cared for. She and her mum used to visit John here. He was already getting on in years by then, already thinking of retiring. Oh, yes, I re-member little Fifi well, a high-spirited lass, always want-ing to see what the servants were doing, insisting she could help. A good sort, that one."

"She sounds lovely, sir. But about the fortune?"

"Fortune?"

Oh, dear. Poor Mr. Willikins hadn't been the only butler suffering from the forgetfulness and confusion of old age. She gently reminded Mr. Giles, "The hidden fortune. I be-lieve Mr. Willikins told you something about it?"

"Ah, yes. It was when I visited him at his great-niece's house. His nurse brought us tea and John fell to talking about the old days. He became rather incoherent for a stretch, and then said something about the former Lord Wroxly hiding something of great value here in the house."

"Did he say where?"

"No. I don't believe he knew. Well, to be honest, I be-lieved he made the whole thing up. Probably came from a book he'd read, or perhaps one his nurse had recently read to him."

"Did you mention it to his great-niece?"

"Didn't have a chance. She wasn't there at the time. In fact, she was never there the few times I visited. A busy woman, that one. Oh, but as I said, I didn't put much stock in the story. Besides, whatever the previous earl did is none of my business, is it? His fortune was his to do with as he liked, assuming it wasn't part of the entail. And I certainly don't think he would have cheated his own son, the present Lord Wroxly, out of his rightful inheritance, now would he?"

"No, I don't suppose he would, sir. Thank you, sir." Eva came to her feet. "This has been very interesting."

"You're not going treasure hunting through the house now, are you, Miss Huntford?" She could tell by his tone he was teasing.

"No, sir," she replied with a chuckle. "Rest assured I won't be doing that. Good day, sir."

As she stepped into the corridor, she nearly collided with Dora, the young scullery maid. The girl was standing just to the right of the doorway, holding a teacup. She lurched a step backward and peered up at Eva through loose strands of nut-brown hair, made dull and slightly frizzy from standing over hot water and scrubbing pots.

Startled, Eva placed a hand on her bosom. "Dora, what are you doing there?"

"Just bringing Mr. Giles his tea, Miss Huntford." The reply came just a tad too quickly, making Eva wonder.

"How long have you been standing there?"

"I only just got here, just this moment."

Eva stepped closer to her and lowered her chin to meet Dora's gaze. "Were you listening?"

"No, Miss Huntford! Honest. Um . . . if you'll excuse me, I don't want Mr. Giles's tea to grow cold."

With that, she ducked her head, circled Eva, and disappeared through the doorway. Eva stared at the place she had been and shook her head. She wondered how much Dora had overheard, and how much she would relate to the rest of the staff.

As there was nothing at present she could do about it, she went on her way. A narrow stone staircase brought her to the subbasement, where the laundry facilities were located. She found the neatly stacked piles for Ladies Phoebe and Amelia and on her way back up stuck her head into the preparation room, where the head laundress pre-treated stains and readied garments for the washtub.

"Hullo, Mable."

The plump laundress, in her faded housedress and kerchief, smiled up at Eva from behind her workbench. "Miss Huntford, anything I can do for you?"

"No, no, just wanted to thank you for these." Eva held up the clean shirtwaists and silk tunics. She always made a point of thanking the unsung heroines of the subbasement, who ensured clean wardrobes and fresh linens for the entire household. "Can I get you anything? Tea? A bite to eat?"

"I'm fine, thanks, Miss Huntford. Besides, I'll have another pile for you shortly, the delicates, and you'll be needing to fire up your irons for them."

"That's well enough, Mable, I'll be ready." While much of the ironing was accomplished here, by Mable's assistants, Eva always personally ironed her ladies' finer garments, such as blouses adorned with ruffles and lace, or party frocks of costly silk. She was about to turn and go when an odor made its way to her nose and drew a sneeze.

"Bless you," Mable said absently as she continued her work.

Eva thanked her just as absently, too absorbed in trying to identify what continued to make her nose itch. It was so familiar, and so out of place here. She glanced at the clothing waiting to be tended. Along the closest workbench were a few piles of shirts, neckties, trousers, and coats worn by the footmen. Their names had been sewn into the collar of each coat, shirt, or waistcoat, the waistband of trousers, and on the back of each necktie. The neckties lay closest to her, a snaking pile of white linen.

She reached for one, held it close, and breathed in. The odor assaulted her olfactory senses, bringing tears to her eyes and a sticky sweetness to her throat. She whisked it away, then slowly brought it back again. Another sniff had the same result, but also strummed a chord of memory. Turning the necktie over, she read the name embroidered along the seam in back: *K. Stevens.*

She moved along the workbench, searching among the

tailcoats for the one belonging to Stevens. She lifted it by its collar, and the odor she expected wafted from the worsted wool: gin. She lay the coat back down beside the others. A glance at Mable assured Eva the laundress hadn't noticed. Nor would she notice now as Eva tucked the necktie into the pocket of her dress and made her way upstairs.

CHAPTER 12

"I've never heard of any such thing. A secret fortune. Why, it's absurd."

Phoebe sat with her grandparents in the Rosalind Sitting Room, on the first floor, off the same corridor as the family bedrooms. A recording of Caruso played quietly on the gramophone. It was an aria from *La Bohème,* one of Grams's favorites. She and Grampapa were spending nearly all their time upstairs now, except for meals, as they no longer felt safe on the ground floor after what happened to Grams, not to mention Arvina Bell. Phoebe hardly blamed them. She wished she could urge them to leave Foxwood Hall, perhaps join Julia and Amelia at Lyndale Park in Staffordshire.

They would never go, never leave their home because some brute had frightened them in the middle of the night. They'd see leaving as allowing themselves to be bullied, and that would never do. No, better to stay and take precautions than turn tail and run.

"Are you sure, Grampapa?" Phoebe didn't doubt his word, but surely there must be some record of this rumor, somewhere. Mrs. Bell couldn't have gotten it out of thin air. And if John Willikins knew of it, then someone else at Foxwood Hall must have heard of it, too.

"Your grandfather is most certain, Phoebe," Grams chided. "I've never heard so much as a breath about this, either. Why on earth would your great-grandfather wish to hide away a piece of the family fortune?"

"Perhaps because it wasn't part of the family fortune," Phoebe suggested. From where she sat, she could see out the garden-facing windows to the forests that separated the estate from the tenant farms and the rolling hillsides beyond. She imagined the scene had changed very little through the years—or through the centuries. Her great-grandparents, and indeed the many generations before them, had looked out over the same countryside, sometimes blanketed in snow, at other times flaming with fall colors, or bursting with spring blossoms, as now.

That unchangeability of life, from one generation to the next, was what had sustained Foxwood Hall and estates like it since they had first come into being. The unbroken chain from son to son, each merely a temporary custodian of the property and wealth.

There had been uncertain times in the past, but never more so than now, in the aftermath of the Great War. The country's economy and its traditions had been left in tatters. Could her great-grandfather have foreseen such times and hidden something away as a kind of insurance that the family—and the Foxwood estate—would continue long into the future?

"Could the reason for the secrecy," she said, voicing the turn her thoughts had taken, "have been because Great-Grandpapa feared for the future, and wished to keep something tucked safely away, where it could not be taken by the tax collectors?"

"Are you suggesting your great-grandfather sought to

cheat Her Majesty's government when he passed away?" Grams raised a thin silver eyebrow.

"Not *cheat,* not exactly. But protect future generations, yes."

Grampapa shook his head as Phoebe spoke. "It doesn't make sense, though, not to have told anyone. Not to have told me, his heir."

"But he died prematurely, didn't he?" Phoebe reminded him. "Unexpectedly. Perhaps he meant to tell you, but didn't have the chance. But somehow John Willikins knew."

"John Willikins was a very old man when he told Arvina Bell about this supposed secret." Grams once again lifted that eyebrow, the one that always made Phoebe feel as though she were about to fail an important examination. "It was likely a figment of his imagination."

"Then what about the missing photograph?" Phoebe pressed on. "What about Mrs. Bell being murdered in the library at the very same time the photograph went missing? And then someone breaks into the house. It's all connected—it must be—and obviously the individual in question is after *something.*"

"Now, Phoebe, listen to reason." Phoebe sensed her grandmother's patience stretching thin, but before Grams could go on, Grampapa spoke.

"Perhaps the issue isn't whether this hidden fortune exists, but that others believe it does. The intruder may very well be intent on finding something that doesn't exist, and might stop at nothing to find it." He went silent a moment, then concluded, "And that could put us in as dangerous a position as if this so-called fortune were real."

Phoebe left her grandparents with that warning weighing heavily on her mind. In her bedroom she took up the duplicate photograph. Surely, there must be some clue here if only one looked closely enough. It had been taken in the library, with bookshelves forming a backdrop. Jumping up, she went to her writing table and snatched up the magnifying glass she always kept there, beside her letter opener. Bringing the photo to the brighter light of the window, she tried to make out the titles on the spines of the books. Perhaps there was some message to be deciphered . . .

The books were little more than a blur, and a dark one, at that, being too far from the window that had illuminated her great-grandparents' faces. At a knock on her door she set aside the photo and magnifier.

"Yes, come in."

Eva stepped in and closed the door behind her. She held out a length of rather limp white linen.

"What's that?"

"Stevens's necktie." Eva crossed the room to her. She held the tie up with both hands so Phoebe could read the name embroidered onto the back. "I don't believe Stevens was drinking last night. Can you smell it?"

Phoebe leaned in closer and inhaled. A sharp, cloying scent made her pull away. "Oh! That's awful." She leaned closer and sniffed again, more cautiously. "Ether?"

Eva shook her head. "I believe it's chloroform. When my brother was a small lad, he sliced his knee open and needed stitches. He was so upset, crying hysterically, really, that the doctor had to put him out so he could attend the wound. I was there. I remember the smell."

Phoebe took the necktie from Eva, letting it dangle from her fingertips. "So whoever broke in probably used a cloth soaked in chloroform on Stevens, and some of it got on his tie."

"That's what I believe. And then he doused a bit of gin on Stevens's clothing to mask the odor."

"Goodness, talk about forethought. I suspect it didn't

take much to realize we would have footmen patrolling the house at night, and our culprit came prepared." She shook her head at the ingenuity of their intruder. "This is good news for Stevens. He certainly won't be sacked, once we show this to my grandfather."

"I'm glad of that much, at least," Eva agreed. "Now the question is, who has access to chloroform?"

It wasn't really a question, and Phoebe didn't need to think about it. "Doctors. Dentists too, I suppose, but we didn't have a dentist on the house tour, did we?"

"We most certainly did not. And while Dr. Bishop remained within our sights the entire time, it doesn't mean he hasn't been helping someone."

"Driven to murder by unrequited love?" Once again, not a question. She and Eva had learned already, from the doctor's own lips, that he had cared deeply for Arvina Bell. Had those feelings turned lethal when the woman showed little reciprocal interest? Could love do that to a person in real life, and not merely in penny dreadfuls?

"Driven to be an accessory—perhaps." Eva regarded the necktie as Phoebe handed it back to her. "Or coerced, bribed, tricked . . . who knows?"

"There is, of course, more than one doctor in the area, but it makes sense to begin with the one who already has a connection to Arvina Bell's murder."

"Then let's hope the doctor is in."

Lady Phoebe pulled up beside the doctor's house and cut the engine. "Here goes," she said. "I hope he'll speak with us. Honestly, I mean." She opened her driver's-side door.

Eva opened her door and swung her feet to the ground. "The more I think about it, the more I'm convinced some-one either coerced the doctor into giving them the chloroform or they stole it outright. I cannot believe Dr. Bishop could have voluntarily helped in Arvina Bell's murder. His feelings for her appeared too genuine to have been an act."

"I hope you're right, for the doctor's sake."

Eva knocked on the door. A moment later the same housekeeper who had brought them tea last time greeted them with no small surprise. "Why, I'm so sorry. I hadn't realized you had an appointment with Dr. Bishop this morning. I keep his appointment book for him and I don't recall seeing your names."

"Yes, well, we don't exactly have an appointment," Lady Phoebe said, "but we're here about a matter of no small urgency. If we might have a few moments of the doctor's time, please."

"I'll have to see . . ."

"There aren't any other vehicles here, so Dr. Bishop can't be terribly busy at the moment." Eva gave the woman a determined look and set her foot on the threshold. "And as Lady Phoebe said, it's urgent."

Eva left the woman with no choice but to step aside and allow them entry into the foyer. "Please wait here," she said stiffly, "and I'll see if Dr. Bishop has time to see you."

She didn't have far to go. Eva remembered from their last visit that the surgery was in the front of the house, directly across from the parlor. The housekeeper knocked on the door. As there was no answer, she tried again and softly called the doctor's name. "Dr. Bishop? Are you there?"

Again, she received no reply.

"That's odd." She turned back to Eva and Lady Phoebe with a clearly puzzled expression. "He's always in his surgery this time of day. Perhaps he stepped out for a moment. Please have a seat in the parlor and I'll try to find him."

Once ensconced in the parlor, they could hear the

woman's tread on the stairs. Eva whispered, "I assume *stepped out* means we caught the good doctor in the WC."

It wasn't long before the housekeeper returned downstairs, looking more perplexed than ever. "I can't understand it. He doesn't appear to be in the house. I looked out back. He's not there, either."

"Perhaps he went into Little Barlow or Redvale?" Lady Phoebe suggested.

The woman shook her head, her frown growing tight. "That's impossible. He *always* tells me when he's going out. There is something very wrong about this, I tell you."

Eva and Lady Phoebe came to their feet. Eva said, "Perhaps you should check the surgery again. Is the door locked?"

"It shouldn't be, but he doesn't like me to enter that room. I never do unless he asks me to clean in there."

"I think you had better," Eva said.

The housekeeper about-faced and crossed the foyer. Eva and Lady Phoebe hurried after her. She knocked again, and when no answer came, she tried the knob. The door opened and she stepped inside. Lady Phoebe and Eva peered in after her.

Her sudden scream brought them up short. Then they scrambled across the threshold, and then each came to a horrified halt.

A scarlet plume arced across the back wall of the room. On the floor, sticking out from behind the examining table, lay a pair of tweed-clad legs, the feet encased in brown leather oxfords. A sharp breath knifed at Eva's lungs, and though her instincts urged her to flee, she held out one arm to hold Lady Phoebe back before she herself moved forward and peeked over the table. Dr. Bishop lay faceup in a pool of congealed blood, his eyes gawking up at the ceiling. A scalpel lay on the floor beside him. A grisly gash scored his throat.

"Is he . . . Is he . . ." The housekeeper covered her mouth with her hands and dashed from the room. From somewhere at the back of the house, presumably the kitchen or water closet, came the sounds of violent retching.

Lady Phoebe came up beside Eva and stared down at the body. "He is," she said, answering the housekeeper's unfinished question. "Killed by his own scalpel." She reached for Eva's hand, wrapping trembling fingers around it.

"I believe we can safely say he was an unwilling participant in last night's break-in at Foxwood Hall," Eva whispered. Then she noticed something and went to the counter beside the sink. On a metal tray lay some wads of cotton—also bloodied—a bottle of carbolic acid, a needle, and a spool of thread. "Come see this," she said to Lady Phoebe. Her mistress came to her side. "He had a patient here. It looks as though he stitched a wound. And the fact that he never properly cleaned up suggests his patient"— she glanced down at the body, then looked quickly away— "did this."

"Our intruder. Grams drew blood with that candelabra." Lady Phoebe stood between the examining table and the counter, clearing the body by several feet. "He must have turned around to place the used cotton on the tray, and his killer came up behind him and—"

Eva nodded. "Poor Dr. Bishop. I can't help but believe he was a kindly man who didn't deserve this. We need to let Miles know. There must be a telephone in the house."

"Yes. And we need to check on the housekeeper, poor woman."

They found her in the kitchen, sitting at the small oak table beside an arching inglenook fireplace, where the cooking would originally have been done. Now a coal-fired range stood within its stone walls. The housekeeper sat with her head in her hands. She raised her eyes, but not her face, as Eva and Lady Phoebe approached the table.

Eva pulled out a chair and sat beside her. "I'm so sorry, Mrs . . . ?"

"Dixon." She drew a shaky breath. "Laura Dixon."

"It seems Dr. Bishop attended a patient right before he died. Do you know who had been here to see him?"

"I've no idea. There's been no one here this morning, not since I arrived."

"Then you don't live in?" Eva asked her.

"Goodness no. I couldn't spend my nights here, under the same roof as an unmarried man. I live in Redvale with my sister and her husband. They drive me back and forth."

"I see." Eva considered, and then asked, "When was the last time you saw the doctor? Did you bring him his breakfast this morning?"

"No. The surgery door was closed when I arrived. He sometimes does that, closes himself in to work on, well, whatever it is he does when there are no patients. I always leave him alone until he comes out. Heaven help me!" She raised the hem of her apron to her eyes, dabbing at tears. "If only I had checked on him earlier."

Lady Phoebe came closer to the table. "I don't think it would have made any difference. We have reason to believe whoever did this came in the very early hours of the morning. Dr. Bishop was probably gone before you ever came to work."

Eva turned to look up at her, and they exchanged a brief nod. They had obviously reached the same conclusion— that after breaking into Foxwood Hall and tussling with Lady Wroxly, the culprit had come here for medical help— and then murdered the doctor to ensure his silence.

"Do you have a telephone? We need to call the police," Eva said.

The woman stood on shaky legs and led the way into a small office, probably once a pantry, that connected to both the kitchen and the surgery. "Right there." She pointed to the candlestick telephone on the desk.

Miles and Chief Inspector Perkins arrived some twenty minutes later. Not surprisingly, the chief inspector looked distinctly annoyed to find Eva and Lady Phoebe on the premises.

"Did you touch anything?" he demanded after barely offering them a civilized greeting.

"Not a thing," Lady Phoebe said.

"*Hmph*. Wait here in the parlor, I might have questions for you." He started to turn away, but stopped and added, "Such as what the two of you are doing here."

He didn't wait for an answer, but pivoted on his heel and disappeared into the surgery. Miles went in after him, his notepad at the ready. But just before the door closed behind him, he tossed a commiserating glance at Eva over his shoulder.

"We've been told to wait here, but I think the difference between here and the kitchen is an academic one." She came to her feet. "Let's go talk to Mrs. Dixon, shall we?"

"And get a look at the doctor's appointment diary." Lady Phoebe stood and smoothed the front of her frock. "She said she handled his scheduling, so she must have it somewhere handy. I'd like to know who had seen the doctor recently."

"My thoughts exactly."

"I think you should do most of the talking," Lady Phoebe said. "She'll feel more comfortable with you. I'll only discomfit her further."

They found the housekeeper where they had last seen her, at the kitchen table, looking haggard and shaken. She looked up at them with red-rimmed eyes. "That chief inspector could use some lessons in manners, couldn't he? He was beginning to make me believe *I* was a suspect."

They took seats at the table on either side of her, and Eva leaned to place her hand over the other woman's work-roughened one. "He's always that way, brusque and impatient. Don't let it bother you too much." Eva allowed a brief pause before asking, "Did he wish to know who had been to the surgery recently?"

The woman had replaced her apron hem with a proper handkerchief, with which she dabbed at the corner of her eye. "He asked if I knew who had been here this morning, and as I told you, I said I had no idea. He took no pains to conceal his exasperation that I couldn't be more helpful."

"What about earlier this week? And even last week? Did the inspector ask about that?"

Mrs. Dixon looked thoughtful. "Now that you mention it, no, he didn't exactly. He did ask if Dr. Bishop had seen any new patients recently. And if anyone was in arrears with their payments. But I don't know anything about Dr. Bishop's finances. He handled all of that himself. I only saw to the appointments."

"Could we, do you think, see the scheduling book?" Eva asked this in her most nonchalant tone, as if it had only just occurred to her.

The housekeeper hesitated. "Ordinarily, I would say absolutely not. That book is confidential. But . . . under the circumstances . . ." She came to her feet and went into the adjoining office. When she returned, she carried a notebook and set it before her on the table. "Dr. Bishop saw a rather good number of patients in the past several days."

"Is that unusual?" Lady Phoebe asked.

As they had predicted, even that simple query had an unsettling effect on the woman, who stuttered her reply. "Well, um, y-yes, Lady Phoebe, it was, rather. You s-see, the doctor moved here to enjoy a kind of s-semiretirement and—"

Eva once again covered Mrs. Dixon's hand with her own, having an instantly calming effect. "We understand. You say recent days were busy ones for him? Could I have a look?" She moved her hand to the appointment diary, lightly touching it with her fingertips.

Mrs. Dixon slid it across the table to her. Eva opened the cover and used the ribbon in place to find the most recent appointments. What she saw left her startled and disconcerted. She glanced over at Lady Phoebe.

"This practically reads as a who's who of the historical society. Look at this." She pointed to the first name that caught her attention: Arvina Bell.

CHAPTER 13

Phoebe inched her chair closer to Eva's and peered down at the entry for Arvina Bell's visit to Dr. Bishop. The day and time were carefully penned next to her name, along with the reason for the appointment: *Indigestion.*

"Next is Hayden Bell." Eva read the entry. "Headaches. That must be related to the head wound that left that scar on his brow."

"Yes." Phoebe trailed her fingertip down the page. "Vesta Hawkhurst . . . here because of heart palpitations. And her husband, Abel, for a rash."

"Primrose Scott, nerves," Eva continued. She sat back. "That's rather vague. As for the rest of the names on the page, I don't recognize them."

"The doctor had two other visitors this week," Mrs. Dixon supplied. "One is a regular, ever since Dr. Bishop met him through the historical society. Mr. Sadler."

"The bookshop owner?" Eva was surprised to hear this. "What do you mean by *regular*? Is he a hypochondriac?"

"No, no, they play—er, *played*—chess together. Weekly."

"I see." Phoebe tucked this information away for later. "And the other? You said there were two."

"Yes. Miss Chapman. She wished to see the house, which is quite historic. I believe it dates back to the late sixteenth century, although it has been modified and refurbished over the years."

"I suppose she wishes to include the house in her articles?" Phoebe asked.

"That is what she said," the housekeeper confirmed, and then jumped to her feet. "I'm so sorry. I completely forgot to offer you something. Tea? I've a lovely Bakewell tart in the larder. It was to be for Dr. Bishop's dessert tonight." She drew in a sudden, tremulous breath and raised the handkerchief to her eyes. "Oh, poor Dr. Bishop. I simply cannot believe he's gone."

Phoebe's heart went out to the woman. She had not only lost her employer, and, perhaps, a friend, but also her livelihood. She considered if there were any positions to offer her at Foxwood Hall, but Mrs. Sanders had held the housekeeper's position for years now and wouldn't likely appreciate a rival who could boast similar skills, albeit on a smaller scale. Perhaps something in the village, then . . .

"What will you do now?" Eva asked Mrs. Dixon, coming right to the point.

"Oh, you mustn't worry about me. My husband, God rest him, took good care of matters and I've a tidy sum laid by. Truly, I only took this position for something to do. I like to keep busy and out of my sister and her husband's way. And I was fond of Dr. Bishop, such an amiable man to work for. Now, the girl who comes to clean thrice weekly is another matter . . ."

Phoebe made a mental note to get the girl's name. A maid would be far easier to place than a housekeeper.

From down the corridor came the creaking of the surgery door opening. She and Eva rose from the table and hurried to meet the policemen in the foyer. "Have you discovered anything?" she asked before thinking better of it. The chief inspector's scowl reminded her of the fruitlessness of such an inquiry.

"If we did, it's surely none of your business, Lady Phoebe. If you'll excuse us. Come, Brannock."

"One moment, sir."

Mr. Perkins's scowl landed next on the constable, but the latter gave a shrug. "I need to obtain Mrs. Dixon's home address, sir, in case we need to speak with her further."

"Right. Go ahead, then. I'll wait for you by the motor-car." Before Chief Inspector Perkins was quite out the front door, Constable Brannock made a show of trudging down the hallway to the kitchen, passing Phoebe and Eva without a word. As he had said, he wrote down Mrs. Dixon's address in Redvale. Phoebe heard the woman again ask if she could provide any refreshments, but the constable indicated they were ready to leave.

On the way back to the front door, he ducked into the parlor and gestured for Phoebe and Eva to follow. "What did you learn?" he murmured, obviously mindful of the open front window.

"Several of the historical society members have been here in recent days." Eva spoke just as quietly and handed him the appointment diary. "All of them that were on the house tour, in fact."

"All?" The constable took on a pained expression. "That doesn't make things any easier, does it?"

Phoebe quickly explained the circumstances that brought Eamon Sadler and Ophelia Chapman to visit the doctor. Then she asked him, "Did you find any fingerprints in the surgery?"

"Plenty, but that's to be expected, isn't it? None, unfortunately, to point to any one person as our murderer. Just like at Foxwood Hall." He heaved a breath, looking grim. "I'd better go. Thank you for this." He indicated the diary and took his leave.

When they were back at home, Phoebe and Eva went over each member of the historical society and the reason they had been to see Dr. Bishop. The day had turned chilly, with scatterings of raindrops sweeping the lawns. That didn't stop them from donning mackintoshes and strolling down the tiered gardens and across the footbridge to the pond. They wanted privacy, and they would have it here, uninterrupted. Unless, of course, Grams happened to glance out a window, noticed the drizzle, and sent Vernon or another footman out to retrieve them.

"Hayden Bell's war wound is not only visible, but it must be well documented," Phoebe said as they skirted the largest of the willows bowing over the pond, the tips of its branches caressing the water. "But he could have been lying about the headaches, simply making an excuse to see the doctor."

"And Vesta Hawkhurst's heart palpitations would certainly be verifiable with the use of a stethoscope," Eva said, "which, I'm quite sure, the doctor would have used. I don't see any possibility that she could have lied about the condition and gotten away with it. Her husband's rash would also have been visible. Again, easily verifiable."

Phoebe nodded. They stopped at the mossy bank of the pond, regarding the droplets making patterns across the surface of the water. "Lady Primrose's nerves, however, unless manifested by a racing pulse, would be more difficult to diagnose beyond her claimed symptoms. She could have been lying, again an excuse to visit the doctor. But any of them might have waited for a moment when the doctor became distracted and snatched a bottle of chloroform."

"Then there are Eamon Sadler and Miss Chapman."

Eva gazed down at the daisies at their feet, little puffs of scarlet, fuchsia, or white petals surrounding bright yellow centers, planted to appear like random wildflowers. They glistened like jewels in the misting drizzle—like a fortune in plain sight, Phoebe mused.

Eva went on. "Either of them might have contrived to slip away from the doctor's company and into the surgery, where he or she could have stolen the chloroform."

Phoebe adjusted the hood of her mackintosh. "It's also possible the doctor knew all about it, that he was somehow coerced or persuaded to hand it over."

Eva gave a solemn nod. "Remember how eager he was to praise all of his fellow society members. Too eager, if you ask me."

"Yes, like he was covering for someone and terribly afraid he or she would be found out. Perhaps someone was blackmailing him."

"And if so, my lady, then he would have been covering for himself, too, wouldn't he?"

"Why, you're right." Phoebe considered the possibility. "But what could an elderly physician—an amiable one, according to Mrs. Dixon—have to hide?"

"I don't know, but whatever it is, he might have tried to leave it behind in London. Perhaps Miles can find out more about him. I'll telephone him as soon as we go in."

"Speaking of which, we'd better get back before Grams sends Mr. Fairfax to find us."

Eva stepped outside Henderson's Haberdashery, her shopping bag laden with several yards of lace and ribbon, silk and cotton threads in half-a-dozen colors, and several sets of buttons. She had also selected a new set of sewing needles and a pair of trimming scissors to replace the old ones, which had been sharpened time and time again.

Lady Phoebe had dropped her outside the shop before

driving on to the church. She and the vicar's wife were once again conferring about the latest donations for Lady Phoebe's charity promoting the Relief and Comfort for Veterans and their Families. With the summer months upon them, they especially wished to make certain the local population understood that suffering and want didn't dissipate along with the cold weather. Men—and women— who were no longer able to work due to their war injuries continued to struggle to feed and clothe their children.

Eva breathed in the morning air, fragrant with the roses growing in the window box of a newly opened tea shop, and set out toward St. George's. She had reached the nearest corner when angry voices brought her to a halt. Those voices were familiar. Though she couldn't see the speakers, she continued to listen. Thank goodness the earliness of the hour meant there were few people about and no one stopped to question what on earth she was doing.

She was, in fact, spying, and eased her way to the end of the storefronts. Down the side lane that branched off from the High Street, Lady Primrose Scott and Able Hawkhurst stood in the doorway of the tobacconist. The sight of two historical society members chatting together should not have given Eva pause, and she certainly would have continued on her way if not for the near-beet redness of Lady Primrose's complexion and the fury flashing in Abel Hawkhurst's eyes.

The discussion appeared to become even more heated, with Lady Primrose craning her neck to toss sharp—albeit from this distance, unintelligible—words at Mr. Hawkhurst. Eva started as Mr. Hawkhurst took hold of Lady Primrose's arm, while he, in turn, leaned down and issued a whisper that made the woman recoil.

Eva nearly made her presence known. But at that precise moment Mr. Hawkhurst pulled back with what she could only describe as a wolf's grin, and after a tense hesitation Lady Primrose smiled as well—with all the warmth of a glacier.

They were coming toward her, prompting Eva to back up all the way to the window of the tea shop, closed at this hour, where she pretended to be studying the interior. In actuality, she saw nothing of the newly refurbished room as she heard the rapid *clip-clipping* of Lady Primrose's pumps. The woman nearly ran into Eva as she came around the corner. Mr. Hawkhurst also reached the top of the lane and turned in the opposite direction along the High Street, moving so quickly as to make it necessary to hold the brim of his bowler to prevent it from being taken by the breeze.

"Miss Huntford." Lady Primrose stopped suddenly, wobbled slightly, and breathed in audibly through her nose. "What are you doing here?"

An odd question, considering Eva carried a shopping bag. But she calmly replied, "I did a bit of shopping while Lady Phoebe visited with the vicar's wife at the church. I'm going there now." She gestured into the tea shop. "Have you been in yet? It looks lovely."

"No, I . . . uh . . . no. Not yet. Well, good day to you, Miss Huntford." She gave the belted jacket of her walking suit a tug and hurried along the pavement. She also wore lace gloves and a hat—effectively concealing any wounds she might have received from Lady Wroxly's candelabra last night.

Up ahead, Mr. Hawkhurst had slowed to a stroll and came to a stop outside the post office. The door swung open and Mrs. Hawkhurst came out. They spoke some words, he offered her his arm, and they walked on together. Eva wished she had had a closer view of him. Had *he* broken into Foxwood Hall last night and tussled with Lady Wroxly?

And could that have anything to do with what transpired between him and Lady Primrose this morning? Had he threatened her when he grabbed her arm? Had she threatened him, and he grabbed her arm in protest? Both were considered upstanding members of the community. Had neither of them worried about being seen or over-heard—which, indeed, they had been? Apparently, whatever they had argued about had made them forget about propriety and public image.

Eva hurried along on her own way to St. George's, heading to the side entrance and down the steps to the basement. There she found Lady Phoebe and Violet Hershel, the vicar's wife, presiding over neatly folded stacks of summer clothing and boxes of household supplies.

"Ah, Eva, there you are," Lady Phoebe called to her. "Did you find everything you needed at the haberdashery?"

"I did, indeed." Eva held up her shopping bag. The haberdashery was, to Eva, like a sweetshop to a child or a jewelry store to a society lady. As a lady's maid, she delighted in the tools of her trade, the very items that helped her keep her ladies' wardrobes fresh and in style.

"And how is Mr. Henderson?" Lady Phoebe's demeanor sobered slightly as she asked this, and no wonder. Myron Henderson had come home from the war minus a leg and could only walk now with the use of a cane and a clumsy prosthesis. Despite this, he was one of the lucky ones, having a business to run, which kept him both useful and well-to-do.

"He seems quite well and offered to donate some lightweight flannels to the RCVF."

"Oh, that's splendid of him. Well . . ." Lady Phoebe turned to the vicar's wife, a slender woman in her midforties who never suffered a wrinkle or a hair out of place. Come to think of it, Eva mused, she rather reminded her of Lady Primrose that way. Lady Phoebe said to the woman, "Thank you so much for all of your help, Mrs. Hershel. I'll be in touch to arrange the distribution."

They took their leave of the woman and headed outside to the motorcar. Eva quickly filled Lady Phoebe in on what she had witnessed between Lady Primrose and Abel Hawkhurst. They were just opening the doors to climb into the Vauxhall when a voice stopped them.

"Phoebe! Miss Huntford."

They both peered out from beneath their hat brims. Farther along the High Street, Eva spotted Ernie Shelton hurrying toward them. She was surprised to see the fashionable young journalist, Ophelia Chapman, strolling at his side.

"Those two know each other?" Lady Phoebe murmured to Eva across the roof of the Vauxhall.

"Perhaps they just met," Eva suggested. "They're both staying at the Calcott Inn, after all." Eva narrowed her gaze on the young woman. "Miss Chapman doesn't appear too broken up about Dr. Bishop."

"No, she doesn't. Perhaps she doesn't know yet." Or perhaps she had done the deed. She and Lady Phoebe watched the pair approach, chatting and laughing together as they came along the street.

"They've certainly become chummy rather quickly, haven't they?" Lady Phoebe observed. "What is Ernie still doing here?"

Eva shook her head and shrugged. They shut the Vauxhall's doors and walked to meet the other pair partway. Eva hung back a pace or two, happy to let Lady Phoebe do the talking—while she did the observing.

"Good morning, Ernie, Miss Chapman. I . . . er . . . wasn't aware you two were acquainted."

"Quite well, as a matter of fact," Miss Chapman said with a little peal of a laugh.

"Yes," Ernie said, "we met in Staffordshire, at Lyndale Park. She featured the area and the estate in her magazine."

"I see. What a coincidence that you'd meet again here, of all places."

Eva could hear in Lady Phoebe's voice that she found this coincidence exceedingly dubious, as did Eva herself. Ernie Shelton had deceived the Renshaws in the past, and she didn't doubt he would do so again.

"Yes, it is quite a quirk of luck, isn't it?" Miss Chapman gave that bell-like laugh again, and when she did, tossing her head like a coquette, Eva studied her closely. Like Lady Primrose, she wore lace gloves, and Eva could perceive no wounds beneath them. She appeared sound enough, fresh and fashionably dressed, with a close-fitting hat sporting a colorful array of lace and silk flowers.

Eva turned her attention to Mr. Shelton. But he, too, seemed healthy enough and displayed no signs of having recently been bludgeoned by Lady Wroxly's candelabra.

"Tell me, Miss Chapman," Lady Phoebe said as if she had already dismissed the matter and moved on, "how are your fellow members of the historical society faring?"

"We're all muddling through," the young woman replied. "It doesn't help that we're all considered suspects in Arvina Bell's death."

"*Suspects?*" Ernie turned to her with an incredulous look. "Are you serious?"

Miss Chapman released a sigh. "Not serious suspects, but we were all there in the house at the time. Unfortunately, our zeal to learn as much as possible sent us into places we shouldn't have been."

"I think some of you must be doing better than others." Lady Phoebe stepped closer to them and lowered her voice. "Did either of you happen to see Lady Primrose and Abel Hawkhurst arguing outside the tobacconist's shop a short while ago? Any idea what that could have been about?"

"*Hmph.*" Miss Chapman arched an eyebrow and smirked. "I don't believe that would have had anything to do with Arvina. Those two are forever at odds over society business."

"Do tell," Lady Phoebe said, sidling closer still, as if she were the village gossip eager to sink her teeth into the latest scandal. Eva had to school her features not to betray her amusement.

"Yes, Ophelia, do tell," Ernie urged as well, and Eva made a mental note of his use of her given name, a familiarity that suggested more than mere acquaintance.

"Well," the young woman said with a salacious grin, "I've seen looks pass between them—you know, *significant* looks—and then there are those sudden silences whenever they notice anyone observing their conversations. I'm not suggesting anything, I'm only relating what I've seen. You may draw your own conclusions."

Whatever conclusions Miss Chapman thought they might draw, Eva did not believe the pair's behavior outside the tobacconist's shop could be explained by a flirtation or even an illicit affair between them. No, it could not have been that simple.

Unless, of course, Arvina Bell had discovered their affair and threatened to expose them.

CHAPTER 14

"But surely you don't mean to insinuate that two married people—that is, two people who are each married to someone *else*—are conducting themselves in a manner not in keeping with the vows they took?" Phoebe used all her guile to convince Miss Chapman that she was hopelessly naïve in such matters. Ernie, she could plainly see, wasn't fooled for an instant; his pursed lips and narrowed eyes told her that much.

"As I said, I'm not suggesting anything." Miss Chapman winked as she transferred her handbag from one forearm to the other, the very same darling little bag she had carried that day at Foxwood Hall.

"Although, if it *is* true," Phoebe went on, "theirs wouldn't be the first romance to blossom within the historical society, would it?"

Miss Chapman tilted her head. "I'm sure I don't know what you mean."

"Dr. Bishop and Mrs. Bell. Oh, it appeared to be one-sided, but the poor doctor was smitten. Isn't that so, Eva?"

"Yes, he admitted as much to us the last time we saw him. He thought most highly of Mrs. Bell."

"He truly did." Phoebe kept a close watch on Miss Chapman's features, the color of her complexion. So far, neither had changed in any significant way. "And now they're both gone, to a better place, one hopes."

"*Gone?* As in *dead*?" Ernie blurted this with a look that accused Phoebe of somehow being responsible. His next words confirmed it. "Events of this sort follow you everywhere, don't they, Phoebe? I heard about Mrs. Bell, but who is this other person?"

"Dr. Bishop, George Bishop." Though Phoebe answered Ernie's question, she spoke directly to Miss Chapman. "Found dead in his surgery only yesterday. Had you heard, Miss Chapman?"

"Yes, I did actually." Her face took on a somber look— too little, too late, in Phoebe's estimation. "It's incomprehensible. Two society members in so short a time. It leads one to wonder, and worry, who will be next."

As if he'd been poked in the back, Ernie pulled up sharp. "Egads, do you think someone is stalking your organization? Just what is it you people do?"

"Nothing out of the ordinary, I can assure you," Miss Chapman protested. "We merely acquire and archive information. Or, in my case, write about what we learn."

"In Mrs. Bell's case, too, let's not forget," Eva murmured, and Phoebe caught the slight pinkening of Miss Chapman's cheeks.

Phoebe decided to be direct. "I understand you visited Dr. Bishop not long ago."

"Me?" Miss Chapman raised a hand to her bosom.

"Yes, his housekeeper mentioned you were interested in the house for your article."

"Oh, yes, that's true. Goodness, with everything that's happened, I'd nearly forgotten."

"I hope you took good notes, then, since you'll not have

another chance now," Ernie interjected, earning him a withering look from Miss Chapman.

"How did he appear to you?" Phoebe asked. "Did he seem nervous or upset about anything?"

"Why, no, not that I recollect. He took me through the house and chatted endlessly about how lucky he felt to have come upon the property at just the right time."

"I see." Phoebe paused, pretending to consider her next question. "Did he show you his surgery?"

"Of course. Why shouldn't he have? He was quite proud of it."

"And exactly what day were you there? Think back," Phoebe urged. "It could be important."

"The day before the tour of Foxwood Hall." Miss Chapman smiled. "I remember it well. But if you'll excuse me, I've work to do back at the hotel. Ernie, a pleasure to see you. Lady Phoebe. Miss Huntford." She started briskly on her way.

"It would seem you frightened her off." Ernie laughed, but despite his attempt to make light, he gave an awkward shuffle of his feet and cleared his throat. "So, er, has Julia come home yet?"

That again? Phoebe fought the urge to huff and roll her eyes. "No, Ernie, she hasn't. I've told you, she's gone to Lyndale Park. That hasn't changed. We are not hiding her."

"Oh, but I'm afraid you're quite wrong about her being at Lyndale Park." A triumphant note entered Ernie's voice, as if he'd just won a difficult challenge. "I called Cousin Veronica earlier this morning. Julia *was* there, but she's off again somewhere. Was very mysterious about it, too."

Phoebe's heart jolted. "What? Are you absolutely certain?"

"Of course I'm certain. There's nothing wrong with my ears and I heard Veronica as clearly as I'm hearing you now."

"What about Amelia? And the baby?"

"I understood that she took the baby with her, but Amelia remained behind."

Why would Julia leave, and without a word to the family? She'd made no mention of a change in plans yesterday. Had Grams heard from her again today? Part of Phoebe knew it was none of her business what Julia did. But Julia and mysteries were historically not a good combination. What could she be up to?

Eva appeared as worried as Phoebe felt, and nodded her approval as Phoebe said, "We need to get home. Ernie, if you'll excuse us." His mocking salute and cheeky smile followed her as she and Eva made their way across the High Street.

Phoebe's worries mounted as she listened to Veronica Townsend's voice across the wires. "No, as I told Ernie, she packed up early this morning and left in the motorcar they came in. Took the baby and her maid with her. No, she didn't tell us where she was going. I'm quite surprised she didn't inform the family of her change in plans."

Phoebe heaved a great sigh. "Thank you, Veronica. Is Amelia there?"

"I'll get her . . ."

Moments later Amelia's thin voice traveled through the earpiece. "Hello, Phoebe. I'm afraid I can't tell you more than Veronica already has. Julia said she'd be back for me in a few days, and . . ."

Phoebe heard, quite plainly, her sister's reluctance to go on. "And what, Amellie? You've got to tell me."

"It's only that she told me not to volunteer the information to Grams that she'd left Lyndale Park."

"She asked you to lie to Grams?" The shock of it sent a

judder of outrage through her. "She had no right to do that to you."

"Not *lie,* exactly, Phoebe. That's not what I said. Julia simply didn't want me to say anything unless Grams telephoned and asked outright where Julia is."

"And *do* you know where she is?"

"I've no idea, and that is the truth." Amelia sounded weary. "I do wish she hadn't gone, and I wish she hadn't taken Charles. I have to confess, I'm feeling rather alone here. It's not as if Veronica or Mildred are my direct relatives."

"I'll ask Grampapa to send Fenton for you in the Rolls-Royce."

"No, Phoebe, don't. I'll be all right and Julia did say she'd be back. Grams and Grampapa don't need any further worries." Phoebe couldn't argue with her sister there. "I'm a little worried about her, but I suppose if anyone is capable of taking care of herself, it's Julia."

Phoebe ended the connection and sat staring into space for several moments. While she shared Amelia's concerns about Julia, as well as agreeing their sister could take care of herself, a growing anger nipped at the heels of that reassurance. What happened if—or when—her grandparents discovered their eldest granddaughter had absconded to parts unknown with their great-grandson? Good gracious, especially Grampapa. On account of his unreliable heart she couldn't possibly let him know Julia had left Lyndale Park. It could put him in hospital.

She picked up the earpiece and tapped the hook switch several times. When the operator replied, she gave her the information and waited. She repeated this several times in the next half hour or so. But no one—not their mutual friend Olive Asquith, or Althea Davenport in London, or Pamela Eccleston in Oxford, or Henrietta Montague in

Coventry—could shed the barest light on Julia's where-abouts. Henni, in particular, had sounded alarmed by Julia's apparent disappearance. Olive, on the other hand, had brushed it off and insisted she would turn up in her own good time.

Julia's own good time, however, could prove disastrous. Phoebe needed to think of something, and fast. She summoned the operator again.

Eva deposited a basketful of shoes on the boot room worktable and realized immediately something was wrong. Disarray surrounded her. Shoe cleaning supplies, which should have been neatly lined up along the shelves, were strewn across the table. Not only that, but the shelves themselves had been pulled away from the wall and left at an odd angle.

Now that she thought of it, something had felt wrong—*sounded* wrong—the moment she alighted from the bottom step of the back staircase. Voices had been raised. Stevens—who had been thoroughly exonerated—had rushed out of the silver room and nearly collided with Connie on her way to the broom cupboard. Young Josh had scampered from the servants' hall and nearly tripped over Dora, which would have resulted in the spilling of the bucket of coal dust and ashes he carried. And an odd *thump-thumping* that didn't sound like a plumbing problem had issued from inside the water closet.

She left the boot room and went into the nearby valet service room, where she found Vernon staring down at the floor, taking small steps, and tapping his heel against the flagstones every couple of paces.

"What on earth are you doing?" she demanded, utterly flummoxed by his behavior. "And why have the shelves been moved away from the wall in the boot room and all the supplies scattered over the worktable?" She noted that here, too, several cupboards had been left gaping. "What is going on down here?"

Looking annoyed at the interruption, Vernon continued his heel tapping. "Searching. What else?"

"For what?" But even as she asked the question, she knew. Dora, who had apparently eavesdropped on her conversation with Mr. Giles, had gone telling tales.

"The previous Lord Wroxly's missing fortune, of course." Vernon tapped the floor again, this time with his toe, apparently looking for a loose or hollow-sounding flagstone.

"Be sensible." Eva crossed her arms in front of her and leaned a hip against the workbench. She didn't know whether to be amused or worried that he'd taken leave of his senses. "It's not a *missing* fortune, it's a *rumored* hidden fortune. And considering the source, it's very likely a figment of the imagination."

"That may be, Miss Huntford, but we'll never know for sure unless we give this house a good going-over. Did a little tapping and thumping in the dining room earlier."

Shaking her head, Eva about-faced. She found the kitchen deserted, until muffled voices led her to the dry-goods storeroom, where she found Mrs. Ellison and one of her assistants rearranging shelves and exposing sections of wall.

"You too?" Eva demanded. "What *do* you expect to find among sacks of flour and sugar? Doesn't everyone see how ridiculous they're being?"

Mrs. Ellison turned and stood with her back to the wall she had been rapping on. "Not so ridiculous, Miss Huntford. Remember the source—Mr. Willikins, the former butler. If he knew about it, perhaps it's because he helped the former Lord Wroxly hide the fortune down here, where no one would ever expect to find it. It makes perfect sense, if you stop to think about it."

"Good gracious." Once again, Eva pivoted. Similar thuds and bumps sounded from the larder, but she didn't bother to learn who was poring through the milk, butter, and baked goods. She was on her way back into the boot room when Mrs. Sanders came down the stairs.

"Miss Huntford. Do you understand what's going on here?"

"I'm afraid I do, Mrs. Sanders."

"Then I would appreciate it if you'd tell me. I'd been speaking to the countess about the evening's menu when Mr. Giles met me in the upper level of the pantry. He told me everyone below stairs had suddenly gone amok. What's got into them?"

"Haven't you heard the rumor?"

A flush suffused the housekeeper's face and her eyes sparked with anger. If there was one word that raised Mrs. Sanders's ire and her blood pressure, it was the word *rumor*. Another word went right along with it: *gossip*. Both were expressly forbidden to the staff of this household, on pain of dismissal. She gritted her teeth for good measure. "What rumor?"

"Actually, perhaps you *have* heard of it, since you've been here a good number of years. It concerns a fortune supposedly hidden somewhere in the house by the previous Earl of Wroxly." Eva quickly filled in the details.

Mrs. Sanders said nothing during Eva's explanation. She said nothing as she turned away and walked briskly into the kitchen. Her voice came as a murmur as she apparently spoke to Mrs. Ellison and her assistants. Next Mrs. Sanders rounded up the footmen, along with Connie and the underhousemaid.

"Into the servants' hall, everyone." Mrs. Sanders pointed an imperious finger while the servants, Eva included, filed in. Mrs. Sanders waited patiently until the last of them had gathered around the table, looking like a garrison about to be taken to task by their commanding officer.

Which they were.

After berating them for nearly a quarter of an hour, Mrs. Sanders ended with, "Even if such a fortune exists and one of you found it, what on God's green earth do you plan to do with it? It belongs to Lord and Lady Wroxly, doesn't it? Nothing, and I do mean *nothing,* entitles you to a penny of anything to be found in this house."

Before the housekeeper could utter another word, someone coughed—Eva didn't see who—and a hand went up. The fingertips appeared first over Vernon's head. Eva shifted slightly to see around the tall footman. It was Dora, and Eva guessed the cough had been meant to prompt her. Mrs. Sanders shot a dagger-sharp gaze at the girl. "Yes? What?"

"If you'll forgive me, ma'am, p'haps Lord Wroxly'll offer a reward."

Mrs. Sanders's expression sent Dora's head ducking for cover. "You'll find your reward along the High Street if you persist in this foolishness. That goes for the rest of you. Now, I want order restored immediately and I don't wish to see so much as a tea leaf out of place again. Dismissed."

Eva headed back to the boot room. She'd yet to polish a single shoe for Lady Phoebe. Murmurs filled the corridor, fading as the staff dispersed. Mrs. Sanders might have given them what-for, but Eva didn't believe the matter would be dropped that readily.

Phoebe had been hiding out in the drawing room ever since her unsuccessful inquiries into Julia's whereabouts. With both Grams and Grampapa keeping mostly to the first floor, she deemed the ground floor drawing room the safest place to avoid having to answer questions.

Or so she thought. She had re-read the same paragraph in the book open on her lap when suddenly Fairfax came trotting into the room. He greeted her with a few snuffling snorts, then put his front paws on her knees and stretched forward to lick her hand.

"Phoebe, there you are." Grams came in, her long skirts sweeping the floor, and sat beside Phoebe on the settee. The onyx brooch at her throat caught the lamplight and shimmered like moonlit water. Other than her wedding ring, Grams tended to wear onyx and jet, along with a locket that contained a lock of Papa's hair. When news had come that he had died in the war, Grams had put on mourning and worn little but black ever since.

Phoebe closed the book, having no idea what its pages contained. "Have you been looking for me, Grams?"

Fairfax lowered his paws before shifting sideways to rest his chin on Grams's knees. She settled in, stroking him absently. "I don't suppose you've spoken to Julia?"

"No, Grams, I'm afraid I haven't." Phoebe found herself clenching her teeth while she hoped Grams would ask no more questions. But, of course, Grams being Grams, she did.

"How about Amelia?"

Phoebe drew a breath to steal herself. "I did. She's fine."

"And the matter concerning Julia? Am I right about that? *Is* she troubled by something?"

"Grams, I wish you wouldn't worry so."

"You're not answering my question. Why is that?" Phoebe had no sooner angled her face away than Grams placed her forefinger beneath her chin and turned her back around. "Phoebe? What are you not telling me?"

And there it was: Grams's uncanny ability to read each of her grandchildren like a book. "All right, Grams. Please promise you won't be upset."

"I will make no such promise. Phoebe, out with it. Now."

"Julia left Lyndale Park this morning."

"Oh." After a pause Grams added, "Are she and Amelia on their way home?"

"Not exactly. Amelia is still there."

"What on earth do you mean?" Grams's bluntness had Fairfax raising his head and staring up at her as if to ask if she needed his assistance. "Julia dropped Amelia at Lyndale Park and left? Why?"

"I'm not sure, exactly. Perhaps she decided she needed to do some shopping. Or visit a friend."

"And the baby?" Phoebe could hear the alarm brewing in Grams's voice.

"She took him with her."

"And have you inquired with any of her friends?"

"I did, at least the most likely ones. They haven't seen her."

"Why would she go off alone like that? She could be endangering Charles . . ."

Phoebe placed a hand on Grams's wrist. Grams had taken on a high color and a vein throbbed in her temple. "Don't do that. Don't think the worst."

"How can I not when there are two people whose lives were so recently cut short? Phoebe, there are dangers all around us."

"But that's just it, Grams. That happened here, in Little Barlow, and Julia's not here. She's somewhere else, safe. She and little Charles. And don't forget she's got Douglas driving her. And Hetta is with her. They wouldn't let anything happen to Julia and Charles."

"No doubt she's sworn them to secrecy," Grams muttered. "Julia pays Hetta's salary now, but Douglas knows it's your grandfather who pays his. I've a good mind to see he gets the sack."

"Don't blame Douglas. Or Hetta. You know how Julia can be."

Grams pursed her lips. "How could she do this . . ."

Before Phoebe could respond, Fairfax, apparently grown bored of the conversation, sidled away to lie down in a pool of sunlight near the terrace doors. He rolled onto his side with a great, openmouthed yawn.

Grams's gaze had followed him, but now slid back to Phoebe with a defiant gleam. Suddenly, however, she seemed calmer. "Why the four of you must grow up is beyond me. I liked it much better when you all did as you were told."

"Sorry, Grams. But you know Julia is quite capable of taking care of herself—"

"Don't you dare patronize me."

Phoebe should have known platitudes wouldn't help, not with Grams. She tried another tack. "Grams, we must keep this to ourselves. Grampapa would become ever so upset if he knew."

"You're quite right." Grams clutched the arm of the settee beside her. "He must not know they're missing."

"Not missing, just . . . elsewhere," Phoebe corrected her.

"Yes, well, your grandfather's heart might not be able to withstand such worry. Here's what we must do. We must continue telephoning everyone who knows Julia and her habits. In fact, give Owen a call."

"Owen, in Yorkshire?" Phoebe contemplated the notion of Owen being familiar with Julia's habits. A tiny lump that should no longer exist pressed against her heart. She had once believed the two to be enamored of each other. Discovering that not to be the case, that Owen actually preferred Phoebe, apparently hadn't banished all remnants of jealousy. She tried to keep the sullenness from her voice. "I don't see what he'll be able to do."

"No one is more capable than Owen Seabright. We both know it. Call him, Phoebe. He'll find her."

Phoebe decided not to bother Owen. But mere mention

of him got her thinking, and suddenly she believed she might know where Julia had gone. She waited until Grams had retreated upstairs with Fairfax shadowing her, before hurrying to the ground floor telephone. This time she didn't have to wait long for the connections to be made, and no wonder. She had asked for a local number.

A manservant answered and hesitated when Phoebe identified herself and asked to speak with Theo Leighton. "His lordship is not at home, I'm afraid."

"Can you tell me when he'll be back?"

"Not for several days. May I take a message?"

Phoebe paused, thinking. "Is his mother or aunt at home?"

"Lady Allerton is presently in London. However, Lady Cecily is in residence."

The Lady Allerton, to whom the butler referred, was Theo Leighton's mother, Lucille, Marchioness of Allerton. Lady Cecily was his great-aunt, quite elderly and not in possession of all her wits. Still, Phoebe had little other choice. "Do you think Lady Cecily would be able to come to the telephone?"

"I think she'd be delighted." Phoebe could almost hear the smile in the man's voice. She waited several minutes before a slightly tremulous female voice crawled across the wires.

"Phoebe? Phoebe Renshaw? What an absolute pleasure, darling. I don't often receive calls these days, neither over the telephone nor in person, more's the pity. Are you well? How are your grandparents?"

Lady Cecily paused for a breath and Phoebe seized the opportunity. "We're all quite well, Lady Cecily," she lied. She saw no reason to upset the octogenarian with news of murders and midnight intruders. She almost rushed head-long into the subject she'd called about, but Lady Cecily's mention of never receiving calls spoke of loneliness and tugged at her heartstrings. "And you? I hope you are also well?"

She sighed quietly as Lady Cecily launched into a long and detailed description of aches and pains and all the little matters she had caught herself forgetting lately. Phoebe remembered the Leighton family's Christmas visit two years ago, and how they had learned that a confused Cecily had once stolen a screwdriver and began loosening the screws in furniture, door hinges, and even lamps throughout the family home, until they'd finally caught her at it.

The elderly woman finally fell silent, and Phoebe said, "I understand Theo is away."

"Yes, I believe he left yesterday. Or was it today? Yes, today, I think."

"Was he . . . alone or accompanied?"

"I couldn't say. But it was oh so lovely to see Julia again. And the little one. What a handsome child."

Phoebe's pulse beat faster. Her hunch had been correct. "Please think back, Lady Cecily. Did they leave together?"

"I would say not. I do remember watching their motorcars proceed down the drive. Yes, there were two of them. Hers and his."

Then perhaps Julia was already on her way back to Lyndale Park. Dared Phoebe hope? But why such an abbreviated visit with Theo?

Poor Theo. Julia might have married him instead of Gilbert Townsend, if only Theo had inherited money along with the title of Marquess of Allerton from his brother. Now that Julia had her inheritance from Gil, was she reconsidering?

"Thank you, Lady Cecily. It's been lovely chatting with you."

"And you, too, dear. Shall I tell Theo you rang us up?"

"No, that's not necessary. Unless you happen to see Julia again."

Phoebe ended the call, wondering how much to tell Grams. Julia had gone alone to see Theo, but with Lady Cecily there, they hadn't been unchaperoned, giving tongues no reason to wag. And they had left separately, going their own way in their own motorcar. But if all had been above-board, why had Julia kept the visit a secret?

That was certainly a question Grams would ask. Phoebe decided to continue hiding on the ground floor as long as possible.

CHAPTER 15

Eva found herself back in the Vauxhall shortly after breakfast the next day. What she had witnessed between Primrose Scott and Abel Hawkhurst, along with Miss Chapman's insinuations, had led her and Lady Phoebe to conclude that they should revisit Mrs. Hawkhurst and see whether she had reached the same conclusions about her husband and the other woman.

"Lady Primrose, for all her efforts to appear the staid English matron, could be hiding more than people might imagine," Eva observed. The state of the woman's parlor continued to niggle at her. It simply showed no hint of individual personality, but rather a carefully assembled tableau of everything an MP's parlor should be. Staged and artificial.

"If so, that staid English matron would have much to lose, wouldn't she?" Lady Phoebe said, her hands tightening on the wheel in preparation of hitting a patchy stretch of road. "Not to mention her husband. It's fairly certain a scandal would cause him to lose his seat in Parliament."

"And Abel Hawkhurst would lose his marriage and everything that goes with it." Eva didn't have to explain that *everything* meant whatever money his wife had brought into the marriage. By the looks of their estate, they needed every penny available.

"Neither would have a leg to stand on socially."

Yes, Eva thought, if Lady Primrose and Abel Hawkhurst were engaged in an affair, they would have ample motive to do away with anyone who found out, whether or not that person threatened to betray their secret. Neither would have risked taking that chance.

"Of course we can't come right out and ask Mrs. Hawkhurst about it." The road having smoothed, Lady Phoebe took one hand off the steering wheel to change gears as she accelerated. "We could be wrong about this, and we wouldn't want to put a mistaken notion in Mrs. Hawkhurst's head. I'll have to ease into the matter carefully."

"And while you do that, I'll look for any signs of injury from your grandmother's attack with the candelabra." Eva kept an eye on the road, as she usually did. Not that she didn't trust Lady Phoebe's driving skills, but one never knew when a deer or sheep or heaven knew what might decide to run across the road. "Clothing hides a multitude of sins, though. A pity we can't ask the entire historical society to disrobe."

Lady Phoebe emitted a sound that was part snort, part gasp, and part laughter.

They arrived at Sunderly just as the sun was angling over the slate rooftop and pouring over the honey-golden stone façade. The effect was enchanting, like a painting. They hoped they had been correct in their timing. Before exiting the Vauxhall, Eva took up the notebook she had brought along.

The same housemaid who had admitted them previously bade them welcome and escorted them to the drawing room, with its cobwebs and cracks and, visible in the morning sunlight, bare patches in the Turkey carpet.

They hadn't long to wait for Vesta Hawkhurst to greet them. She eyed them warily as she shook Lady Phoebe's hand and offered a cordial nod to Eva. "Please make yourselves comfortable. May I offer you tea?"

"No, thank you, we've only just breakfasted." Lady Phoebe made a show of arranging her skirts while Eva settled the notebook on her lap, her handbag beside her. This time she sat beside Lady Phoebe on a Queen Anne settee rather than on a side chair on the fringes of the room, the indication being that she had come in a more official capacity. "I hope we're not disturbing you too early, Mrs. Hawkhurst."

"Not at all. I've been up for nearly an hour. We rise early here at Sunderly. Mr. Hawkhurst is on his estate rounds."

Eva caught the slight upturn at the corner of Lady Phoebe's mouth. This was exactly what they had hoped for, the reason they had come at this most unsociable hour.

"What might I do for you, then?" Mrs. Hawkhurst took on a solicitous expression, as befitted the lady of a great estate. But then a shadow crossed her features. "I do hope it doesn't have to do with poor Arvina. And, goodness, Dr. Bishop. I was thoroughly shocked to hear about his death."

"As were we." Lady Phoebe did not say any more about it. No need, they had decided beforehand, to mention their having been at the doctor's house when his body was discovered. "No," she continued, "our visit has nothing to do with that. I'm here concerning my charity, the RCVF. The Relief and Comfort—"

"Of Veterans and their Families," Mrs. Hawkhurst finished for her. "Yes, I'm familiar with it. If you'll remember, I contributed last spring."

"Just so. My assistant, Miss Huntford, brought along our record book, where we keep track of donations and

dispersals, as well as a list of our regular contributors."
She paused long enough for Mrs. Hawkhurst to take
this in.

The woman's hand went to her collar and tugged
slightly. "And what can I do for you?" she repeated.

Lady Phoebe smiled and gestured to Eva, who opened
the ledger, and then her handbag to extract a fountain pen.

"What may we put you down for? Our categories are
virtually endless and include household items, kitchen
supplies, bedding, adults' and children's clothing . . . Or
perhaps you'd prefer to make a monetary donation?"

"Monetary?" The woman swallowed.

"Yes. However much you feel would be helpful."

Mrs. Hawkhurst compressed her rouged lips, her eyes
growing as large as the buttons down the front of her silk
cardigan. Her hand strayed to her collar again, then
drifted to the brooch pinned at her shoulder. Eva followed
that hand, though when it sank back to her lap, her gaze
remained on the brooch.

Its geometric design distinguished it as a contemporary
piece, consisting of a long rectangular sapphire in a white
gold—or perhaps platinum—setting, rounded at the corners and trimmed with small rubies. To Eva's eye, the
stones appeared real and not paste, and the modern styling
suggested the piece had been made more or less recently,
and was not, in fact, something Mrs. Hawkhurst could
have inherited from her mother.

Such a piece of jewelry would have been costly. Were
she and Lady Phoebe wrong about the Hawkhursts' financial situation? She glanced around the room and didn't
think so. She returned to studying Mrs. Hawkhurst.

The poor woman had turned a vivid scarlet color and
clutched her hands together in her lap. "I suppose we
could spare some household items and perhaps some
cooking supplies. Would that serve?"

No, then, Eva thought, their money difficulties could not be imagined. She almost felt sorry for Vesta Hawkhurst and experienced a twinge of guilt for being the source of her present mortification. She opened the ledger, found the most recent page, and filled in Mrs. Hawkhurst's name on an empty line. Beside it she wrote, *household items,* leaving room to fill in the specifics, although she had a feeling the donation would never materialize.

"I can arrange for your donation to be picked up at your convenience," Lady Phoebe said, her smile unwavering. "Is there a particular day you have in mind?"

"Er . . . no . . . at the moment I really couldn't say. Can I have my housekeeper telephone over to Foxwood Hall, once we've had a chance to see what we can . . . er . . . donate?" Eva had the distinct impression the woman had been about to say *spare,* but at the last instant had changed it to the more agreeable term.

"Of course." Lady Phoebe signaled to Eva again, and Eva flipped to the second section of the notebook. "Shall we put you down as one of our regular donors? We have several drives a year, typically before the Christmas and Easter holidays, before the school term begins, and at the start of the summer holidays. We also administer aid to individual families throughout the year." Lady Phoebe's brows arched in question.

"Oh, yes, I suppose . . ."

"Splendid! Eva, please put Mrs. Hawkhurst down as a regular." Her expression turned more serious. "Now, I wonder if you'd mind letting Lady Primrose Scott know of your involvement with the RCVF."

"Primrose? Why ever for?"

"Because I'm also going to appeal to her generosity, and knowing that a friend and colleague has already signed on as a donor will encourage her. Don't you think so?"

Mrs. Hawkhurst's expression became shuttered. "I don't

know that my actions will have any influence on Primrose at all."

"No? Aren't you friends?"

"Not particularly."

"Oh, goodness. Forgive me, but I assumed you and your husband were socially active with the Scotts. Of all the members of the historical society, you and they do seem to have the most in common."

"We have very *little* in common." Mrs. Hawkhurst's nose had become pinched so tight that bright white lines appeared on either side. Lady Phoebe had struck a nerve— several of them from the looks of it. Yet despite Mrs. Hawkhurst's evident anger, Eva was taken aback in the next moment to see tears glittering on the woman's lashes. "As for a donation from that quarter, I wouldn't count on it, Lady Phoebe. That woman is not what she pretends to be. Lady Primrose is no *prim rose*." Her voice broke and she surged to her feet. "Please excuse me. I don't feel quite well."

She ran from the room.

"Good heavens, Eva," Lady Phoebe whispered, her fingertips hovering over her lips. "That went much worse than I expected. I feel like the worst sort of heel, to use an Americanism. I might as well have come right out and asked if she knew whether her husband and Lady Primrose were having an affair."

"The answer is obviously yes, she knows, or she never would have responded that way. You mustn't blame yourself. You're not responsible for the problems in the Hawkhursts' marriage."

Lady Phoebe didn't look convinced and merely said, "Come, we'd better let ourselves out."

They came to their feet, Eva gathering the notebook and her handbag. They were stepping into the main hall as Abel Hawkhurst came down the staircase. Eva and Lady Phoebe stopped short.

"I thought he was making his estate rounds," Lady Phoebe whispered.

"Maybe we could slip out a side door," Eva suggested. If the man was on his way down the stairs, then he must have passed his wife on her way up. Surely, he would know their visit had upset her.

"Lady Phoebe," the man called, not bothering to acknowledge Eva. "I do apologize for my wife. It seems she took suddenly ill." He came toward them, smiling apologetically. He shook Lady Phoebe's hand, while continuing to ignore Eva. In a lower voice he continued, "It's her nerves, you see. Ever since poor Mrs. Bell's death . . . well, you know."

"Mrs. Bell's *murder,*" Lady Phoebe corrected him. "Not to mention Dr. Bishop's."

He winced at her bluntness and only then appealed to Eva. "Your mistress doesn't hide behind niceties, does she?"

"No, she doesn't," Eva replied. She thought Lady Phoebe would bid the man good morning and take her leave of him. Eva was more than ready to go, having already looked the man over and finding no apparent signs of his having been battered by Lady Wroxly. But Lady Phoebe showed no sign of moving, holding her ground before the much taller Abel Hawkhurst and pinning him with her gaze.

"There are reasons to suspect that an illicit affair led to Arvina Bell's murder, Mr. Hawkhurst, that perhaps she had learned a secret about someone and was permanently silenced as a result. What do you think about that?"

"What do I think?" He snorted a laugh. "I think you've been reading too many lurid novels, Lady Phoebe. I think your grandmother should keep closer watch on what books come into Foxwood Hall."

It was all Eva could do not to let her mouth drop open. Of course, if it did, there was no telling what words would come roaring out as she took the man to task for speaking so to her lady. One look at Lady Phoebe, however, assured her she need not intervene, for her gaze never wavered and her posture never slackened.

"I don't need poorly written fiction to convince me all is not well among the members of your historical society, Mr. Hawkhurst. Take you and Lady Primrose, for instance."

A muscle in his cheek jumped. "What about Lady Primrose and me?" His voice took on a rumble of warning.

"You and she were seen arguing in the village yesterday."

"That's none of your business, is it?"

Lady Phoebe shrugged. "I didn't say it was."

"Then you've no cause to bring it up." He shook his head as if at a naughty child. "Really, you two, upsetting my wife and practically accusing me of goodness knows what, and before I've even had a proper breakfast. I believe it's time for you to leave." He held out an arm as if to scoop them both up and toss them out the front door.

They voluntarily crossed the hall. He walked ahead to open the door, and as they made to step over the threshold, he leaned in. "If anyone has anything to hide, it's Primrose Scott. Try asking her about the Paris Roses."

"The what?" Lady Phoebe's frown mirrored Eva's own puzzlement.

"Never mind." He nudged them outside and shut the door.

Once back in the Vauxhall and safely on the road, Phoebe breathed a sigh of relief. "That was certainly interesting." She darted a glance at Eva and then back at the road. "I'm sorry, I know it took you by surprise when I spoke plainly to Mr. Hawkhurst."

"To say the least." Eva chuckled wryly. "But I'm glad you did. His reaction was telling."

Phoebe headed the Vauxhall back toward the village. "What were your impressions?"

This was a game they had played in the past, with Phoebe questioning suspects, while Eva sat silently, almost invisibly, all the while observing and taking mental notes.

"Nothing to link them to the break-in at home, I'm afraid. But they're both hiding something." Eva turned to gaze out her window. "He as much as she, though I can't decide if they're both attempting to conceal the same thing or not."

"What do you mean?"

Eva turned back and fingered the edges of the RCVF ledger. "When you brought up the possibility of Mrs. Bell dying as a result of someone having an affair, he seemed more relieved than worried. That laugh—it seemed genuine. Unplanned."

"Interesting. So then, if not an affair gone wrong, what do you think he and Lady Primrose could have been arguing about?"

"I don't know, but both Mr. and Mrs. Hawkhurst agree that Primrose Scott is not what she seems. And I tend to agree. She works too hard to maintain appearances."

Phoebe nodded her agreement. "What else did you notice?"

"I don't need to tell you the Hawkhursts are strapped for cash. That much is obvious. But the brooch she was wearing—I'd stake my reputation as a competent lady's maid that it's real. Sapphire, rubies, and unless I miss my guess, a platinum setting. And it's relatively new, judging by the design."

"So not an inherited piece." Phoebe tightened her hands and applied the brake as a rabbit skittered across the road up ahead. "How could they have afforded it?"

"Very possibly, Mr. Hawkhurst bought it on credit to reassure Mrs. Hawkhurst all is well."

"Your hunch about buying on credit rings true. It's so common for men of his standing to run up debts almost indefinitely, until their estates come crashing down around them. But how can Vesta Hawkhurst believe such a lie when they obviously can't afford enough help to keep the house clean?"

Eva shrugged. "People believe what they wish to believe."

"True," Phoebe agreed with a nod. "So, if Abel Hawkhurst and Primrose Scott *aren't* having an affair, what else could he be hiding? Any clues?"

"The obvious answer is his finances."

"You don't sound too sure of that," Phoebe pointed out.

"I have a nagging sense it's rather more complicated. After all, it wouldn't explain what they were arguing about—unless, of course, he owed her money."

Phoebe considered this a moment before replying. "If that were so, why would he bring up her name? Unless the historical society finances are in question. Perhaps Lady Primrose has been skimming."

Eva raised an eyebrow in speculation. "Perhaps Mr. Hawkhurst has been skimming and wishes to throw suspicion onto Lady Primrose."

"That would actually make more sense, wouldn't it?" Phoebe thought back on the conversation. The man had been condescending and dismissive. And he had spoken cryptically. "Whatever could the Paris Roses be? A new breed of rose?"

Eva inclined her head. "Could be. Roses *are* a lucrative business. Then again, it might not be actual roses. It could be jewelry, or some form of artwork, such as a carving, painting, or even tapestry."

"Also lucrative. Perhaps someone has more in mind than a bit of the historical society's petty cash. It's time for another visit with Primrose Scott."

* * *

What had been intended as a brief stop at home to check on the family resulted in Eva staying behind when Lady Phoebe set out to visit Primrose Scott.

A summons came via Mrs. Sanders, who, by her harried appearance, must have run all the way up the back staircase to find Eva in Lady Phoebe's bedroom, where they had continued discussing the Hawkhursts. "Excuse me, my lady. Miss Huntford, Miss Chapman is waiting to see you in the servants' hall." The words rushed out of her as she smoothed iron-gray hairs back into the bun at her nape.

"Miss Chapman? Wishes to see me?"

"Yes, yes, you. Must I repeat myself? There's been a minor catastrophe in the kitchen and I've more important things to do than entertain unexpected visitors. Lord and Lady Wroxly asked that you handle whatever Miss Chapman wants in any way you see fit."

"Did they?" Eve wondered what that meant. "What could there be to handle?"

"You're full of questions, aren't you, Miss Huntford?"

"Sorry, Mrs. Sanders, I'll go down presently."

Mrs. Sanders disappeared the way she had come, leaving Eva and Lady Phoebe mystified.

"Whatever could have happened in the kitchen?" Lady Phoebe wondered aloud.

Eva shrugged. "A minor catastrophe could mean anything from the range not firing properly to an order not being delivered, to one of the assistants falling ill. Between the two of them, Mrs. Sanders and Mrs. Ellison can handle it, so I shouldn't worry. But this matter of Miss Chapman . . . it's most curious."

"I'm curious, too." Lady Phoebe placed her hat back on her head and secured it with a pearl-tipped pin. "But I don't wish to put off my visit with Lady Primrose. I want to speak with her before she is somehow warned of my coming. It helps to catch people off their guard."

"I'm not best pleased at the thought of you going alone."

"Nonsense. What can happen in the middle of the day, especially when Lady Primrose is so adamant about keeping up appearances? I shall come to no harm."

With that assurance—which did little to put Eva's mind at rest—they parted, with Eva hurrying belowstairs. She found Ophelia Chapman sitting at the table in the servants' hall. She stood as soon as Eva entered the room and held out her hand.

"Miss Huntford, thank you so much for seeing me."

Eva couldn't help taking an instant to admire the woman's outfit. An almost waistless frock of butter-yellow crepe skimmed her figure, culminating in a bold Oriental floral pattern beneath the knees, making both a subdued yet dramatic statement. House of Paquin, Eva decided, but not an original, for she judged the crepe to be cotton and not silk. Miss Chapman had also subtly changed her coiffure, deepening the part on one side so the hair dipped just above one eye. Eva envied the woman's ability to put together a chic look without spending the kind of money society women did to look virtually the same, and without appearing as though she had tried too hard.

She grasped Miss Chapman's offered hand. "It's very nice to see you again, Miss Chapman. What can I do for you?"

"There's been a development. I'm not only writing a series of articles on the region anymore. Hayden Bell has asked me to complete his mother's book to honor her memory."

"I see." Eva still didn't understand what Miss Chapman needed. "And how can I be of help?"

"Can you pave the way for me to be able to continue studying the house and its contents? I wouldn't need much time—a day or two, nothing more. I merely need to fill in the gaps in Arvina Bell's research—and, of course, my own—from the house tour. Do you think the earl and countess would object?"

Eva hesitated. On the one hand, Lord and Lady Wroxly might very well object to a veritable stranger having the run of the house, especially with Mrs. Bell's murderer still at large. For all she knew, Miss Chapman, who had gone her own way at least once during the tour, might have committed the deed.

On the other hand, Miles had verified that Miss Chapman did have the proper credentials and was a fairly well-known journalist within her particular field. Lord and Lady Wroxly hadn't objected to Mrs. Bell's plan to include Foxwood Hall in her book, and, moreover, this *was* a lovely way to honor the woman's memory. It might also draw more interest in house tours, although Eva wondered whether the earl and countess would ever allow another one, considering.

According to Mrs. Sanders, the earl and countess wished Eva to handle the request in any way she saw fit. She made her decision. "I think we can accommodate you, Miss Chapman, at least as far as the ground floor is concerned. Would you need to see more than that?"

The woman frowned and compressed her lips as she considered. "What if I were allowed upstairs, but with a member of the household? You, for instance. And then we can finally attend to that interview we talked about."

"I suppose that might be all right."

"Good. At any rate I'll review the ground floor first, and the surrounding gardens, which should certainly be included. From what I glimpsed out the windows, they're lovely. Shall I return tomorrow, around nine? The sooner the better, I say."

"Yes, tomorrow at nine should be fine." Eva hoped Lady

Phoebe wouldn't need her elsewhere. If she did, perhaps Vernon could be spared to keep an eye on Miss Chapman.

"Wonderful. See you tomorrow, then."

Eva smiled. There was one other benefit to having Miss Chapman here: Eva would be able to question the young woman about her visit to Dr. Bishop's house before he was murdered.

CHAPTER 16

"Thank you for seeing me again, Lady Primrose." Phoebe sat across from the older woman in the same immaculate parlor she and Eva had seen on their first visit here. "Some new questions concerning Mrs. Bell's death—and the doctor's—have arisen recently."

"I can't imagine why you're troubling yourself about such things, Lady Phoebe, dear. Why would a nice young lady such as yourself wish to become entangled in such an unwholesome matter? Leave it to the police. Surely, your grandparents can't approve."

Phoebe detected a note in the woman's voice as she spoke those last words, a subtle threat, perhaps, that Lady Primrose would enlighten Grams and Grampapa as to Phoebe's recent activities if she didn't back away.

Well.

"It's not as though I have any notions of tracking down the killer myself. No, I'm more than happy to allow the police to solve the crime. But if I can help them in any way, I surely must."

Lady Primrose's mouth resembled nothing so much as a

prune as it tightened into a ball of disapproval. "Very well. What are these questions?"

"Well, ma'am, let me begin by asking if all is well with the historical society."

"Of course. Whatever could you mean?"

Phoebe made a show of appearing reluctant to speak plainly. "There are some rumors flitting about that there might be some internal problems."

"*Internal problems?* We're a local-interest group, Lady Phoebe. The society exists as a way for us to amuse ourselves, and to keep records of interest to the local community. We don't have any such thing as *internal problems*. We're not that important." She let out a brittle laugh and worried the edge of the silk scarf draped around her neck. "The very idea."

"But your group has funds, does it not? And you *are* the treasurer. Have you noticed any discrepancies?"

The woman gasped. "Are you accusing me of stealing from the society? Because if so, I am dreadfully offended."

"Lady Primrose, you and Abel Hawkhurst were seen arguing in the village yesterday. Did it have anything to do with historical society business?"

Ire burned in the woman's gray eyes. "You've been spying on me?"

"No, I haven't been, I assure you."

"Then it was that sneaky maid of yours. Do you think I didn't notice how she sat right there last time, in the very spot where you are now, not saying a word, but taking in every last detail about this room—and about me? Do you think I'm both blind and stupid?"

Actually, Phoebe didn't think either of those things, but she did wonder why Lady Primrose was becoming so distraught if she had nothing to feel guilty about. "I do understand why these questions might unsettle you, but you seem highly agitated and I can't help but wonder why."

"Why? *Why?*"

Phoebe ignored her growing hysteria and calmly continued. "Quite contrary to suspecting *you,* my thought is perhaps Mr. Hawkhurst might be pinching funds. I find it strikingly obvious that he's having financial difficulties, so it's not an outlandish notion. Given that, and his argument with you yesterday, I can't help but suspect you might have discovered a discrepancy in the books, brought it to his attention, and received a warning to keep the knowledge to yourself."

Lady Primrose stared back with something akin to horror dawning in her eyes. She jumped up from her chair so suddenly, Phoebe flinched. She feared the woman might run from the room, as Mrs. Hawkhurst had done earlier, but she instead began pacing with heavy steps that left ruts in the carpet. She was so distracted she nearly smacked her hip on the side of the piano.

"Have I guessed correctly, Lady Primrose? Has Mr. Hawkhurst threatened you?"

Lady Primrose came to an abrupt stop beside a lovely escritoire of inlaid rosewood. She propped a hand on it and said in a low, trembling murmur, "I would like you to leave. Now."

"Don't you see?" Phoebe came to her feet and faced the woman. "Two people are dead, and those deaths are connected. If you know anything at all about it, you had better come clean."

Lady Primrose wrenched around to face the desk, and when she turned back toward Phoebe, she held a letter opener in her hand. "I told you to leave. Now get out!"

Phoebe gasped, but stayed put. It was just a letter opener, after all, not a dagger. Then again, the steel was long and thin and came to a rather intimidating point. "Lady Primrose, have you ever heard of the Paris Roses?"

With a guttural sound Lady Primrose charged her,

wielding her weapon as if to plunge it into Phoebe's heart. Her face had turned fiery, her eyes glazed. Phoebe hesitated another instant—an instant that brought the irate woman that much closer—before turning on her heel and retreating. She was somehow able to snatch her handbag from the settee before fleeing the room and the house.

Once she was back in the motorcar, she sat clutching the wheel with both hands. Tremors raced through her while her heart thumped wildly. She fixed her gaze on the front door. Would Lady Primrose come bursting outside and continue her assault?

The door remained shut and Phoebe's pulse and breathing slowly calmed to something approaching normal. Only then could she attempt to maneuver the Vauxhall onto the road. As she headed for home, she wondered whether Lady Primrose would have carried out her threat.

At home she found Grams in the Rosalind sitting room. Grampapa, she had learned from Mr. Giles, had retired to his study after hearing the morning report from Mr. Gregory, the estate manager. Unlike Mr. Hawkhurst, Grampapa no longer went on rounds of the estate on a daily basis, but relied on others for his information.

Today, Phoebe would rely on Grams for the information she sought. Grams was the one person she knew to be versed in society gossip, while never being one to pass it along.

"Oh, Phoebe, there you are." Grams seemed not only pleased to see her, but delighted. She set aside the embroidery she had been working on.

Phoebe came into the room and smiled down at the delicate handiwork framed in its hoop. The gold flowering vines on black silk was meant to be a pillow cover, though it might never grace an actual pillow. Grams's projects often went unused, finding a permanent home in a drawer in her dressing room. These days embroidery was, for her, merely a source of relaxation. "Your stitches are so perfect, Grams. I don't know how you do it."

"Patience," Grams instantly replied with a significant look. They both knew it was a virtue Phoebe lacked, at least when it came to such ladylike pursuits. "But never mind that. Wonderful news. Julia telephoned while you were out."

"Thank goodness. Where is she?"

Grams pursed her lips. "She was a bit evasive, but she did mention Henni Montague. Apparently, they've spent some time catching up. Julia apologized for forgetting to telephone about her change in plans and said she'll be returning to Lyndale Park in a couple of days."

Phoebe nodded and didn't mention that she knew for a fact Julia hadn't been with Henni Montague at all, because Phoebe had checked with Henni. Nor did she think it wise at that precise moment to inform Grams of Julia's visit with Theo. Instead she said, "That's one worry off our minds."

"Indeed. She even held little Charles near the phone and I could hear him cooing. All is well." She tipped her head. "Is there something you wanted?"

"Yes, there is. Have you a few moments, Grams?"

Grams patted the cushion beside her. The room was silent, the gramophone in the corner still. Phoebe sat and noticed how her fingers still trembled slightly from her encounter with Lady Primrose. She folded them together in her lap.

"How well do you know Primrose Scott?" she began.

"Primrose?" It was obvious the question took Grams by surprise. "In recent years, not well at all. But I knew her when she was young. When we were *all* quite a bit younger," she said wistfully. "Why do you ask?"

Did a bit of suspicion accompany the question? Knowing Grams, probably. "I ran into her today and she acted strangely." As much of the truth as Phoebe wished to divulge.

"How so? And what do you mean, you *ran into her*?"

Phoebe wanted to sigh in frustration at Grams's perceptiveness. She focused on the first question and tried to ignore the second. "I was asking her about the historical society and she became very defensive and standoffish." An understatement, though technically not a lie. "It was almost as if she didn't wish to talk about it. Like something greatly troubled her."

"I can't imagine what it could be. Well, except for the death of her friend, Mrs. Bell."

"Yes, but I wasn't asking her about that."

Grams took on something of a faraway look. "Primrose Scott—or Primrose Whitley, before she married—was always something of an enigma, for a girl of her breeding. Always contrary to the other girls her age. I knew her parents, who were of an age with your grandfather and me. They always despaired of Primrose ever marrying, ever settling down. She was something of a bohemian in those days. She even disappeared for a time."

"Did she? Where did she go?" Phoebe couldn't imagine the very proper Primrose Scott as a bohemian, someone who abandoned traditional society in favor of an artistic and less restricted lifestyle, especially at the turn of the century, when such ways were looked upon as scandalously indulgent.

"Apparently, she traveled abroad with a great-aunt, which I suppose is nothing unusual. This was in the final years of the last century and the early years of this one. Then, one day, there she was again, looking none the worse for wear and every bit the proper lady. Not long after her return, she married Conrad Scott and began a very conventional life as the wife of a career politician."

"And the aunt?"

"I couldn't say." Grams shrugged. "I'd never met her."
Her silver brows arrowed inward. "What has it to do with
how she behaved toward you today? Phoebe, are you
meddling in things that are none of your business again?"

"Don't worry, Grams." Phoebe decided a swift change
of subject was needed. "I'm just so happy Julia telephoned."

"I can't tell you how relieved I am." Grams looked
down at her hands, veined and wrinkled, the long fingers
thin and fragile-looking. Yet Phoebe knew better. The vul-
nerability of those hands belied the strength of will at
Grams's core. "It wasn't like her to worry us that way. I
kept telling myself she's a grown woman and we can't expect her to keep us apprised of her every move. But I don't
mind admitting I haven't slept well."

"You will tonight, Grams." Phoebe kissed her grandmother's cheek. But as she headed toward her bedroom,
she wondered why Julia had lied about her whereabouts,
and what was really going on.

Eva listened in alarm and growing outrage as Lady
Phoebe related the events of her visit to the Scott residence. Her hand tightened around the handle of the clothing iron she held until her knuckles whitened. "She
actually threatened you with a letter opener?"

"She did. I doubt she actually would have used it, but
she did present the very image of a madwoman coming at
me with her blazing eyes and that daggerlike letter opener
waving high in the air."

Lady Phoebe had come below stairs to find Eva catching up on her ironing. Presently she had one of Lady
Amelia's silk frocks stretched flat across her board, lightly
sprinkled with a starch solution. It had taken a couple of

years, but Eva had finally gotten used to the electric iron with its long cord that plugged into a socket in the ceiling, and now she had to admit the chore went faster than when she had used the old cast-metal irons that needed to be heated on a hot stove.

She resumed working, taking meticulous care around the seams. "She truly sounds desperate to keep her secret, whatever it is."

"I just spoke to Grams, who told me, interestingly enough, that Lady Primrose was a bit of a bohemian in her younger days, around the turn of the century." Lady Phoebe related a story that, while rousing Eva's curiosity, didn't sound terribly scandalous. A young lady traveling with her aunt? It happened all the time. But then she remembered something.

"The Paris Roses," she murmured, then set the iron down. "Mr. Hawkhurst said we should ask her about that."

"And so I did. That's when she came at me with the letter opener."

"I'll wager she spent at least some of her time away in Paris, and *something* happened."

"Something that could damage her reputation," Lady Phoebe suggested.

"Something she's desperate to keep secret, especially from her MP husband and their constituents." Eva considered the likely possibilities. "A romantic liaison gone awry, leaving her compromised, perhaps. And one may suppose Mr. Hawkhurst knows about it."

"And is blackmailing her," Lady Phoebe concluded. Her eyebrows reached for her hairline. "Perhaps she disappeared with *him,* and the story about the aunt was just a cover-up."

"But if that was the case, why would he have waited until now, if he's indeed blackmailing her? Why not years ago, when she first returned from her travels?" Eva shook her head. "No, it seems more likely this is something he learned recently. Perhaps stumbled upon by accident."

"When we ran into him at Sadler's bookshop, he seemed awfully startled to see us there," Lady Phoebe said, her eyes wide with speculation again. "And there were those photographs of French showgirls from the turn of the century. Eva, you don't suppose . . . ?"

"No. Certainly not." Eva picked up the iron, but held it aloft as she considered. She shook her head. "The idea of a gently born girl running off to become a dancing girl in Paris? It's beyond absurd, isn't it?"

"Then why did Mr. Hawkhurst tell us to ask Lady Primrose about the Paris Roses?"

"I don't know . . ."

"I think we need to have another look at those photographs."

"Do you really think we'll just happen to find Lady Primrose hanging on that wall? And even if she was, how would anyone recognize her from over twenty years ago, wearing theatrical makeup and a feathered headdress?" Glancing down, Eva realized she'd been ironing the same frock over and over again. She took it off the board and carefully hung it on a wooden hanger she herself had padded and covered in satin. She placed it on a bar next to several other garments she had already pressed.

"I suppose you're right." Lady Phoebe leaned on her elbows on the worktable. "Still, though. Perhaps Mr. Sadler has already sold such a photo to Mr. Hawkhurst, and he's using it to blackmail Lady Primrose."

Before Eva could respond, there came a light rap on the open door. She was happily surprised to find Constable Brannock standing on the threshold. He held his police helmet in his hands. "Miles! What brings you here?"

"Have I come at a bad time?" His gaze lighted on Lady Phoebe. "I can come back . . ."

"Nonsense, Constable Brannock. Come in." Lady Phoebe pushed away from the worktable. "We were actually discussing the members of the historical society. Did you know it's possible Abel Hawkhurst has been blackmailing Lady Primrose? He might have discovered something about her past she would not wish to become common knowledge."

"That's interesting. How did the two of you happen upon that?"

"I went to see her today." Once again, Lady Phoebe described her visit to the Scott residence, as well as her conversation with her grandmother when she returned home. Then Eva explained about the photographs she had discovered in Mr. Sadler's shop.

"I think it might be a good idea to see if Mr. Sadler will admit to having sold a photo to Mr. Hawkhurst," Lady Phoebe said. "Or, at the very least, whether Mr. Hawkhurst had shown an uncommon interest in them. We can go today."

"Sadler's place is isolated," Miles said, shaking his head. "You went there once. I don't like the idea of you going again."

"It's merely a bookshop." Lady Phoebe chuckled.

"Owned by a man who may or may not have murdered Arvina Bell," Miles reminded her, and Lady Phoebe conceded his point with a nod. "But I do agree that it's a good idea to question him again. I'll ride out there this evening."

"Splendid. We'll meet you there," Lady Phoebe said happily. "He closes at six o'clock. I should think five forty-five would be a good time. He's unlikely to have any customers then, not that he ever has many, by the looks of it."

Miles narrowed his eyes at her in censure, but didn't bother arguing.

Eva snatched up a shirtwaist to be ironed and spread it flat on the board. "You never answered my question. What brings you here?"

"Another matter of blackmail, actually." He walked to the worktable and set his helmet down. "I've made some inquiries. It's very possible someone had been blackmailing Dr. Bishop, if not for money, then for his cooperation."

"Just as we suspected," Lady Phoebe blurted, then gestured for Miles to go on.

"Dr. Bishop practiced as a surgeon in London at several of the city's hospitals. Had a very distinguished career and ran in some important circles. Was well known among cabinet ministers and other government officials."

"I predict a dramatic downfall," Eva said.

"Quite dramatic," Miles confirmed. "Seems about a year and a half ago he botched a simple appendectomy on the wife of an assistant to the undersecretary of the Home Office. She died." Miles paused to let them take this in. "It was hushed up for some reason—I haven't been able to find out why, though I suspect money changed hands."

"Money from Dr. Bishop's pocket." Eva raised an eyebrow and pursed her lips.

Miles nodded. "Probably. Anyway, he disappeared for a time, only to show up in the Cotswolds and set himself up as a simple country physician."

"A physician who stocked chloroform in his surgery." Eva released a breath. "Who might have known his secret?"

"It'll be difficult to find that out, but I'm working on it." Miles watched a moment as Eva put the finishing touch on the shirtwaist. "We're trying to trace who might have been in London at the time of the incident, and who has ties to the government."

"Excuse me." Lady Phoebe raised a hand as if in the classroom. "Lady Primrose has ties to the government through her husband. And she conveniently remained here in Little Barlow while her husband is currently in London. Here, where she could keep an eye on Dr. Bishop and wait for the perfect opportunity to permanently silence him."

"True." Miles picked up his helmet. "But that's all circumstantial. We need something more definite and that's what we're working to find." He gave a low whistle. "Who would have thought this little historical society would be so rife with intrigue and deceit?"

CHAPTER 17

Phoebe brought the Vauxhall to a standstill on the side of Sadler's Rare Books Emporium. No other motorcars were in the vicinity.

"Miles isn't here yet, my lady." Eva stared out the windscreen before turning to Phoebe. "Odd, as he's always so prompt. Perhaps we should wait."

Phoebe craned her neck to glance over her shoulder at the road. "I'm sure he'll be here any minute. I say we go in and get Mr. Sadler talking."

Eva shrugged and opened the passenger-side door. Phoebe came around the boot to join her, before together they traversed the walkway to the shop door. She raised her hand to knock, then remembered they were calling at a place of business and not a private home, though it appeared more like the latter.

The bell tinkled as they stepped in. Mr. Sadler, across the main room sliding books onto a shelf, turned to greet them. The smile he wore faded the moment he realized the identity of his customers. "Oh . . . er . . . Lady Phoebe. Miss Huntford. What can I do for you? It's *very* close to closing time."

He emphasized that last, almost making it an admonition.

"Don't worry, we won't keep you long." Phoebe waved away his concerns. But as she did so, she looked him over, searching for signs he might be the culprit injured by Grams during the break-in. She detected nothing unusual, or that she hadn't noticed the last time she saw him.

"Another book of poetry, perhaps?" he suggested as he came toward them. "Another fashion guide?"

"Not exactly." Phoebe started past him, toward the little hallway that housed the photographs. "I'd like another look at these."

"Oh, I don't think . . ." He swiftly followed on her heels, and she could hear Eva taking up the rear. This wasn't what they had agreed upon. Phoebe was to have kept him busy while Eva stole into the hallway to study the photographs, but Phoebe had changed her mind. Once again, she thought a direct approach might yield more immediate results.

She pulled the chain on the overhead light, bringing the showgirls in all their photogenic splendor to life. Their lack of attire brought a surge of heat to her face, just as when she had first viewed these images. But now, she could also appreciate the glamour, and along with it the sense of freedom that must have marked these women's lives. Phoebe had once heard someone say there was liberation in casting off society's restrictions, in not caring about one's reputation. Judging by the grins and the spirit glinting in the dancers' eyes, there was truth in that.

They were young and undeniably beautiful. They must have held men spellbound with their charms and dancing talents. But what happened when youth and beauty faded? Where did such women go then? If Primrose Scott had been among them, she had been one of the lucky few who escaped while still young enough, and her reputation still

intact enough to find a husband. At the turn of the century—in fact, at any time before the present—there would
have been few other paths for a woman to pursue.

One other occupation came to mind—the most likely
one for a former showgirl—and she grimaced to think of
it, to consider both the danger and the humiliation of it.

She became aware of Mr. Sadler standing in the doorway behind her, his puffing breath reminding her of his
discomfiture at having her view what he reserved specifically for gentlemen customers.

She turned to him. "Have you ever heard of the Paris
Roses?"

"I . . . I . . . er . . . yes, I have, Lady Phoebe. But I hardly
consider that a fit topic to discuss with a young lady of
your standing. Why, your grandparents would be—"

"Mortified. Yes, I know. It's just that I heard the term
recently and I wondered about it. It makes sense to me
that the term might refer to women such as these." Even as
she spoke, she heard the tawdriness in her words, uninten-
tional though it was. If a woman of that time had chosen
such a profession, Phoebe believed she'd had good reason.
"You said they were showgirls in Paris around the turn of
the century. Tell me, have you sold any such photograph in
recent months?"

The question plainly threw him off balance. He stuttered some more before frowning like a schoolmaster at an
errant pupil. "I'm sorry, Lady Phoebe, I cannot divulge
that information. Now I must insist you come away from
here. I see I shall have to move these photographs to a
more secure location. I never imagined any young lady
would be so interested in them." He stood with one arm
extended to usher her back into the main room. Eva stood
aside to allow them to pass. Phoebe caught her eye and
winked. It was time to implement their original plan.

In the main part of the shop, Phoebe drifted to a wall of

shelves. "You mentioned poetry. Have you anything by Byron?"

The man pursed his lips in disapproval. "May I recommend Elizabeth Barrett Browning?"

"Oh, all right. Where would I find her?" While Phoebe kept Mr. Sadler busy searching out volumes, Eva slipped back into the hallway. Soon enough, however, she reappeared, and Phoebe made her selections. Mr. Sadler carried them to the register. While she dug into her handbag for her purse, Eva drifted to the front window to stare outside, wondering where Constable Brannock was. Indeed, what could have held him up?

"Thank you so much, Lady Phoebe." Mr. Sadler handed her the shopping bag. "Now, then, ladies. Closing time. Good evening to you both."

As he spoke, a lorry rumbled down the road toward the shop. When Phoebe expected it to pass by, it instead turned in. She could hear its rumbling motor circling the building.

Mr. Sadler scrambled around the counter and practically shooed them out. "I have a delivery to take. If you'll excuse me, I'll be locking up now so I can attend to that."

Back in the Vauxhall, Eva said, "I'm worried about Miles."

"So am I." Phoebe backed the motorcar onto the road and straightened it out. But she drove only a few yards, stopping where she could see the lorry that had brought Mr. Sadler's delivery where it stood behind the building. "Curious."

"What? That the delivery should be taken through a back door? I don't see anything curious about that." Eva spoke a bit testily and fidgeted with the straps of her handbag. Phoebe didn't blame her; she knew how worried Eva must be about Constable Brannock.

"Not that." Phoebe pointed to the lorry. "It's the size

that I find curious. Why would a delivery of books need a vehicle so large? Mr. Sadler's shop can only hold so much."

"Perhaps they're making deliveries at other shops as well." Impatience ringed each word. Again, Phoebe didn't blame her lady's maid.

"Perhaps." She drove on, but for only a few dozen more yards, where she could then pull onto the verge. She switched off the motor. "I want to take a look. You can wait here if you wish. I shouldn't be long."

"Absolutely not." Eva opened her door and slid out. It was to her credit that she didn't try to talk Phoebe out of this latest change in plans, however much she wished to find out what had delayed the constable.

"Thank you, Eva." Phoebe drew in a deep breath and stepped into the trees bordering the road. If they kept within them, they could backtrack without readily being seen. She pointed the way, grateful they had both worn comfortable shoes and somber colors that would blend in rather than stand out against the foliage. "Let's go."

"My lady, slow down. You're making too much noise." Eva followed Lady Phoebe through the trees. She didn't so much mind the underbrush snagging at her hem, nor the way her low-heeled pumps sank into the moist earth beneath them, nor even the mosquitoes just now waking up in the warmth of the evening air. No, it was the possibility of being apprehended, should this lorry turn out to be something other than an ordinary delivery.

And Miles. Where was he? Only a matter of vital importance or personal injury would have kept him from meeting them tonight. She prayed it was the former. But even at that, she believed he still would have found a way to either get there or have a message delivered to them.

Lady Phoebe finally came to a halt. From their location they could peer through the fringe of the trees onto Mr.

Sadler's rear property. The lorry stood with its motor idling, a loud rumble that would cover any footsteps.

She and Lady Phoebe positioned themselves behind the low-hanging, bushy branches of a yew tree—the perfect cover for observing. And what they observed soon had Eva scrunching up her features in puzzlement.

"They're not delivering books at all," she whispered. She brushed trailing leaves aside and watched a pair of men carry an oblong object covered in a drop cloth. When they reached the open rear gate of the lorry, they slid it inside. Then they returned to the back door of the shop. A few moments later they reappeared, each holding an item once again wrapped in cloth. These, too, they placed inside the lorry. "They're *taking* things. Why would Mr. Sadler lie about having a delivery? Or did we misunderstand?"

"Oh, I don't believe we misunderstood anything," Lady Phoebe murmured, almost to herself rather than to Eva. "I had a funny sensation when that large vehicle showed up, and I believe I'm right. In fact, I wonder if it was those photographs at all that made Mr. Sadler nervous about us wandering into the hallway."

"What do you mean?" Eva asked without taking her eyes off the scene outside the shop.

"I think he worried about our being too close to his storeroom and what they're now loading into their lorry." Lady Phoebe gestured with her chin at the laboring men. "Stolen goods, if you ask me."

"Then we need to leave. Immediately. We must find Miles and let him know."

"I agree. Let's be off."

They pushed away from the tree, but Eva's heel caught on a rock wedged into the ground. Her ankle turned. As she swallowed a yelp of pain, she went down, stirring the undergrowth beneath her.

"What was that?" came a call from the lorry.

Eva picked herself up with Lady Phoebe's help. The two men doing the loading stopped in their tracks, and the driver pointed out his side window toward the woods. "I heard something. Go check it out."

Lady Phoebe still had a grip on Eva's forearm, and now she tugged her into motion. They set out running, no longer mindful of the terrain, heedless of the brambles scratching their ankles and the low branches slapping their faces. Eva's ankle throbbed, but she ignored the pain, telling herself she could moan over it later.

The ruckus of their pursuers crashing through the trees behind them sped them faster. When the Vauxhall came into view, they dove for it, wasting not a second in tugging the doors open and ducking inside, though first Eva went round the bonnet to turn the crank while Lady Phoebe started the engine. The rear tires spun in the grass, and the motorcar lurched onto the road. They headed for Little Barlow at top speed, and for once, Eva didn't think to complain of Lady Phoebe's driving or even clutch at the seat. She was too relieved to have gotten away relatively unscathed.

The vehicle bucked slightly as Lady Phoebe changed gears. "Did you hurt yourself back there?"

"Not much. I'm fine." Eva's breath came in pants. She pressed a hand to the base of her throat and made a conscious effort to calm herself. "You?"

"Just a tad shaken."

"I'm sorry I slipped. If I hadn't, they'd have been none the wiser about our being there."

"Never mind. I'm taking us straight into the village and to the police station."

"I do hope Miles is there. I cannot imagine what kept him. We shouldn't have gone in alone."

Lady Phoebe shook her head, her hands gripping the

steering wheel. "No, our mistake was in going back. That was my fault and I'm sorry, Eva. They must surely know it was us."

"Does it matter, really?" Still feeling shaky, Eva hugged her arms around her middle. "They're obviously guilty of something, and Miles will see they're dealt with accordingly."

"Guilty of theft," Lady Phoebe clarified, and Eva nodded her agreement. "No wonder Eamon Sadler chose such a lonely stretch of road for his shop. And no wonder that shop is as dusty as it is—I'm sure it's a rare day he actually has customers. The place is nothing more than a depository for stolen goods. My guess is they store them there until they're ready to transport the lot to London or another of the big cities."

Everything Lady Phoebe was saying made perfect sense. "And Mr. Sadler's membership in the historical society is terribly convenient for gaining access to the area's manor houses."

"Exactly. I'll wager he does the initial scouting and those other men do the burgling. Why, Eva, this explains the break-in at Foxwood Hall. He must have told his cronies what we had and where to find it, and they came later for the spoils." Lady Phoebe shuddered. "When I think what might have happened to dear Grams . . ."

Eva glanced over at her young lady. Yes, Phoebe Renshaw would shudder to consider the safety and well-being of those she loved, but for herself? Hardly a blink in the face of two men chasing them through the woods.

They were nearing Little Barlow, but still on the Old Gloucester Road, a tree-lined lane that meandered up and down hills and snaked around sharp bends. Beyond the windscreen, something caught Eva's notice. She pointed. "What's that?"

"Where?"

Eva craned forward and strained her eyes to see in the deepening twilight. "Up ahead and across the road. By those trees. There's a motorcar on the verge and it looks to be at an odd angle." She gasped. The black sedan, which nearly melted into the darkness of the overhanging branches, faced the wrong direction, as though the driver had lost control and swerved to the other side of the road. The two side doors visible were emblazoned with a single word: PO-LICE. "That's Miles's motorcar. I *knew* there had to be a good reason he didn't meet us."

Lady Phoebe pulled to the side of the road, and Eva jumped out the moment the Vauxhall came to rest. Fear lodged in her throat as she hurried to the other motorcar. It seemed too still. Too silent. The very air around them felt weighted and hushed. All except for Eva's heart, which thrashed loudly in her ears. "Miles? Miles, are you in there?"

A note of growing hysteria clung to her shouts. She reached the driver's side and cupped her hands around her eyes to peer through the window. A gasp escaped her, and she tugged the door open. Miles lay slumped on his side across the seat. Eva reached in.

"Is he all right?" Lady Phoebe stood just beyond her. Eva could sense her hovering, trying to see over her shoulder.

"I don't know. He's not conscious. And . . . Oh, there's blood. On his brow. He must have hit his head."

"Yes, his window is cracked."

Good heavens. "Miles? It's Eva." She gently grasped his shoulder as she bit back an urge to weep. "Miles, *please* wake up."

"The front corner is rumpled," Lady Phoebe called out. She had moved to the side of the motorcar facing away from the road. "He hit a tree."

A tree on the wrong side of the road. Eva shook her head. Not Miles. He would never lose control of an automobile, especially in fine weather. He was too steady, too careful. He had flown aircraft missions over Germany in the worst of conditions and survived them all.

Miles groaned—more of a whimper—and all thoughts fled Eva's mind except one: his welfare. She ducked out of the vehicle and ran around to the other side, where she opened the door as wide as the trees would allow. Here she could run her hand over Miles's hair and speak into his ear.

"Miles. It's Eva. I'm here. You're going to be all right." But would he? Were those empty words? He was so very pale—much paler than his usual Irish complexion. And beneath the shock of russet hair that had fallen over his brow, a bruise had blossomed. At its center a small cut scored the skin. It seemed to have stopped bleeding, but had crusted in his hair and eyebrow, and the faint lines creasing his forehead.

He shifted ever so slightly, and Eva's heart did a little flip. "Yes, Miles. Wake up. I'm here."

A breath stirred his lips. His eyelashes fluttered, and he let out another groan. "Eva . . ." It came as no more than the faintest whisper.

"Yes, Miles. That's it. Keep coming back to us. You're almost there."

Eva glanced up to see Lady Phoebe at the driver's-side door, her hands clutched in front of her, an urgent look on her face. Their gazes met, and Eva gave a nod of relief.

Miles's arm pressed the seat and he leveraged himself up several inches. Eva helped by grasping his shoulders and keeping him from collapsing. In another moment he was upright against the seat. He leaned his head back and compressed his lips, his features etched with pain.

"Are you all right?" Eva couldn't think of anything else to say, except that she was so very happy he was alive. But speaking the obvious wouldn't be of any help.

"Where are we?" He raised a hand to touch his brow.

He winced, released a breath, and touched the wound again with his fingertips. "What happened?"

"We're on the Old Gloucester Road. You must have been on your way to Sadler's shop when . . . Well, we don't know what happened. Do you?"

He scrunched his eyes tight, bottom lip slipping between his teeth. He bit down so hard Eva feared he would bite clear through. "I was on my way to meet you and Lady Phoebe." His eyes burst wide and he lifted his head from the back of the seat. "Are the two of *you* all right? Did you go to the shop? I hope you didn't talk to Sadler without me . . ."

"You mustn't worry about us, we're fine," Eva assured him, tempted to cross her fingers at the white lie, or rather the implied one, for while they *were* perfectly fine, they *had* gone into the shop alone, and they *had* nearly been apprehended by apparent thieves. Speaking of which . . .

She drew in a breath, realizing what might have happened. "Miles, could you have been run off the road?"

"Yes . . . yes . . . I remember now." He made an effort to sit up straighter, then gave it up and remained slumped against the seat. "There was a lorry."

"A large one?"

"Yes." His gaze swerved to collide with hers. "How did you know?"

"We saw it," she admitted quickly. "What happened?"

He eyed her suspiciously, but replied, "It came up behind me, close. I remember thinking, *Doesn't this chap realize I'm a copper?* The next thing I know, he rams me from behind. More than once. The last time . . . the motorcar spun out. I went all the way around, and then there was a jarring stop, and . . . that's it. Then you were here." He found her hand that was resting on his forearm and held it tightly. "I woke up to you, Eva, telling me to come back to you."

His lips twitched, the corners rising in a smile that made him appear almost a boy who had accomplished a special feat—except that it produced in Eva a response only a man could prompt. She felt a lovely warmth inside, tumbling around an immense tangle of relief.

"Constable Brannock, I'm so glad to see you awake and talking," Lady Phoebe called from outside the motorcar. "You gave us a dreadful fright."

He nodded at her and smiled again. "It'll be full dark soon. We need to get out of here. Can you see how badly my motor is damaged?"

"Lady Phoebe said the front corner is rumpled."

"Then with any luck it should still be drivable."

"And just who do you propose does the driving?" Eva asked with a wry chuckle. "We have the two motorcars, and neither you nor I can drive."

"I think I can." He released her hand and shifted over behind the steering wheel.

"Miles, you mustn't. You're in no condition."

"What else is to be done? We can't all squeeze into that little Vauxhall."

"We've done it before, with Lady Annondale or Lady Amelia."

"Three wee ladies are another story." He drew in a deep breath, then several more, his hands wrapped firmly around the wheel. "No, I think I'll be all right. But just to be sure, you and Lady Phoebe follow me in the Vauxhall."

"I'll ride with you," Eva said.

"No, you won't. I believe I'll be all right, but I'm not willing to take the chance with you. We go separately." Eva opened her mouth to protest, but he reached over to press his fingers to her lips. "Separately. That's final."

CHAPTER 18

❧

At the police station in Little Barlow, Eva and Lady Phoebe went over every detail of their visit to Sadler's Rare Books Emporium. Luckily for them, Chief Inspector Perkins had gone home for the day, and Miles seemed in no hurry to inform him of today's adventures. He made no secret, however, of his disapproval that she and Lady Phoebe had gone inside Sadler's shop without waiting for him, and he very nearly seethed as they described returning to the property to observe the activity surrounding the lorry.

"You took an awful chance. This is exactly the sort of thing I don't wish you to do."

Eva withered ever so slightly on the hard-backed wooden chair. She didn't like having worried him, albeit that worry occurred after the fact. But if they hadn't gone back to the shop, they would have found Miles that much sooner, and perhaps he might have been able to catch the thieves in the act of loading their lorry. Then again, perhaps not. A phantom pain stabbed at her temple as she regarded the sticking plaster she herself had placed on his cut minutes ago. Thank goodness he hadn't appeared to need stitches.

"We're very sorry, Miles," she said, "but we simply didn't know what had kept you, and had we not gone back, we wouldn't know that Mr. Sadler was involved in shady dealings."

"That's very true, Constable." Lady Phoebe eagerly took up Eva's argument. "Based on the activities at the shop, it's obvious the men in the lorry saw you traveling toward Sadler's and decided they couldn't risk allowing you to arrive there. If you ask me, they're on a tight schedule and couldn't wait it out if the shop had been your destination."

"Is that your professional assessment, Lady Phoebe?" If his steely gaze was an effort to make her cringe, it failed. Lady Phoebe merely smiled and nodded.

"And don't blame Eva," she added. "Our activities were entirely my fault."

"Now, that isn't true at all," Eva contradicted her. While returning to the scene hadn't been her idea, nor had she approved of it, she and Lady Phoebe were far past the days when either of them expected Eva to blindly obey in such matters. If she had wished to argue the point, she could have, and if she had wished to remain behind, she could have done that, too. Not that she'd ever allow her lady to walk into danger alone.

Miles held up a hand to cease their protestations. "Never mind. I want the two of you to go home and stay there, and please stay out of trouble. I'm going to the post office now to wire our fellow stations to be on the lookout for this lorry." He picked up the sheet of paper on which he had written the descriptions of the lorry and the men. "I'm sure they're long gone from the area, but we might be able to track them down before they reach a city. I should

think we'll concentrate on roads leading to London, Gloucester, and Bristol." He started to rise from his chair, but
sank back down when Eva spoke.

"Obviously, there's more to this than a mere burglary."

He inclined his head. "Perhaps, perhaps not."

"It couldn't be mere coincidence that all of these things
have happened in the space of so short a time," Eva insisted. "Arvina Bell, Dr. Bishop, the hostilities between the
Hawkhursts and Lady Primrose, and now this business at
Sadler's shop. It must all be connected somehow."

"If it is, we'll find the link between them. For now, I've
got probable stolen goods on one hand, and two murders
on the other. Not to mention assault on an officer and a
hit-and-run motor incident." He pushed out a breath.
"Can you manage to get home safely?"

"Of course we can," Eva assured him, but he looked
less than convinced. She stood, and Lady Phoebe followed
suit, as did Miles. "Let us know if you discover anything."

He didn't reply to that, but instead said, "Go straight
home."

After helping Lady Phoebe prepare for the day that next
morning, Eva went below stairs to meet Ophelia Chapman, who would be arriving at nine. If Eva guessed correctly, she would be there at nine sharp, and not a moment
later. Miss Chapman struck her as a well-disciplined professional. Women had to be if they were to succeed.

Sure enough, as the mantel clock in the servants' hall
struck nine, Miss Chapman was escorted in by Stevens.
She approached Eva with a cordial smile and her hand extended. "Miss Huntford, how lovely to see you this morning." She spoke as if they had accidentally run into each
other on a village lane. "I hope you don't mind, but I
brought along a friend. Ernest, do come in."

Eva's jaw dropped as Ernest Shelton sauntered through the doorway. "Good morning, Miss Huntford. May I call you Eva? Nice to see you again. I trust all is well?"

That he would ask such a question, knowing a woman had been murdered in this house, almost directly above their heads, rendered Eva speechless.

"Ernie is going to man the camera while I take copious notes." Miss Chapman removed her gloves, folded them, and slipped them into her handbag, a larger one than she usually carried. Eva assumed she had brought along more tools of her trade. Once again, she had dressed smartly, with that same chic, almost coquettish, sweep of hair over her brow. Eva couldn't help wondering if she had made the change to appear more attractive for Mr. Shelton. If so, she wished Miss Chapman good luck in that arena—she would need it.

"We collaborated on my research into Lyndale Park, so Ernie knows how I operate," Miss Chapman went on to explain. "And since he's practically a member of the Renshaw family, I thought his being here would alleviate any qualms the earl and countess might have about my having the run of the place."

"Oh, I don't know . . ." It certainly wouldn't alleviate any qualms Lady Phoebe might have.

"We can begin down here and then proceed to the ground floor." Miss Chapman turned to Mr. Shelton. "Is your camera at the ready?"

He held up the box model draped by its strap around his neck. "Primed and ready to go, Ophelia."

"We'll start right here. What a charming room, especially one put aside for the staff. Not all servants' halls are this homey." She walked to the end of the room to study the board bell on the wall. With astonishment in her voice she asked, "Are these still used?"

"Yes, they are," Eva said. "Despite buzzers having taken

their place in most houses nowadays, Lord and Lady Wroxly prefer to keep this system as it is. It's more traditional."

"How quaint. I assume there is another board somewhere?"

"In the corridor, of course."

They went room by room, including Mrs. Sanders's parlor, Mr. Giles's pantry, the kitchen, storerooms, and even the coal room. Eva couldn't help noticing, as they progressed, the stealthy way many of the staff seemed to be moving about their daily tasks. At first, she thought perhaps they didn't wish to disturb Miss Chapman's observations. But when they entered the scullery, Dora started and came to her feet, looking like a startled fox. She had been crouching at a lower shelf, and now Eva noticed some pans had been pushed out of place.

"Working hard, Dora?" she asked with a pointed lift of her eyebrow.

"Yes, ma'am, I am. Just putting away some baking pans." She rushed by them and hurried through the scullery into the main kitchen.

"These vaulted ceilings certainly reveal the age of the house, its origins from the Tudor period," Miss Chapman remarked, "along with the thickness of the walls. And those cupboards, my goodness. Look at those doors and hinges. They could keep invading marauders from getting at the stores." She ambled back out into the kitchen, with Ernie in her wake, but Eva took another moment to see what Dora might have been up to.

A spatula lay on the bottom shelf, and she detected scape marks on the stones of the wall behind it. A suspicion formed in her mind, not only about what Dora had been doing, but the rest of the staff who moved so gingerly about. Mrs. Sanders had warned them not to continue searching for the previous Lord Wroxly's hidden treasure, but evidently her admonition had failed to leave a lasting impression. All it had done was make them more circumspect about how they searched.

She could only imagine what took place above stairs when the maids and footmen readied the house each morning.

She found Mr. Shelton and Miss Chapman waiting for her at the bottom of the service staircase.

"May we go up now?" Miss Chapman gestured above.

"Certainly." Eva led the way to the upper level of Mr. Giles's pantry, and the buttery that led into the dining room. Miss Chapman made note of the benches, cupboards, and shelves, and continued into the dining room. But as she stepped over the threshold, she cried out, "Oh!"

Eva hurried to her side. "Miss Chapman, have you hurt yourself?"

"Silly me, it's nothing." She lifted her foot and reached down to massage her ankle. "Tripped on the corner of the rug. I must take better care to watch where I'm going."

"Please do," Eva cautioned her, as much for Miss Chapman's own good as for the room's breakable treasures, should any come toppling down on them.

Miss Chapman spent a good deal of time in the dining room, and had Mr. Shelton take countless photographs of the architectural details: the fluted pilasters, the elaborately carved window casings, the cornices, the medallion from which the tiered crystal chandelier dangled. From there, they moved on to the drawing room, chatting as they crossed the Great Hall.

"Is that Miss Chapman, I hear?" Lady Phoebe came down the Grand Staircase with a cordial smile on her face, until her gaze landed on Ernest Shelton. "Good heavens, Ernie. What on earth are you doing here?"

* * *

Phoebe would have grimaced at the rudeness in her own voice, had it not been Ernie Shelton she was speaking to. With hands on her hips she waited for an answer.

He held up the camera hanging from around his neck. "Taking pictures. For Miss Chapman."

"Since when are you a photographer?"

"Oh, good morning, Lady Phoebe. I've brought along an assistant today." Miss Chapman offered her a pleasant smile. "Did you know your cousin had photographic talents?"

"No," Phoebe replied tightly. "I did not know that about my *cousin*." That last word she pushed out from between gritted teeth. Is that how he had described his connection to her family? As a cousin? "So then, Ernie, you really haven't come to try to catch Julia at home?"

"Not at all." His upper lip curled in something approaching a smile, but was more of a smirk. "I know Julia isn't home."

"You finally believe me, then."

"I do, because I happen to know exactly where she is." He studied his fingernails as he added, "And we both know it's not Lyndale Park."

He thought he knew a secret, did he? Phoebe tilted her chin at him. "Yes, I know all about it."

"Do you? You know where she is?"

"My sister's exact whereabouts are her own business."

"Really?" Ernie held up a hand and studied his fingernails again. "Are your grandparents at home?"

"Yes, but what's that got to do with Julia?"

"I would prefer to tell *them* what I know." Ernie pivoted on his heel to follow Miss Chapman into the drawing room.

Eva waited outside the doorway for Phoebe to cross the hall to her. "That man is always up to something. Did you hear what he said? He knows where Julia is, but he'll only tell my grandparents."

"I shouldn't have let him tag along with Miss Chapman. I should have known he had his own reasons for doing so. Photographer, indeed."

"It's not your fault." Phoebe placed her hands on her hips again as she considered what to do. "I just might call his bluff and refuse to allow him upstairs to talk with Grams and Grampapa. I don't have a good feeling about this, and they might be better off not knowing where Julia is until Julia herself is ready to tell them."

"Do you think it's wise?" Eva's worries tightened her brow. "Your sister could be in trouble. Danger, even."

"If that were the case, I should think even Ernie would come clean about her circumstances without playing these games." Phoebe shook her head. "No, we should wait for Julia and trust that she has good reasons for her silence. Whatever they may be," she added, wishing Julia would stop playing games and be forthcoming. "Do you want me to stay down here and help keep an eye on them?"

"No, that's all right. I'll watch them closely, and I'll let you know when they've gone."

Phoebe went back upstairs and returned to her room, where she once again went over everything they had learned about the historical society members since Arvina Bell's death. It all seemed to lead in circles, from the Hawkhursts to Lady Primrose to Eamon Sadler and back again to the Hawkhursts. Which of them could have known about Dr. Bishop's malpractice incident?

That question aimed guilt directly at the very woman examining the house today: Miss Chapman. She might work for an architectural magazine, but she was still a journalist, and she probably had her sources when it came to serious news. But surely any of the others might have discovered Dr. Bishop's secret as well and used it to their advantage. Lady Primrose's husband worked for the government, so he might have known about the death of the wife of the assistant to the undersecretary of . . . Hmm. She'd forgotten the exact position of the woman's husband. And the Hawkhursts were also well connected and had friends among London society.

Again, the evidence led her in wide circles, precisely because the killer had left little-to-no evidence behind. No fingerprints. A door left ajar. A windowpane in another door broken—with no indication of what the individual had used.

A knock on her door brought her thoughts skidding to a halt. "Yes, come in."

Eva opened the door, a grave expression on her face. "My lady."

"Have they gone already? Goodness, I hadn't realized so much time had passed."

"It hasn't. It's Ernie. He asked to use the lavatory. I gave him directions to the one below stairs, but he's not there. I'm sorry, but I don't know where he's gone."

"Oh, good heavens." Phoebe shot up out of her desk chair and headed for the corridor. Eva stepped aside to allow her to pass. A smidgeon of panic pressed against her breastbone. "Do you think he came up here?"

"I don't know. I'm very sorry I let him out of my sight."

They started down the corridor together, their strides brisk. "You couldn't very well follow him to the lavatory."

Voices drew them across the gallery, past the billiard room and to Grampapa's study. Phoebe's pulse pounded out the notes of her rising fury as she beheld Ernie sitting in front of Grampapa's desk, Grams beside him, both of them facing Grampapa.

She couldn't see Grams's or Ernie's faces as their backs were to her, but Grampapa held a shocked and dismayed expression, his skin a shade of crimson his physician would entirely disapprove of.

Oh, Ernie, what have you done? And why?

He must have heard her footsteps, for he glanced over his shoulder. "Ah, Phoebe, there you are. I was just catching up with your grandparents." He came to his feet. "Lord and Lady Wroxly, it's been a pleasure. I wish you both continued good health. But I'd better rejoin Miss Chapman, or she'll wonder if I haven't abandoned her entirely."

Phoebe wanted to smack the smile off his face as he squeezed past her into the corridor. How dare he come up here on his own and upset her grandparents—as he had obviously done. As he retreated, she moved swiftly into the room. Eva, however, slipped away, obviously following Ernie to be sure he went where he said he would.

No one spoke a word for several moments, and the stifling nature of the silence made Phoebe want to slip away, too. Instead she lowered herself onto the chair previously occupied by Ernie. "What did he want?"

Her grandmother turned a pale face toward her. "Did you know?"

"Know what?"

"Where Julia is," Grams pressed.

At least Phoebe could answer truthfully, even if she had known the general nature of what Ernie had come to tell them. "No. Quite honestly, I don't. Where is she?"

Grampapa's hand came down on his desk with a *thwap*. Phoebe jumped, not at the sharpness of it, but at how uncharacteristic such an act was for him. "Your sister is . . ." He stopped and swallowed, as if a bitter taste filled his mouth.

"She's with Theo," Grams blurted. "Can you believe it, Phoebe? I happen to know that his mother is in London presently, and his aunt Cecily, I'm sorry to say, is no fit chaperone. Which means—"

"Which means they are together, *un*chaperoned," Grampapa concluded. A throaty sigh pushed through his lips. "Our Julia . . . what could she be thinking?"

"How does Ernie know this?" Phoebe asked. True, she had known Julia visited Theo, but according to his aunt Cecily, they had both left, going separate ways in separate motorcars. She supposed that only proved Grams's point about the elderly lady not being a fit chaperone.

"Ernie said he had suspected as much and telephoned over to the Leighton estate and simply asked for her." Grams clucked her tongue and shook her head.

"Perhaps it's not as it seems." Phoebe desperately wanted to reassure them, even while inwardly berating her sister for such a lapse in judgment. Didn't she realize how much her actions would hurt Grams and Grampapa? They were adherents of the old school, of Victorian traditions. For them, the war had changed nothing—at least nothing to do with how men and women conducted themselves, especially with one another.

"How could she do this to us?" Grams lifted a trembling hand to her throat. "How can she risk her own reputation, as well as ours and that of the Townsend family? She is exposing her own son to the taint of public scandal. She—" Grams pulled a black-edged handkerchief from her sleeve and dabbed at her eyes.

Even more than Grampapa's palm to the desk, Grams's tears frightened and unsettled Phoebe. As a rule Grams didn't cry. She strode through life with stoic calm, steady logic, and unfailing dignity.

Oh, Julia, what *have* you done?

"We'll go and get her." Grampapa came to his feet. He reached for the telephone on his desk. "I'll have the Rolls-Royce brought around and we'll go at once."

"Yes," Grams agreed. "We'll drag her home if we must."

"No, wait." Phoebe reached over to press her hand to Grams's, at the same time meeting Grampapa's determined, if infinitely sorrowful, gaze. "Do you think that's a good idea? Grams, you yourself said we should trust Julia. She's an adult and has the right to do as she thinks best."

"How can carrying on with a man—in his home, and with her infant son present—be best for anyone?" Grams's breathing became labored, raspy, sending fresh fears through Phoebe. "No wonder she didn't telephone to tell us where she was."

"Hadn't she?" Grampapa asked. It was clear Grams had kept the truth from him, as she and Phoebe had decided would be best. Now Phoebe regretted the omission, as now he must learn of Julia's mysterious behavior all at once.

"We don't know the circumstances," Phoebe said, "and going there now would mortify Julia. It could drive her farther away. And . . . you know she's had feelings for Theo for years, that she might have married him if not for the . . ." She hated to say it, but it needed voicing. "If not for the financial necessity of her marrying a moneyed man. Perhaps she didn't feel she could tell you about visiting Theo now."

The arrow shot home. Grams blanched. "Then this is my fault. Oh, Archibald, what have I done? I've pushed her to commit an impropriety because she felt she couldn't confide in me."

"No, Maude, I won't let you take the blame for Julia's actions."

"Grams, Grampapa, perhaps there is no blame here. Perhaps all is well, and Julia will be home soon, and she'll tell you everything you wish to know." Phoebe scrambled for the right reassurances, but felt herself coming up short. "Please, I beg you to do nothing."

"How can we do nothing, when we're so worried about her?" Grams appealed to Grampapa, who somberly nodded his agreement.

"Because," Phoebe said, "Julia has never let you down before, has she?"

They each responded to that with silence, their brows furrowing.

"Because she has always put duty ahead of her own needs." Phoebe hadn't always thought so. Her relations with Julia had been tenuous at best these past several years, tempestuous at the worst. She had at times considered her eldest sister selfish, self-absorbed, stubborn, and contrary. And yet . . .

Phoebe had spoken true. When they had needed her, Julia had never disappointed the family, even going so far as to sacrifice her own happiness.

"All right, Phoebe." The leather chair creaked as Grampapa sat back down. "We'll wait for Julia."

Grams nodded. "We don't like it, but we'll wait. She never *has* let us down, and neither have you. We're trusting both of you now."

CHAPTER 19

"Where is he?" Phoebe demanded of Eva in the ground floor corridor. Eva flinched in response. Phoebe softened her tone, but not her intentions. "I'm sorry, Eva. But I need to speak to him this instant."

"In there." Eva unnecessarily pointed the way into the garden room, and both Ernie and Miss Chapman moved into Phoebe's view as they examined the room's ornamentation. "They just finished in the Petit Salon. Don't worry, this time I haven't left either of them out of my sight for an instant."

Phoebe went to stand in the doorway. "Ernie, a moment, if you please."

He looked over and smirked. "Yes, Phoebe?"

"Not here," she replied, and beckoned with a hooked finger. "Come with me."

"Oh, all right." With much huffing to signify what an inconvenience he found Phoebe's request, he apologized to Miss Chapman and promised to be right back. She nodded absently as she continued studying the pattern of the ceiling tiles.

Phoebe led him all the way to the Great Hall and beyond, into the drawing room. Not that she wished to spare him the embarrassment of being taken to task in front of Miss Chapman, but she thought he might speak more honestly without an audience to play to.

Upon reaching the middle of the long room, she stopped, whirled, and placed her hands on her hips. "How dare you upset my grandparents? What kind of cad are you?"

"I upset them? My dear Phoebe, you sister has upset them with her actions. I was merely the messenger."

"As you were the messenger last autumn when we were at Lyndale Park and you telephoned Grams and Grampapa to tell them Julia had been ill, and had been putting her unborn child at risk?"

"Well, they deserved to know, didn't they?"

"Nothing about this family is any of your business." She stepped closer to him, prompting him to back up. "I cannot believe that a year ago at Julia's wedding to Gil, I believed you to be a kindly, well-meaning gentleman. Until you proved me thoroughly wrong."

"Again, I only conveyed the message. Don't you see your argument is with your sister?"

"No, Ernie, I'm quite sure this argument is with you. Why did you do it? You know my grandfather does not enjoy the best of health. Are you trying to make him ill? Is that the only reason you came here today?"

He raised his chin in a self-righteous gesture. "I came here to be of service to Miss Chapman."

"Why? How on earth did you ingratiate yourself to her? What do you know about architecture?"

"I'll have you know she and I established a friendly rapport when she researched Lyndale Park. I proved helpful to her then. We maintained contact because she has an elderly aunt who lives in Staffordshire and Ophelia visits her regularly."

Phoebe rolled her eyes. "Ophelia now, is it?"

"Yes, and why not? I'll tell you that I also proved useful to her a few months ago when she brought her aunt's dog to me in hopes I could help it. It had a dangerous intestinal blockage and might have died. Neither Ophelia nor her aunt had the money for a veterinarian's services and hoped I might assist them out of friendship. Which, I might add, I was only too happy to do. So you see, Phoebe, I'm not quite the monster you believe I am."

"I never said you were a monster," she mumbled in reply. "Only that you seem never to do anything without an ulterior motive."

With a good deal of Foxwood Hall's ground floor explored, Miss Chapman and Mr. Shelton left for the day. Miss Chapman said she wished to review her notes and begin organizing them for her articles. They would be back the following morning, so Eva could relax for now.

In theory, at any rate.

She and Lady Phoebe sat together now in the Petit Salon over tea and a tray of finger sandwiches. In such situations Eva couldn't help remembering how, only a few short years ago, she could never have occupied the same table as her lady, as if they were equals. It still made her mildly uncomfortable, but in times like these, when they had important matters to discuss, it simply made things easier.

Lady Phoebe had just finished telling Eva about the havoc Mr. Shelton caused in Lord and Lady Wroxly's minds when it came to their eldest granddaughter. When she had finished, Eva let out a low whistle between her teeth. "It truly shouldn't surprise any of us what Mr. Shelton is capable of. He's revealed his character often enough in the past. And yet . . ."

"And yet he does continue to astonish." Lady Phoebe shook her head and stared at the artful arrangement of crustless sandwiches. "I've never met a more devious individual. No, I take that back. We've both met more devious individuals, but most of them are in prison now."

Eva added a trickle of cream to her second cup of tea. "I suppose it's lucky for everyone that Mr. Shelton stops short of committing true crimes, even if only just. But the question remains—why did he insist on upsetting your grandparents so?"

It made Eva's blood boil. Did the man thrive on making others miserable? Or was there some other, deeper motive for intruding on an already-difficult situation here at Foxwood Hall?

"I don't know," Lady Phoebe said. "Perhaps it satisfies something in his embittered soul. Or perhaps he's up to something."

"My thoughts exactly." Eva often found it almost eerie how similarly they had come to think. "Do you suppose he knows about this hidden treasure?"

"Perhaps he does. If so, the next question is whether Miss Chapman also knows, and are they working together?" Lady Phoebe obviously considered the matter as she sampled a bite of a fish paste and watercress sandwich. "I do believe he's telling the truth about working with Miss Chapman at Lyndale Park. It's far too easy to verify, since all we have to do is check with Veronica and Mildred."

"Excuse me, my lady, you have a visitor," Mr. Giles said from the doorway. "Lady Primrose Scott. Shall I show her in here, or would you prefer to receive her elsewhere?"

Lady Phoebe's startled gaze locked with Eva's and for a moment they were both speechless. Then Eva said, "Perhaps you should have Mr. Giles say you are not at home."

All too well did Eva remember Lady Phoebe's last encounter with the unpredictable Lady Primrose—not to mention her very near encounter with Lady Primrose's letter opener.

"No . . ." Lady Phoebe spoke slowly as she obviously considered her options. "I think I should see her. I cannot imagine that if she wished me ill, she would come to my home to harm me."

"Nonetheless, I think *we* should see her. Together. I judge it ill advised for you to see her alone."

"Very well." To Mr. Giles, still hovering in the doorway, Lady Phoebe said, "Show her to the drawing room and tell her I'll be there presently. Oh, and, Giles, have Vernon on hand in the Great Hall, please."

They waited a few minutes, no longer than was proper, before starting down the corridor and across the Great Hall to the drawing room. Lady Primrose was seated on one of the armchairs near the hearth, but not comfortably. One glance revealed to Eva how ill at ease she felt, tugging on her handbag straps and compressing her lips as she waited for them.

"Lady Primrose, to what do I owe the pleasure?" Despite that last word, Lady Phoebe's voice conveyed little pleasure. In fact, Eva had never heard her take such a curt tone with any guest, except for Ernest Shelton

Still gripping her handbag, Lady Primrose came to her feet. "Thank you for seeing me, Lady Phoebe." Her gaze darted to Eva. "May we speak alone?"

"No, we may not." As Lady Phoebe strode into the room, Eva kept pace with her. "Can you blame me, after our last meeting?"

Lady Primrose blushed furiously and stared down at the floor. "That is why I'm here. I wish to explain. I feel I must. But . . ." She gazed around the room, and then over their shoulders to the doorway. "Could we go somewhere more private? What I have to say . . . I cannot have it overheard."

Eva shook her head no, but Lady Phoebe took the request in stride. After a brief hesitation she said, "We can go out to the gardens. That will have to suffice. Eva, please have Vernon come in and stand at the windows. Your actions will be observed, Lady Primrose, and should you become violent, help will be quick in coming."

"I understand," the woman murmured.

Eva spoke to Vernon, who followed her back into the drawing room. From there, she, Lady Phoebe, and Lady Primrose stepped out onto the terrace and descended the steps to the uppermost level of the gardens. The breeze carried a waft of sweetness from the recently watered rose garden. They chose a footpath that led away from the house. Lady Phoebe took the lead, with Lady Primrose following her, and Eva at the rear.

"Well?" Lady Phoebe prompted. She stopped and turned. "No one will overhear us here."

Eva glanced over her shoulder at the house. The sight of Vernon's figure standing at attention brought a measure of reassurance. But she hoped this would be quick.

"Can you at least promise me this will remain among us?" When Lady Phoebe nodded, adding that neither she nor Eva would breathe a word, Lady Primrose cleared her throat. "You were right about something. Dead on, actually. Abel Hawkhurst *has* been stealing from the historical society funds."

"I can't say that's much of a revelation." Looking thoroughly unimpressed, Lady Phoebe crossed her arms in front of her and tilted her head.

"Perhaps not. But I haven't yet told you all." Lady Primrose gestured down the path. "May we continue walking? It will make this all easier to say."

"If you wish." Lady Phoebe led the way, moving to one side to allow Lady Primrose to walk beside her. Eva once again took up the rear, her lady's sentinel, ready to intervene if necessary.

"I can prove nothing," Lady Primrose said. "He's been doctoring the books, so it's his word against mine."

"You're the treasurer. Why would you allow him access to your records?"

"He gave me no choice. He's been blackmailing me for months."

Lady Phoebe hesitated a step before continuing along the path. "How?"

"That is what I will explain." Lady Primrose drew a long and deep breath. "He knows something about me, from the years I spent in Paris when I was young."

Lady Phoebe craned over her shoulder to trade a significant look with Eva. That look was rife with the theory they had already devised. Now they would see if they had guessed correctly.

"In my younger days I did things . . . things I'm not proud of. I'd left home, you see. Left England thinking I might never return. As I said, I was young and idealistic and thought I understood the world. Thought I could be the mistress of my own fate." She shook her head, studying the vibrant delphiniums beside her. "What a fool I was. I came to see that, but for a time I believed myself to be free."

She fell silent, contemplating the flowerbeds, the sculpted hedges, the winding course of the footpath. Then she straightened her shoulders. "I went to Paris and became a dancer. No, more than that. I performed on the burlesque stages all over the city. And I was good. All the rage with the gentlemen. Oh, the costumes I wore! They called me *La Rose de la Seine,* and I was the toast of the Parisian nightlife, part of a group of dancers known as the Paris Roses. I—" She broke off, her gaze narrowing first on Lady Phoebe, then Eva. "You don't seem at all shocked. Or even surprised."

"We aren't," Lady Phoebe said. "We've been able to piece

it together, for the most part. We never would have if Abel Hawkhurst hadn't told me to ask you about the Paris Roses, and if we hadn't seen him at Sadler's Emporium."

"Sadler? What has he got to do with it?"

Lady Phoebe compressed lips and then said, "Are you aware that he trades in old photos of burlesque performers?"

Lady Primrose's mouth dropped open, and a look of horror crept across her features. "That's how Abel got it. The photograph he has of me. It's how he's been blackmailing me."

Eva and Lady Phoebe could only nod. Then Eva said, "I wonder how he recognized you. Those photos are decades old."

"Yes, but what I never knew until several months ago was that Abel Hawkhurst was in Paris at the time and saw me perform—more than once. He remembered me well enough to find me familiar when we met again years later. I had married by then, was completely changed from the young woman I had been. It took him a good while to place me, and even then, he couldn't prove anything."

"What brought you home?" Lady Phoebe asked. "From Paris and that life, I mean."

Lady Primrose gave a low, humorless laugh. "An incident. One that left a man dead. I won't say more than that, as the only bearing it has on today is that it sent me home to my parents, and eventually to the man who became my husband."

Eva's mind churned with this information. Lady Primrose Scott, born an aristocrat and married to a conservative MP, once a Paris dancing girl? And . . . and a man with some connection to her had *died*?

"Mr. Hawkhurst must have seen those photographs at Sadler's," Lady Phoebe said, "and perhaps asked him to find one of *La Rose de la Seine*."

"Perhaps. However Abel came by it, he's been holding it over my head these many months. I could lose everything. *Everything.* My husband, my sons, my entire life." A choking sob escaped her. She opened her handbag and fished out a handkerchief, and took a moment to compose herself. "I cannot let this come out. I will do anything to prevent it from becoming known."

"Abel Hawkhurst has much to lose as well," Eva pointed out. "Should it become known he's been stealing funds, he'll lose his position in society. His creditors will come after him. No one will ever do business with him again."

Lady Primrose nodded her agreement. "He'd lose his wife as well. I don't believe she has any idea how depleted their resources are. He's doing everything he can to hide it from her."

Eva nodded, remembering Mrs. Hawkhurst's costly-looking brooch. Had her husband stolen it?

"Oh, she does have some inkling," Lady Phoebe said. "Perhaps she's trying to deny it to herself, but the lady is well aware of the trouble they're in. She also believes her husband to be having an affair—with you."

If either Eva or Lady Phoebe supposed Lady Primrose would react to this news with shock, she disappointed those expectations with a shrug. "I'm not at all surprised that she might think so. She has come upon us more than once, interrupting his threats and my protestations. It's no great stretch to misinterpret fury as passion. Poor woman." She glanced into the distant trees. "Poor me. Abel's made victims of us both."

A silence fell, which Eva used to study Lady Primrose. The woman stood stiffly upright, her hands gripped around the strap of her handbag. Her bottom lip had disappeared between her teeth, and the ridges above her nose looked positively painful, they were so tight.

"You have more to say," Eva concluded out loud.

Lady Primrose's mouth relaxed a fraction. "Yes, but I have no proof, no evidence. Only an ill sensation in the pit of my stomach."

"You might as well speak your mind," Lady Phoebe urged.

After another hesitation Lady Primrose said, "I believe Abel murdered Arvina. That woman stuck her nose into everything, and it's highly likely she discovered his thievery. And I'm terribly frightened I'll be next."

"Have you brought your suspicions to the police?" Lady Phoebe asked.

"Of course not. I don't dare. My secret will come out and my life will be destroyed."

"Did Mrs. Bell know of your past activities?" Eva asked her evenly.

Lady Primrose paled, her nostrils flared. She held Eva's gaze and just as evenly replied, "I understand your meaning, Miss Huntford. No, I don't believe she did. I therefore had no reason to have murdered her. Does that answer your question?"

"It does," Eva conceded, while silently acknowledging that, of course, Lady Primrose would not necessarily confess to murder. Still, the utter lack of urgency in her denial suggested she had told the truth. But what of her suspicions concerning Abel Hawkhurst?

"You'll find the truth, won't you?" Lady Primrose took on a pleading tone. "Please, Lady Phoebe. I know you've involved yourself in this. You've been going about asking questions of all the historical society members. Don't let that man get away with murder. Don't let him destroy the life I've worked so hard to build."

Once again, a contrary thought popped into Eva's mind: it wasn't so much the life Lady Primrose had built that she needed to protect, but the life she had worked so hard to hide. Lady Phoebe assured her she would do everything she could to find the truth and stop the murderer from harming anyone else.

The woman left shortly after, leaving Eva and Lady Phoebe to mull over everything she had told them. They sat in the warm sunshine on the terrace steps, but they hadn't long to themselves before Vernon stepped outside and beckoned.

"Forgive me for interrupting, Lady Phoebe."

She and Eva came to their feet. Lady Phoebe said, "That's all right, Vernon. What is it?"

Vernon's gaze shifted to Eva. "Telephone call for Miss Huntford. It's the constable."

CHAPTER 20

Phoebe waited impatiently for Eva's return. Had Miles Brannock discovered who killed Arvina Bell? Would this soon be over and they could return to their normal lives?

She couldn't help shaking her head at that last thought. Her life had been far from normal these past several years, what with murder seeming to happen wherever she went, and she and Eva always being dragged into the investigations.

That elicited a wry chuckle. If truth be told, she had never been *dragged* into anything. Compelled to investigate—yes. Driven to find the truth to prevent innocent people from being convicted while killers walked free. Could Phoebe help it if she and Eva had a knack for seeing past the surface to the complex issues and connections beneath, which often eluded their local chief inspector, as well as authorities farther afield? She supposed it was their ability to work together, each with her own personal experiences and points of view, that allowed them to see matters from all sides without the usual biases.

Her heart quickened at the sound of footsteps on the terrace. Eva came down the steps at nearly a run, breathless, obviously having hurried from below stairs, where she had taken her telephone call.

"They found the lorry, my lady, the one from Sadler's shop," she announced in a rush, then stopped to catch her breath and tuck in a strand of dark hair that had come loose. "It was headed to London, just as Miles thought it might be. He said there were stolen goods from burglaries that had been reported from towns and villages all over the Cotswolds. It appears we discovered a theft ring."

"Good heavens! Have they taken Eamon Sadler into custody?"

"They have. He's under arrest as an accessory, but according to Miles, he's not admitting to anything. Maintains the lorry picked up only books that night. Nothing else."

"*Pish,* as Julia would say."

"Exactly. Which is why Miles asked that we both go to the police station today. He'd like to take another statement and have us describe again the kinds of items we saw being carried out of the shop."

"No time like the present." Phoebe led the way up the steps and into the house, where they both collected their things. Phoebe used the estate phone to order her motorcar brought around, and she and Eva met a few minutes later on the drive.

At the police station Eamon Sadler slumped low on a chair, brooding, and looked down at his feet. Chief Inspector Perkins sat at his desk and appeared to be going over notes scrawled across a sheet of paper. Miles Brannock stood between them, his attention on Mr. Sadler.

The chief inspector glanced up as Phoebe and Eva entered. He gestured for Phoebe to sit on the chair across the desk from him. "Thank you both for coming in."

Those words prompted Phoebe and Eva to exchange

surprised glances. Typically, the man told them they weren't welcome and shooed them away. Phoebe sat, and Eva went to stand near Constable Brannock. After an initial glance up at them, Eamon Sadler returned to contemplating his shoes.

"I understand you were at Sadler's Rare Books Emporium the day before last, when a lorry arrived ostensibly to deliver books to the shop," the chief inspector said. Phoebe was about to confirm this when Mr. Perkins continued. "Can you tell me why you were at the shop at the time?"

Phoebe resisted the urge to turn around and appeal to Eva for help with the answer. Admitting they had gone to question Mr. Sadler and view the photos of burlesque dancers seemed ill advised. She said the first thing that came into her mind, a half-truth. "I'd only recently become aware of the existence of Mr. Sadler's bookshop. We were shopping for books."

"I see." He made a notation. "And did you purchase any?"

Phoebe wished to demand what that had to do with anything. "Yes, a thing or two. You see, we arrived rather late, and when the lorry pulled up and Mr. Sadler explained that he had a delivery to take, we left. At least we prepared to leave."

"Prepared? What detained you?"

"As we already told Constable Brannock, we thought it odd that such a large lorry came to deliver books, and upon a second look we noticed they were carrying parcels out of the shop, rather than in." She didn't bother mentioning that they had actually driven away and returned on foot to observe the activity.

"So you spied on them for a time, did you?" Here the chief inspector's shaggy eyebrows rose in his lined forehead, his expression rife with accusation. In short, he once again became the Chief Inspector Perkins whom Phoebe had grown used to in recent years.

"Yes, we did," she replied. "Sort of. Long enough to realize something dodgy was going on. Then we drove away and happened upon Constable Brannock on the side of the road."

"Yes, lucky for him you found him when you did." Mr. Perkins thanked them with a rather reluctant nod. "Can you describe this lorry for me? And the objects you saw carried from the shop?"

Phoebe did, including every detail she could remember, though she once again left out the part where they'd parked the Vauxhall and returned through the woods. When she had finished, Chief Inspector Perkins asked Eva, "Do you concur with everything your mistress has attested to?"

"I most certainly do, sir."

"Anything to add?"

"I don't believe so, no."

"Very good. I'll need you both to sign here at the bottom of the page."

Once they had affixed their signatures to the statement, the chief inspector told them they could go. But Phoebe had other ideas. She came to her feet and approached Eamon Sadler, stopping a few short feet away. She mustered an imperious expression that would have made Grams proud.

"Mr. Sadler, are you and your cohorts responsible for the break-in at Foxwood Hall and the attack on my grandmother?"

"I don't know what you're talking about," he mumbled. He crossed his arms over his chest and drew further inward upon himself.

"I believe you know exactly what I'm talking about, Mr. Sadler. Your membership in the historical society gives you the perfect opportunity to traipse through the great houses in the area and scope out the valuables. Information you pass along to those men in the lorry, no? Or perhaps they merely do the transporting, and there are others involved." She pivoted to address the chief inspector. "Have you considered that there may well be others in on this operation?"

"You may leave the police work up to me, Lady Phoebe," he said tightly.

"Not when people are harming my grandmother," she snapped. But she hadn't finished. "I've heard rumors that Abel Hawkhurst has been skimming funds from the very same historical society. Miss Huntford and I ran into him a couple of days ago at Mr. Sadler's shop, and he seemed rather startled to see us. One might even venture to say he seemed dismayed at being caught there." She turned back to Eamon Sadler. "Is Mr. Hawkhurst part of your ring?"

The man scoffed. "Begging your pardon, Lady Phoebe, but you've lost your wits."

"Where did you hear about this?" the chief inspector demanded of her. "From whom?"

"More than one source," she lied, crossing her fingers behind her back. "I don't like to say, really. It could endanger others. I suggest someone take a careful look at the society finances."

What happened next shocked Phoebe to her toes. The chief inspector, narrowing his eyes on Eamon Sadler, passed a hand back and forth beneath his chin, the backs of his fingers rasping against the obviously rushed shave he'd had that morning. He let out a *hmm* . . . a *harrumph* . . .

Then he pushed to his feet, his rotund belly moving the desk an inch or two out of place. "Eamon Sadler, did you have a hand in Arvina Bell's death?"

"What?" Mr. Sadler slid upright, his eyes bulging.

"You heard me. Did Arvina Bell discover what you—

and perhaps Abel Hawkhurst as well—were up to, and needed to be permanently silenced? And Dr. Bishop, too?"

The bookshop owner sprang to his feet, prompting Constable Brannock to lunge in front of him to prevent him from going any farther. "Look, I'm no murderer," Mr. Sadler insisted over the barricade of the constable's shoulder. "They use my shop as a warehouse—that's all. And as for the break-in at Foxwood Hall, I'd have to be crazy to go there one day and send the crew back the very next night, especially after a murder occurred in the very same house. We're not that stupid."

"That's a questionable claim," Constable Brannock said under his breath as he pulled out his notepad and jotted down this latest information.

Chief Inspector Perkins issued Eamon Sadler a penetrating glare before gesturing to the constable. "Lock him up in the back. And then go find Abel Hawkhurst and bring him in."

With the return of Miss Chapman and Mr. Shelton to continue their research of Foxwood Hall, Eva had her hands full. She had been surprised Lord and Lady Wroxly allowed Ernie Shelton to cross their threshold again after the way he had upset them last time, but apparently they had decided not to penalize the messenger. Their argument was with Lady Annondale and the way she had disappeared without a word to them.

Eva still felt uneasy about that, but she agreed with Lady Phoebe that they simply had to trust that Lady Annondale could take care of herself, had good reason for her vanishing act, and would materialize when she felt the time was right.

Eva had spent the morning trailing after Miss Chapman and Mr. Shelton in the gardens and then up to the first floor. How Miss Chapman had procured the earl and countess's permission to traipse upstairs she didn't know, but she and Mr. Shelton had been told they could only view the common rooms and guest rooms—the family's bedrooms were off limits. Once again, Eva had been tasked with making sure they obeyed the rules.

It wasn't a terribly *interesting* job. But her part in discovering who murdered Arvina Bell seemed well and truly over. With both Eamon Sadler and Abel Hawkhurst in custody, and the burglary ring exposed, the police felt satisfied they had found their murderer. They hadn't yet determined which of the pair had strangled the woman, but even Miles felt fairly certain it had to be one of them—or both. As Lady Primrose had said, Arvina Bell had had her nose in everything. The poor woman—it seemed her curiosity had led her too close to these criminal activities for the culprits to allow her to live.

Still, uneasiness continued to plague Eva and Lady Phoebe, although Eva, for one, trusted Miles's instincts.

In the early afternoon she escorted Miss Chapman and Mr. Shelton down the service stairs to the servants' hall, where they would be served tea, and where they could review their morning's notes. They made themselves comfortable while Connie and Dora brought in the refreshments.

"I should think you'll be finished soon," Eva commented from her seat near the head of the table. "At least with the house. Are you going to visit the stables and carriage house?"

Miss Chapman nodded. "Yes, but they shouldn't take long. Another morning and we'll be out of your hair for good."

"You make it sound as if we're a bother." Mr. Shelton spoke around a bite of custard tart. "When, in actuality, your article will increase the popularity of Phoebe's house tours." He shot a gaze at Eva. "That is, if she deems it wise to continue with them."

Eva didn't reply, not about to fall into the trap of speaking on behalf of a member of the family.

"Miss Huntford?" Stevens hovered in the doorway. "Someone to see you. All of you, I believe." He stepped aside, his place on the threshold filled by Arvina Bell's son, Hayden. He held his hat in his left hand, and in the right were several sheets of paper. His dark hair fell over his brow, effectively hiding the scar left by shrapnel during the war.

Eva came to her feet. "Mr. Bell, how are you?"

"All right, considering. Didn't wish to bother anyone, but I found these notes in my mother's bedroom, while I was sorting through her dresser. Oh, speaking of that, Miss Huntford, please tell Lady Phoebe I'll have a donation for her charity soon."

"I will, and thank you, Mr. Bell." She pointed to the papers. "What do you have there?"

He stepped forward, extending them to Miss Chapman. "They're more notes on my mother's intended book. I thought they might be of use to you in finishing it. It maps out the rest of the houses she planned to include."

Miss Chapman came to her feet, took the pages, and scanned the top one. "Thank you, Mr. Bell. I'm sure they'll prove helpful."

"I also wish to thank you again for doing this. Bringing my mother's book to completion is the best way to honor her memory. She—" The young man choked off, seeming overcome with emotion. When he recovered, he offered Miss Chapman a weak smile. "Thank you for suggesting it. You didn't have to, and I'm grateful."

"Think nothing of it," Miss Chapman said cheerily.

"Of course you'll be noted as coauthor and compensated once the book is released," he added.

Miss Chapman waved a hand in the air, dismissing the notion. "I'm not concerned with that. I'm simply happy to see it done."

"Well, I won't keep you from your tea, or your work." Mr. Bell set his hat on his head and gave it a tilt. "You'll let me know when it's ready for the publisher?"

"Of course, Mr. Bell." Miss Chapman extended her hand. He shook it gently, held it a moment longer before releasing her.

Then he turned to Eva. "Might it be all right if I have a stroll around back of the house? I'd enjoy seeing your gardens."

Eva didn't point out that they were not exactly *her* gardens. She only said, "Take as long as you like, Mr. Bell."

When he had left them, Miss Chapman said, "Poor man. He seems rather lost, doesn't he? He must have been a devoted son."

"He's a veteran," Mr. Shelton said, as if that explained matters. At Eva's and Miss Chapman's quizzical looks, he added, "He fought in the trenches and was wounded. I can tell you, when the bullets flew and the gasses billowed across no-man's-land, men like him on the front lines cried out like little boys for their mothers. Not that one could blame them. Now his mother is gone and he's alone."

For a moment Eva found it difficult to speak. She had grown so used to flippancy from Mr. Shelton, that now, when he not only made a good point, but a compassionate one, he left her dumbfounded. She sought for something kind to say in response. Mr. Shelton drained the last of his tea, broke a digestive biscuit in two, and slipped one of the halves into his mouth as he stood.

"Come, Fee, let's get back to work." He picked up his camera, while Miss Chapman gathered her notes.

Eva followed them back up the stairs, though the entire time they climbed, she felt as if she had forgotten something below stairs. What could it have been? She hadn't brought anything down with her, and she had hours ago collected her lady's laundry and shoes, as well as the flowers Connie had picked in the hothouses and arranged into bouquets for Lady Phoebe and the countess's bedside tables. Anything else could wait until Miss Chapman and Mr. Shelton left for the day.

Still, the sensation accompanied Eva all the way to the first floor and down the corridor to Lord Wroxly's study, where Mr. Shelton took more photographs and Miss Chapman examined the woodwork, bookshelves, and the style of the windows. She took a particular interest in the gun case mounted on the sidewall and the array of hunting rifles visible through the glass.

"A handsome collection. Does Lord Wroxly shoot?" she asked.

"Not anymore," Eva told her. "Not since before the war. He used to host hunting parties here with his son. Vast ones they were, with many guests and lasting for days. There would be dinners and entertainments every night as well, though they ended early. The ride to hounds began each day just after dawn."

Miss Chapman nodded her understanding. "Many a landed family has given up the old ways. So no one ever touches these?" She gestured at the weapons.

"No, not to my knowledge," Eva said. Looking past Miss Chapman to the window, she glimpsed Hayden Bell picking his way down a garden path, stopping here and there to examine the flowerbeds.

"In my opinion it's a good thing." Mr. Shelton took up a position a few feet away from the case, stared down into his camera's viewer, and snapped a photograph. "Never mind the terror experienced by the poor fox being chased, but I've seen too many injuries to both horses and riders. And the hounds, too. Life is precarious enough without people going out of their way to cause injury."

He'd surprised Eva again. "Spoken like a true man of medicine, Mr. Shelton. A physician who vows 'to do no harm.' "

"As a veterinarian . . . that *is* what I am, Miss Hunt-ford."

CHAPTER 21

With Eva busy upstairs keeping watch on their visitors, Phoebe found herself standing outside the closed library door. Eamon Sadler and Abel Hawkhurst were in jail, pending charges of theft and possible murder. Of their guilt, she had few doubts, at least when it came to the burglaries, not to mention Mr. Hawkhurst stealing from the historical society. Constable Brannock had collected the record books from Lady Primrose and had interrogated Vesta Hawkhurst, who had broken down and admitted she believed her husband had squandered their fortune.

Something continued to nag at Lady Phoebe—something that didn't fit neatly into the scenario of Arvina Bell discovering the theft ring and being permanently silenced by either Abel Hawkhurst or Eamon Sadler.

The photograph of her great-grandparents still hadn't been found. They hadn't determined why it had been taken in the first place, or how it fit into the circumstances of Mrs. Bell's death. Somewhere in that photograph a clue existed, but however much Phoebe stared at the duplicate, she could identify nothing significant.

She opened the library door and took a determined

stride inside. After she closed the door behind her, she walked to the center of the room and simply gazed about her. She didn't try to avoid the spot where Mrs. Bell's last breath had been squeezed from her lungs. The draperies and tiebacks had been replaced, but otherwise the scene was the same. Someone might have been standing in the alcove waiting for her. Or perhaps he or she had entered after Mrs. Bell, who, realizing the danger she was in, had backed up into the alcove, leading her killer to the very weapon he used.

Phoebe went to the French doors, unlocked them, and let herself out onto the terrace. She crossed to the dining room, taking a similar route the killer would have. The broken pane in the French door had also been replaced. She regarded it and considered what had been used to break it before the killer had reached in to unlock the door. There had been no blood. No rock found nearby. Nothing else disturbed. The terrace was always kept scrupulously swept and clear, so the killer would have had to run down the terrace steps into the garden for, say, a stone.

A notion drew a gasp. The stolen photo? Had the killer used the frame to break the window? That could account for why the photo had been taken. But it would also mean the individual, discovering the dining-room door locked, had gone back into the library for it, at the risk of being caught. That seemed an unlikely gamble to take.

Perhaps, then, the pane in the dining-room door had been broken with something already on the killer's person, something that had been carried through the house during the tour. And that could be just about anything. Hayden Bell's firearm?

Phoebe turned and started back to the library. Partway there, her foot turned slightly on the edge of a flagstone, as if she'd trodden on a pebble. She bent down to examine the edge of the paving stone, and found, wedged between it and the one beside it, a hunk of something black, indeed about the size of a pebble. She picked it up and studied it, pressing the tip of her thumbnail into the surface. It gave, but only slightly, and she deemed it to be made of hard leather.

A piece of someone's shoe?

After replacing the object exactly where she found it, Phoebe hurried back into the house, pausing briefly to re-lock the outer library doors behind her. Moving through the Great Hall, she came upon Ernie as he reached the bottom of the staircase, his camera hanging from the strap around his neck.

"Ah, Phoebe. There you are. I'm leaving for the day. Ophelia's still working on a few of her notations, but she'll be going soon, too. Says it's such a fine day, she prefers to walk back to the village."

"Well, if she changes her mind, we can arrange a ride for her." Phoebe found herself staring at his shoes, even going so far as to circle him to gain a view of the backs of the heels on his beige oxfords.

"Whatever are you doing?"

She shook her head at her folly. Ernie hadn't been at the house the day of the tour. "Nothing. Have a good day, Ernie."

As he had parked his motorcar in the service courtyard, he headed toward the baize door that led below stairs. Phoebe prepared to search for Eva, but Eva appeared on the gallery above her.

"I have something I need to show you," Phoebe called up to her, and Eva came hurrying down. Together they trekked across the Great Hall to the library. Once inside, Phoebe led Eva onto the terrace and picked up the chunk of leather. "I found this a little while ago. I tripped over it, actually. I think it's a piece of a shoe heel. Do you suppose the police might be able to trace it to the type of shoe it is?"

Eva took it from her and held it up, her eyes narrowing against the sunlight. She held the piece between her thumb and forefinger, turning it this way and that. Nodding, she said, "I can see where it broke off from the rest, and where it's scuffed and worn from coming in contact with the ground." When Phoebe nodded her consensus, Eva wondered aloud, "But is it a man's shoe or a woman's?"

"My question exactly. We need to contact the constable. That's why I put it back where I found it, so he can see it exactly where it lay. I'm surprised it wasn't found earlier." Lady Phoebe set it down in the exact place it had been.

"I'll place the call right now, if you like."

"Please do. I don't know how important it will end up being, but the constable should know about it."

Eva hesitated, shading her eyes with her hand and gazing out over the grounds. "Mr. Bell must have gone already. He wished to walk in the gardens and I said it would be all right."

Lady Phoebe nodded and they reentered the library. Eva stopped so abruptly in the alcove that, after relocking the doors, Phoebe ran into her from behind with an *oomph!*

"Oh, sorry." Phoebe stepped around her and studied her face. "What is it?"

"I remember something. Yesterday, as Miss Chapman entered the dining room from the pantry, she turned her ankle a bit. She said she tripped over the edge of the rug. I didn't have a second thought about it. Do you think . . . ?"

Phoebe's pulse spiked, but she tried to calm herself and not jump to conclusions. "That doesn't prove this bit is from one of her shoes, though, does it? It just as easily could have come from a man's wide heel."

Eva didn't answer. Instead she continued to frown at the bookcases across from them.

Phoebe began to grow alarmed. "What else are you re-membering?"

"He called her Fee," Eva murmured.

"Who did?"

Eva blinked as if awakening from a stupor. "Mr. Shel-ton. He called Miss Chapman *Fee*."

"Short for Ophelia, I would imagine." Phoebe didn't see how that related to the matter at hand.

"Yes, but . . ." The color drained from Eva's face. She grasped Phoebe's wrist. "Mr. Giles . . . he spoke of a little girl, the former butler's great-niece, who sometimes came to visit. He called her Fifi."

"Fifi? Could he have been referring to Miss Chapman? Could she be Mr. Willikins's great-niece?" She broke off, gasping as she remembered something herself. "Eva, her handbag. That little square one I'd admired on the house tour—it's just the right size to have broken the window in the dining-room door. Not to mention the metal frame around it would have made an easy job of it."

They regarded each other another instant before setting into motion. "She's still upstairs. Go below and telephone the constable." Phoebe spoke in a whisper and headed to the Grand Staircase. The closing of the baize door as Eva rushed through it barely registered in her mind. Where was Miss Chapman at this moment?

As Phoebe took the stairs two at a time, she realized something else. Miss Chapman's main alibi was in having been seen below stairs at the approximate time of Arvina Bell's murder. How easily she could have used Mr. Giles's pantry to slip below stairs. That must be how she did it.

At the top of the Grand Staircase, Phoebe paused. At this time of day, and with her grandparents' reluctance to spend time on the ground floor ever since the murder, Grams would either be in the Rosalind sitting room or the bedroom she shared with Grampapa. Grampapa, on the other hand, would probably be in his study, after vacating it to allow Miss Chapman to catalogue the room. Which way? For several seconds Phoebe agonized over the decision.

She turned toward the guest wing and Grampapa's study. Voices told her he wasn't alone.

"Open it for me, Lord Wroxly," the female voice said, the calm yet adamant voice flinging Phoebe's heart against her ribs.

"I'm sorry, Miss Chapman," Grampapa replied with equal calm, "but I don't think that would be a very good idea."

Phoebe stopped a little short of the doorway, out of their view. What should she do? She hadn't thought to summon the footmen—how stupid of her to have raced up here without a plan. Yet if she left now . . . what might happen in her absence? And would rushing back with footmen in tow only endanger Grampapa further?

She considered backing away, hurrying to one of the bedrooms to ring for help, but the corridor itself gave her away, the herringbone floor beneath the Persian runner creaking beneath her weight at the most inopportune time.

Miss Chapman peered around the doorway. "Ah, Lady Phoebe, do join us." For good measure she held up a small handgun. Phoebe let out a gasp—she knew that weapon. It was the very same Amelia had first seen on Hayden Bell's person during the house tour.

Were they accomplices? Had he left as Eva believed, or would Phoebe discover him in the study?

Miss Chapman didn't point the revolver at Phoebe. She didn't have to. The mere presence of the weapon was enough to persuade Phoebe to do Miss Chapman's bidding. Miss Chapman moved farther into the room as Phoebe stepped inside. She saw no sign of Hayden Bell.

"Now," Miss Chapman said, "close and lock the door behind you."

Phoebe looked first at her grandfather, who said nothing but stared back at her with an expression brimming with dread. That, and his current pallor, belied his outward composure. Phoebe quietly shut and locked the door. Once she had turned the key, Miss Chapman held out her hand for it.

"I don't understand," Phoebe lied, not wishing to alert Miss Chapman that both she and Eva were onto her, and that Constable Brannock was on the way. "What's going on here?"

Miss Chapman ignored her, addressing her next words to Grampapa. "As I said, Lord Wroxly, open the gun cabinet."

"I'll do whatever you wish," he said, coming to his feet, but not making a move to walk out from behind his desk, "as long as you allow my granddaughter to leave this room."

"Don't be a fool. You know I won't do that. In fact, it's quite fortuitous that she came along. You would only slow me down, old man, but having Lady Phoebe with me will ensure my safe passage out of this house." She gestured toward the telephone on Grampapa's desk. "I assume that's an in-house phone?" At Grampapa's nod she said, "Good. Order your car brought round. Your own chauffeur will drive me where I need to go."

When Grampapa had complied, Miss Chapman wiggled the muzzle of the pistol toward the gun cabinet. "Unlock it. It must be opened in order to reveal what's secreted behind it."

"*Behind it?*" Phoebe repeated, mystified.

Her grandfather looked equally puzzled. "I don't know what you're talking about."

"I believe you might not, Lord Wroxly. Let's begin with you unlocking the cabinet."

He blew out a breath and reached into his trouser

pocket, withdrawing a ring of several keys. Phoebe knew the key to the gun cabinet to be among them. Grampapa kept it on his person at all times during the day and locked it away at night, his way of ensuring no one had access to the weapons without his permission.

He went to the cabinet framed in mahogany, the rifles hanging from the top rack against a green velvet lining. He turned the key in the lock, and the door swung open readily at his light touch. "They aren't loaded, I'll have you know. The ammunition is kept separately, in another location."

"I don't care about the guns, Lord Wroxly." She waved the muzzle of the revolver again. "Under the velvet, along the right side, look for a latch."

"A latch?" Grampapa shook his head. "There is no latch. There is nothing behind this cabinet but the recess in the wall in which it sits."

"There is, Lord Wroxly. Tear away the edge of the velvet and feel for it."

Threads ripped away as Grampapa used two hands to separate the velvet from the wooden framework. He ran his hands up and down the panel. His brow suddenly furrowed in astonishment, and Phoebe heard a metallic click.

With barely a creak from years of disuse, the gun cabinet swung away from the wall. Grampapa gasped. From where Phoebe stood, the open cabinet blocked her view of whatever lay behind it. She sidestepped, coming to an abrupt halt when Miss Chapman arced the revolver in her direction.

"I only wish to see," she said. Miss Chapman surprised her by softening her expression and nodding. Phoebe rose up on her toes to see over the young woman's shoulder and around Grampapa. A shock of surprise went through her as she beheld a combination safe set into the wall.

"Fascinating, isn't it?" Miss Chapman commented, and turned her attention back to Grampapa.

"Now what?" He held out his arms. "I can't open it. I didn't know it existed. I surely don't have the combination."

"No, but I do. Lady Phoebe, come here." She held out her handbag to Phoebe. "Take out the photograph."

Phoebe gaped at her. "*You* took it. Arvina Bell must have walked in on you. Or was she the original thief, and you walked in on her?"

"The latter, the sneaky thing. Seems Uncle John blabbed to one too many people, but I took care of her, didn't I?"

Phoebe gestured at the weapon in the woman's hand. "How did you get Mr. Bell's gun?"

Miss Chapman sniggered. "Hayden is easily distracted and not particularly good at hiding things. Besides, he felt no reason not to trust the person who took over the writing of his mother's book. Now do as I say." Another flick of the revolver accompanied the woman's words.

Phoebe took the handbag and snapped it open. Among the personal items inside, she found the photograph and slid it out. Her great-grandparents' faces, though not smiling, nonetheless shone with the happiness they must have been feeling on the day of their wedding. Phoebe hastily turned it over. She discovered neat, even handwriting on the back, outlining everything that had happened so far: the opening of the gun cabinet, finding the latch, revealing the safe.

A series of numbers crawled across the bottom.

"Read the combination to your grandfather," Miss Chapman commanded her. "Lord Wroxly, you will open the safe."

Phoebe read off the numbers, but after her grandfather's first attempt, the safe door remained steadfastly shut.

"Do not play games with me, Lord Wroxly."

"Miss Chapman, I assure you I am not." He balled his hands into fists, then opened them, flexed his fingers, and rubbed his palms together. "Perhaps if you pointed that thing elsewhere, I'd not be too nervous to turn the dial properly."

"Would you prefer I point my gun at your grand-daughter?"

There was a taut pause as Grampapa clenched his teeth. "No. That won't be necessary. Phoebe, let's try again."

Phoebe read off the numbers. This time the tumblers fell into place and the latch yielded to the pressure of Grampapa's hand. He hesitated.

"Open it," Miss Chapman said tersely.

Phoebe held her breath, her mind churning with possibilities of what might lay inside. Jewels? Cash? A map to buried treasure? The door opened . . .

"What?" Miss Chapman's sharp outburst startled Phoebe out of her conjectures. The woman moved forward and shoved Grampapa out of the way. "Where is it? It has to be here."

Grampapa collided with the edge of his desk. Phoebe went to him, helped him right himself, and then peered into the safe. To her astonishment, it was empty.

"My father must have had a change of heart and moved it to another location," Grampapa said. "Or he had need of his hidden treasure, and it's long gone."

Miss Chapman backed away from the safe as if someone had slapped her. "All the planning, the effort I've gone to. He said it was here, that you people would never miss it—how could you miss what you didn't know you had? He said I should have it—I deserved it. He—"

As Miss Chapman ranted on, Phoebe and her grandfather stood with their arms around each other, watching in horror as the young woman's hold on whatever sanity she had left slipped away.

"You're John Willikins's great-niece," Phoebe said.

Miss Chapman swiveled her face to regard them. "Of course. He was Mother's uncle."

"*Willikins?*" Grampapa tightened his hold on Phoebe. "When did he tell you these things?"

"Before he died."

Grampapa shook his head in a kindly gesture. "My poor woman, your great-uncle was well into his dotage by then. The back of the photograph suggests that at one time perhaps my father used this safe, but there is nothing else to suggest he secreted away any kind of fortune. I'm sorry, but—"

"Shut up. Shut up, Lord Wroxly She knew about it, too—that Bell woman."

"It appears to have merely been a rumor, perpetuated by an elderly gentleman no longer in possession of his better sense." Grampapa rested his chin on Phoebe's head a moment, imparting the kind of comfort and reassurance only he could bestow. Then he added, in as sincere a tone as she had ever heard from him, "I'm sorry, Miss Chapman."

"No. It's there. It has to be." Miss Chapman bounded forward and nearly stuck her head into the safe. Phoebe saw an opportunity and began to move, but Grampapa held her fast. She craned her neck to peer up at him, and he shook his head in a wordless caution. And a good thing, too. Miss Chapman just as quickly backed away from the safe, her revolver once more trained firmly on them.

Eva knelt outside the door of Lord Wroxly's study, a hairpin clutched between her fingers. Though she had learned the art of picking locks years ago from her younger brother, Danny, her attempt to work as quietly as possible made the task doubly difficult.

"Perhaps we should get a duplicate from Mr. Giles," Miles whispered. He stood beside her, his black uniform trousers like a wall that tempted her to lean on him. But she had no time to spare, and not a moment to rest.

"It would take too much time. Mr. Giles has too many keys to go through." She would request the duplicates be better organized in future, but for now, her hairpin would have to suffice. Thank goodness the woman inside with dear Lord Wroxly and Eva's beloved Phoebe continued spewing words at high volume, hopefully covering any sounds Eva made as she maneuvered her hairpin. Then again . . .

Though muffled by the heavily paneled door, the woman's tirade nonetheless signified an irate and possibly deranged mind. How Eva longed to break the door down and storm inside. How she yearned to tackle the woman and teach her a sound lesson. No one threatened a member of this family on Eva's watch and got away with it.

Finally she heard the click of the lock giving way. She glanced up at Miles, who held his nightstick upraised. She scooted backward, away from the door, and allowed him to grip the knob. Before he could turn it, the blast of gunfire shook the floor beneath their feet.

CHAPTER 22

❧

Her heart in her throat, Eva was on her feet, ready to follow as Miles flung the door open and bounded inside. He came to a halt just beyond the threshold, prompting Eva to grip the door sash to keep from barreling into him from behind and knocking him down.

The acrid odor of gunpowder floated on the air. Her panicked gaze found Lady Phoebe first, standing beside an open cabinet Eva never knew existed before. Lady Phoebe stared as if transfixed at the floor a few feet away from her. Lord Wroxly stood in front of his desk. Eva followed his and Lady Phoebe's gazes to discover Miss Chapman on the floor at Miles's feet. And there was blood . . . coming from her shoulder. A revolver lay several feet from her outstretched hand. Casting off his own bewilderment, Miles lunged and scooped it up.

Eva didn't understand. Had Miss Chapman shot herself in the shoulder? Was that even possible?

"Constable Brannock, I assume you'll want this one, too, as evidence for your investigation." Lord Wroxly held out a small silver handgun and stepped forward to pass the weapon to Miles over Miss Chapman's prone body.

Eva gaped, then recovered enough to say, rather than ask, "You shot her."

"Yes, I did," his lordship affirmed, "and I'd do it again, given the same circumstances."

Lady Phoebe closed the short distance between them and threw her arms around him. "Grampapa, I don't understand."

No, Eva didn't quite understand, either. But two of the people she cared about most appeared unharmed, and that was really all that mattered.

Miles crouched beside Miss Chapman. "It looks like a flesh wound." He glanced around him, pressed to his feet, and went to an oak filing cabinet beside the door. A splintered fissure in the framework revealed the raw wood beneath the dark stain. "Here's where the bullet struck."

Miss Chapman moaned.

Voices filled the corridor. Eva did a hasty about-face, ran out of the study, and met Lady Wroxly, her maid Miss Shea, and footmen Vernon and Stephens as they hurried across the gallery. She saw no sign of Fairfax, and deduced the countess had left him in whatever room they had occupied to keep him safe.

"Eva, I heard a gunshot." Lady Wroxly hurried ahead of the others. "Was my husband cleaning one of his rifles and it went off? Good gracious, was anyone hurt?"

"No, my lady. Not exactly."

"Whatever do you mean, *not exactly*?" Lady Wroxly looked both perplexed and alarmed. She turned to Vernon and Stephens. "Hurry! Go and see what happened."

The two young men trotted down the corridor.

"It's all well in hand now, my lady." Eva glanced over her shoulder, her ears alert for signs that Miss Chapman was giving any further trouble. "There was an incident. Suffice it for now to say our murderer and our thief has been caught. It's Ophelia Chapman, the writer."

"That nice Miss Chapman?" Lady Wroxly held out her hands. "I don't believe it. Do you mean to say she not only murdered Mrs. Bell, but broke in the other night and"— her eyebrows shot up—"I coshed her with the candelabra?"

"That's correct," Eva said, remembering yet another detail she'd noticed about Miss Chapman. "Excuse me one moment, won't you, Lady Wroxly?"

Eva hurried back to Lord Wroxly's study. Miles had gotten Miss Chapman up off the floor and onto a side chair against the far wall. He hadn't cuffed her or secured her to the chair in any way, but with her bleeding shoulder it wasn't likely she would be attempting to fight back or run off. Vernon squeezed past Eva in the doorway, having apparently been sent on an errand. Perhaps for water and linens to address the bullet wound.

Eva strode across the room to her. "I noticed you'd changed your hair not long ago, Miss Chapman. I'd chalked it up to you wishing to be more attractive for Mr. Shelton. But I was wrong, wasn't I?" Before the other woman could react, Eva boldly reached out and moved the sweep of hair off her forehead, revealing the bruise and gash Lady Wroxly had inflicted with her candelabra. Though it wasn't large, several sutures had been needed at the hairline to hold the wound closed. Eva straightened, regarding the woman with a disgust and loathing she was unable to conceal. "And that watch you wore that night you broke in? Lady Wroxly remembered seeing the glowing dial."

"My brother's, from the war," Miss Chapman mumbled, then winced in pain.

"Of course. To keep time so you'd know exactly when to expect Stevens making his rounds of the house. And after breaking in and being clobbered by Lady Wroxly, you went to Dr. Bishop with your bleeding forehead, only to strike him dead to keep him silent. Since you're a journalist, it couldn't have been too difficult for you to discover his secret—the dead patient that made it necessary for him to leave his London practice. So we can add blackmail to your list of crimes, can't we, Miss Chapman?"

The woman grunted in reply. Eva felt a touch at her elbow. Miles had come up beside her. His other hand settled at the small of her back. "Leave the interrogating to me, Eva. Don't worry, she'll be held responsible for everything she's done."

"There's one more thing," Eva countered. "Lift your right foot, Miss Chapman." When the woman reluctantly complied, she said to Miles, "You'll notice a piece of her heel has broken off. You'll find it where Lady Phoebe found it on the terrace, stuck between some paving stones between the library and the dining room, where she obviously made haste to create her alibi of being below stairs at the time of the murder."

She thrilled at the look of admiration Miles flashed her, then turned back to Miss Chapman. "A shame you only packed one pair of shoes for your trip."

"Grampapa, I still don't understand how you came to be holding that pistol," Lady Phoebe said, drawing Eva's attention away from the journalist. "Where was it that you were able to snatch it without Miss Chapman—or me—noticing?"

Eva, too, couldn't fathom how Lord Wroxly had procured the weapon at just the right moment. His policy of keeping his gun cabinet locked—the weapons unloaded—was one of Foxwood Hall's strictest rules.

Lord Wroxly smiled and cupped his granddaughter's cheek in his palm. "It was in my pocket, my dear. And has been since the night that woman attacked your grandmother."

"Archibald? Are you quite all right? Phoebe, my goodness, you too." Lady Wroxly swept into the room with the vigor of a much younger woman. She held out her arms, drawing both Lady Phoebe and Lord Wroxly to her.

"Fine, fine, Maude," he said, gathering them close. "It's all over. Nothing to worry about."

Lady Phoebe caught Eva's eye and grinned. Then the little family unit, each with an arm around the other, walked from the room. Eva heard the countess ask Miss Shea to order a pot of strong oolong sent up to the Rosalind sitting room.

That evening Amelia telephoned from Lyndale Park. She spoke first to Grams, who apprised her of all that had happened at Foxwood Hall earlier in the day. Then Amelia asked to speak with Phoebe.

"I just told Grams that Julia telephoned to say she was sending Douglas back to collect me in the motorcar. I should be home by tomorrow afternoon, barring any unforeseen events. I'm still rather put out that Julia dropped me here and disappeared, but from what Grams just told me, it was certainly safer here in Staffordshire. Phoebe, was it terribly frightening?"

"It *was,* Amellie, yes. But Grampapa was such a hero. And what a shot he is—a regular marksman. I'd no idea. He had no wish to kill Miss Chapman or maim her permanently, in spite of all she had done. The bullet only grazed her shoulder. But that's our dear Grampapa, isn't it?"

"Always the gentleman, even with vicious criminals," her younger sister agreed with a laugh.

"Wait a moment." Phoebe considered something Amelia had just told her. "You said Julia is sending Douglas to collect you, as if she won't be with him. What about her? How is she going to get home?"

Or was she coming home at all? Would Julia do that, simply move away without telling anyone she had no intention of returning? Surely, Julia wouldn't hurt their grandparents that way. Besides, she was a grown woman and a viscountess, at that—she didn't need anyone's permission to do as she wished. Informing the family of her plans would merely have been a courtesy—one a grown woman, and a viscountess, should have recognized.

"Perhaps she hired her own motorcar," Amelia suggested, having no notion of the turn Phoebe's thoughts had taken.

"Perhaps. But you've still no idea where she went after leaving you there?"

"None. She wouldn't tell me anything." Amelia paused, and then added, "You know how she can be."

"All too well. Tell me, how has it been staying with Veronica and Mildred?" One never knew with Julia's sister-in-law and stepdaughter—the latter a woman close to Julia's own age. Like Julia's deceased husband, Gil, their moods seemed to vary with the direction of the wind. "Were they at all beastly to you?"

"Actually, they were rather spiffing. And we got to visit with Trent."

"Oh, wonderful. How is he?"

"Doing quite well, now that he's discovered the family rift had been with his father and never with him. His aunt, uncle, and cousins have been only too happy to reconnect with him."

Trent Mercer, a friend of Fox's from Eton, had lost his father the previous autumn when Phoebe and her siblings had gone to Staffordshire to commission the china service for their grandparents' anniversary. He had lost his mother previously from the influenza outbreak, leaving him now an orphan. After the ordeal, he had accompanied them to Foxwood Hall and stayed on for a time, but Phoebe was happy to hear his relatives had welcomed the boy into their lives.

"Well, I've got to go pack," Amelia said. "I'm sure we'll hear from Julia soon."

Phoebe swallowed a sigh. "Although it will be a relief for Grams and Grampapa, I'm not particularly looking forward to her reappearance. She has a lot to answer for, worrying them the way she's done. See you tomorrow." She rang off.

The following morning Phoebe and her grandparents gathered in the drawing room after breakfast, for the first time since the murder of Arvina Bell. With Ophelia Chapman behind bars, Grams and Grampapa finally felt safe enough to venture down to the public rooms of the house. It came as a relief to Phoebe to see them settle into their favorite spots by the hearth, savoring the cups of tea brought in from the dining room. Soon, she hoped, they would all put the worry and danger behind them and carry on as usual.

But their morning contentment was interrupted by a commotion at the front door. Grams craned her neck, as if that could help her see around the walls into the Great Hall. She consulted the mantel clock. "Could that be Amelia, so soon?"

"I can't imagine." Phoebe set her teacup aside and came to her feet. She took a step toward the Great Hall, but stopped short when a voice called out.

"Grams, Grampapa, I'm home!"

Fairfax, who had been sleeping at Grams's feet—*on* her feet, actually—woke up with a snort and jumped up to all fours. Grams and Grampapa traded astonished glances. Grams said, "Julia?"

As if to answer the question, a baby's laughter and happy babbling drifted to them. Grampapa was on his feet in an instant, and moved to help Grams to hers. Like Phoebe, however, they didn't get far before they stopped in their tracks. From the Great Hall came Julia's voice once again.

"Thank you, Giles. No need to announce me, I'll just go straight through."

Fairfax barked happily and ran out to greet her. A moment later the dog reappeared with Julia as she came through the doorway. Hetta followed, holding Charles in her arms. He broke into delighted grins at the sight of his great-grandparents.

"Hello, all," Julia sang out as if nothing were amiss. "We're back." She regarded them, one by one, smiling broadly. Too broadly, Phoebe judged. "Goodness, what are you all doing standing around? You look as though you've seen a ghost."

Grams strode to her, her long skirts brushing the floor with an angry hiss. "Where on earth have you been? And how dare you worry us these past many days? Julia Renshaw, what *were* you thinking?"

As Grams voiced her displeasure, Grampapa went to her side and took her hand, patting it with his own. "Now, Maude," he murmured, "let's hear what Julia has to say before we start berating her."

"*Berating her?*" Grams snatched her hand back and whirled on him, prompting him to take an instinctive step backward. Fairfax whined. Grams continued, "After what she's put us through? Taking our great-grandson, lying to us about going to Lyndale Park, disappearing off the face of the earth . . ." She trailed off, breathing heavily, the jet pin at her throat catching the light from the French doors and bouncing it erratically.

"Yes, well, I can explain everything. And, actually, I did go to Lyndale Park. You know I did, if only briefly." Julia took Charles from Hetta and brought him to Grams like an offered gift, giving her no choice but to open her arms to cradle the child to her. "There you are, Charles, darling. Here are Great-Grams and Great-Grampapa, to spoil you through and through, as always."

Grams took a moment to coo at her grandson and run her fingertips through his fine curls. Grampapa placed a hand at her back and nudged her toward the chair she had occupied. Phoebe resumed her seat as well, eager to watch this development unfold.

"You did worry us terribly, my dear," Grampapa said after a pause. "But exactly where *were* you?"

"Yes, Julia." Grams pursed her lips before continuing in a tight voice, "Where *were* you?"

"Yes, that." Julia took a moment to fuss with the sleeve of her traveling suit, smoothing what didn't need smoothing. She surprised them all by coming to her feet. "I think the best way to explain is to . . ."

She hurried from the room. From the Great Hall came murmurs, then footsteps—two sets of them, one set a heavy counterpoint to the *clackity-clack* of Julia's heels. When Julia reappeared in the doorway, there was indeed another individual standing beside her.

"Theo!" Phoebe cried out, and jumped up from her seat. She was about to go to him, to embrace him and welcome him to Foxwood Hall after staying away such a very long time.

But then she remembered the reason for his staying away: Julia's marriage last year to Gilbert Townsend, Viscount Annondale, which had so obviously broken Theo Leighton's heart. And Julia's, for that matter, but she had believed marriage to Theo to be impossible. She had been raised to understand her duty: marry well. Which meant marry a wealthy man who would help restore Foxwood Hall, and the estate Fox would one day inherit, to its prewar glory.

Whereas, Theo Leighton had inherited from his elder

brother the illustrious title of Marquess of Allerton and a bankrupt estate to go with it.

And then it struck Phoebe that under the terms of Gil Townsend's will, Julia got to keep her inheritance from him whether she remarried or not. Could they be planning . . .

"Theo and I are married," Julia declared, and the room slammed into silence. Except, of course, for Charles. Oblivious to all but Grams's jet brooch, he had latched on to it with his tiny fingers and tugged.

And tugged some more, until the sound of fine threads ripping joined his babyish chatter. Grams absently reached up and grasped his dimpled wrist, but she didn't dislodge him from her brooch. "What do you mean, *married*?" she asked in a whisper.

Theo looked distinctly uncomfortable. The rippled scars below the left corner of his mouth, extending beneath his chin and along his neck, stretched tighter and redder than usual, the skin having been ravaged during the war by creeping mustard gasses.

"Lord and Lady Wroxly, I apologize for the way we went about this." He took several steps toward them, away from Julia, to stand on his own as he continued to explain. "In the past there was so much against us. My brother. The money—or lack of it. Lord Annondale. We simply thought—"

"You can't be married." Grams pronounced this with complete authority. "The banns haven't been read."

"Theo obtained—" Julia began, but he cut her off.

"A special license. A few weeks ago."

"You planned this?" As he spoke, Grampapa placed a hand on Grams's shoulder, although whether in support or in an effort to prevent her from leaping out of her chair, Phoebe wasn't sure. "Even before everything happened?"

Julia moved to stand beside Theo. She looked both

apologetic and defiant. "Long before. With my mourning period for Gil over, we saw nothing to stop us finally doing what we wished to do years ago. I'm sorry if this has hurt you." Her gaze took in Phoebe as well. "But we wanted it done so that nothing could ever get in the way again. I am no longer the Viscountess Annondale. I am the Marchioness of Allerton."

"Well." Grams leaned her cheek against Charles's downy head. "Nice of you to deprive me of the pleasure of planning a wedding."

"Oh, Grams, haven't you planned enough weddings for me?" Julia went to stand in front of Grams's chair. She reached down to tousle Charles's hair. "It was just Theo and me, the vicar, and his housekeeper and her husband as witnesses. It was perfect. Exactly what we both wanted."

"Well." Grams looked up to meet Julia's gaze. "If it was what you wished, then I suppose it's all right."

"It is, Grams, thank you." Julia leaned low to kiss Grams's cheek.

Grampapa pushed out of his chair. "Julia, my dear, congratulations. I assure you they are heartfelt—this time." He embraced her and kissed both of her cheeks, and then extended his hand to Theo. "I'm delighted, if truth be told. Welcome to the family, my boy."

Julia finally turned to Phoebe. "Well? Haven't you anything to say?"

In truth, Phoebe's throat felt rather too tight for speech, and she blinked several times as she rose and extended her arms to Julia. It was, for them, a rare hug, lovely and earnest, the sort of things sisters do.

Phoebe swallowed and blinked once or twice. "I couldn't be happier for you."

Even with the agreeable development of Julia and Theo's marriage and the return of Amelia—with the promise of

Fox coming home once his exams were done, thus reuniting the entire family—Phoebe continued to feel a nagging sensation, as if something important had been left undone.

It was that silly rumor of Great-Grandpapa's hidden fortune. The safe had proven empty, so why couldn't she let it go?

She simply couldn't, and there it was. She would awaken in the night wondering if perhaps they had overlooked a hint, a clue. Perhaps a step in actually finding Great-Grandpapa's hiding place. True, perhaps he had retrieved the money or whatever it was decades ago and spent it. Or invested it. But if that was the case, why had he left the photograph there, to be found someday and acted upon? Why had the rumor persisted?

Or had he merely forgotten all about it?

"You're far away today, my lady. Is something troubling you?" Eva stood behind her, brushing out the braid she slept in. The tray of hairpins sat on the dressing table in front of her, ready to be put to use.

Phoebe drummed her fingertips on the table's marble surface. "Two people died because of that photograph."

"Greed is a powerful force, my lady."

Phoebe nodded. "It's all such a waste. What could my great-grandfather have been thinking?"

"I'm not sure what you mean." Eva set down the brush and began coiling sections of Phoebe's hair. "He never meant for anyone to know about his secret. That Mr. Willikins somehow learned about the photograph is unfortunate."

"Mr. Willikins, of course!" Phoebe met Eva's gaze in the mirror. "He must have stolen the fortune. Used the photograph, opened the gun cabinet and the safe, and stolen what my great-grandfather had secreted away."

Eva appeared to think that over as she secured the remainder of Phoebe's hair in a neat coiffure that would magically hold throughout the hours of the day. "If that was so, why would Mr. Willikins have told Miss Chapman the fortune was still there?"

"Hmm . . ." Phoebe considered this as well. "He was in his dotage when he told her. He must have forgotten he'd stolen it. Wiped that part out of his mind."

"Perhaps." Eva sounded unconvinced.

Phoebe remained unconvinced as well. Later, after lunch, she tracked down her grandfather in his study. Though he might typically have gone to the library during that time, it was still the one room in the house both he and Grams, not to mention Phoebe and Amelia, still avoided. It would take time before the spirit of poor Arvina Bell vacated Foxwood Hall for good.

He seemed surprised to see Phoebe when she knocked. "Is anything wrong, my dear?"

Phoebe stood gazing at the gun cabinet. "Could we open it again, Grampapa?"

"But why?"

Phoebe heaved a sigh. "I'm not sure. Just to check again, I suppose."

"Check an obviously empty safe?"

"Yes."

He regarded her for several seconds, then stood and went to the cabinet. He opened the glass case. The lining he'd torn to find the latch hadn't been mended yet, so it was an easy task to trigger the latch and swing the cabinet aside to reveal the wall safe. "The photograph is in my right top drawer," he said to Phoebe.

She found it and read off the numbers. Unlike when Miss Chapman had stood aiming her revolver at him, Grampapa managed to open the lock on the first attempt. The safe door opened, once again revealing an empty interior.

"Nothing has changed, Phoebe. I'm afraid there is no magic involved here."

Nonetheless, he stepped aside to allow her access. She stepped close, peering in, then reached in, feeling all around the walls of the safe with her hand. The sidewalls first, then the back.

It shifted, ever so slightly, yielding to her searching fingertips. Her heart went still, then hammered in excitement. "Grampapa . . ."

But she couldn't quite get her fingers round the edges. She backed out, searching the room, the desk. "Grampapa, your letter opener, perhaps."

Without a word he handed it to her, and she went back to work. Using the sharp tip, she pried it between the rear and sidewalls. Angling for leverage, she used two hands to apply greater pressure. The tip of the letter opener found its way between the two surfaces, and Phoebe pried the back panel of the safe free.

"What have you got there?" Grampapa came up behind her and peered in around her.

"A false back. Oh, Great-Grandpapa certainly was clever." She handed him the letter opener and reached in to extract the panel. As she did, a batch of papers behind it fell from their perch where they had stood these many decades, to fall onto the floor of the safe. She reached in and grasped them. "What *are* these?"

Grampapa took the stack of papers from her and walked to the desk.

Phoebe removed yet another packet from inside the safe. "There are several of them. And each bundle seems to have about a dozen or so pages folded together."

"They're bonds, my dear. Very old bonds." Grampapa took up a magnifying glass and held it over the first in the pile. Then he rifled through, glancing at others. "Good heavens, these are from the early years of the last century. Napoleonic War bonds. My grandfather—your great-great-grandfather—must have purchased these."

Phoebe hurriedly brought another bundle to the desk. He took them from her, but he didn't need his magnifying glass to see that these particular bonds had helped fund the Crimean War some fifty years later.

Grampapa held them up to the light. "My father would have purchased these. But why did he hide them? Why the secrecy? It makes no sense. And back then, Foxwood Hall was completely solvent—more than that, the estate turned good profits each and every year. He couldn't have seen any need to hide away money in any form."

"Perhaps for that very reason. Perhaps he didn't need the extra funds then, but he envisioned a time when that might change," Phoebe said, and gently added, "as it has."

Grampapa slipped an arm around her and kissed her brow. "Indeed, it has, my smart, clever girl."

"Are they worth very much, if they were to be redeemed?"

Grampapa continued to study the one he held, and shook his head. "These are perpetual bonds, meaning they can't be cashed in for their principle value until the government is good and ready to allow it, if ever. But the interest is another matter. I would imagine there is a good deal accrued that can be collected, if we are so inclined."

"What will you do, then?"

"Well, my dear, I believe the first thing I will do is discourage you from ever conducting house tours here again. And with these, perhaps you won't have to."

Phoebe wholeheartedly agreed.

NORWEST BANKS

Norwest Bank Indiana, N.A.
Rochester Office

Savings
Withdrawal

Name (please print)

Account number

Address

Date

Please deduct below sum from my savings account on deposit with the above named bank

_____ Dollars $ _____

_____
Authorized signature

NC 86015 TLR 455

⑆0740614⑆ 661